NOTE F

CW01500363

Forgotten Ashes, The Iolite Academy: Book One is an upper young adult fantasy romance that contains content some readers may find disturbing. If you do not wish to receive these warnings ahead of time, please feel free to skip the next paragraph and dive into reading.

This story has scenes containing: animal death (deer), anxiety, blood, bullying, death, dead bodies, depression, loss, misogyny, panic attacks, physical altercations, torture (off-page), violence

If after reading you believe something should be added to this list, please reach out to the author's team at kathryn-covens@gmail.com.

1

THE IOLITE ACADEMY

FORGOTTEN ASHES

KATHRYN COVENS

Cover Design & Chapter Illustrations: Selkkie Designs

Published by: Feeling Through Fiction House

ISBN: 979-8-9901649-0-1 (Paperback)

CONTENTS

To Andy,
for a lifetime of pep talks

SHIFTER TERMINOLOGY

Alpha: Highest ranking male

Luna: Highest ranking female

Beta Alpha: Alpha's second in command

Beta Luna: Luna's second in command

Enforcers: Protectors

Latent: Unable to shift

Mate: Life partner

Pack Rite: Battle for a ranked position

THE ROSE

Someone was following me.

I heard their too-light-to-be-thoughtless, too-heavy-to-be-stealthy footsteps echoing behind from the moment I left the east wing. I let them trail after me as I made my way through the compound toward my bedchamber. If they thought to overpower me by taking me by surprise they'd be sorely disappointed when they were met with my blade instead of my submission. A corner of my mouth raised at the thought.

My patience for insolent pack mates hoping to prove me unfit of my station had met its limit about twenty minutes ago with the most recent grumbling of, "She can't even shift," from someone angry they hadn't gotten their way. The insult was unoriginal at best. I told myself it didn't sting each time it was hissed under someone's breath.

Truthfully, I should have known the day would be less than joyful when I first opened my eyes, body covered in sweat, heart pounding, lungs screaming for air untainted by ash and soot. It took a full five minutes to remind myself there was no debris clinging to my skin. I wasn't stuck in the wreckage. I was in the compound, in my room, in my bed. I wasn't there. They hadn't found me.

They *wouldn't* find me.

The morning marked ten years since Luna Ivy and Alpha Lucas brought me into the pack. Ten years since I was a child wandering the woods alone. At eighteen, I was no longer a child. I was no longer wandering the woods. But even in one of Ivy's warm embraces, receiving one of Lucas' proud smiles, or laughing in the dining hall amongst the pack mates who didn't begrudge my very existence, I still felt alone. I had to be.

If a poor night's sleep was all that plagued me I'd be more amused than irritated by my shadow, but my morning was an omen for the day to come. A spilled bowl of oatmeal on my lap at breakfast. A careless trainee bleeding during this afternoon's weapon training. A fight in the dining hall between two males wishing to claim the same female as their mate—both of whom she'd been pursuing without informing the other.

Each incident frayed my already dwindling patience, but it was the *two-hour* debate over a blade's rightful owner that had me grinding my teeth in frustration. The male whose favor I ruled against was spitting with rage. It meant little to him that the other party's name had been clearly engraved in the blade's handle.

As he stomped away he'd cursed me under his breath and spat, "A Beta Luna who can't even shift acting as though her word is law. If the Beta Alpha were here, this wouldn't have happened."

The only thing saving him from my wrath was my own self-preservation. The distance between us was too far for any normal shifter to hear him. Confronting him would call attention to a truth I'd taken great care to hide over the years—I was anything but normal.

His impertinence irritated me, but what irked me most was he'd been right. If Grayson had been here he may have made the same ruling, but I suspected he'd have reopened the case rather than trusting my judgment. He'd pull me aside and smile his assurance that it was only to keep the peace, not a lack of faith in my abilities, but I knew his true feelings toward me. I'd heard it from his own lips, whether he realized it or not.

Thoughts of Grayson took my day from unfortunate to truly vexing as I considered our impending reunion. Which is why it felt more than reasonable to bring this game of cat and mouse to an end. When I turned the next corner, I slipped behind one of the wooden pillars lining the hallway and melted into the shadows. My follower skulked past my hiding spot. I shot my hand out to snatch their wrist and pull them into the darkness with me.

If I hadn't caught Ivy's sea-breeze scent, I would've had her on her back in seconds. As it was, I showed the middle-aged tiger mercy. I simply twisted her arm behind her back instead, pressing her into the pillar until a fit of laughter shook us both.

"I yield, Briar! I yield!" She chuckled and turned her head to look at me over her shoulder.

"Don't you know better than to try sneaking up on me by now?" I teased in her ear before releasing her arm. Ivy had been trying to take me by surprise for years. When I was younger she would have bested me in under a minute, but the past few years she only pinned me when I allowed her to do it. She liked to say it was part of my training, but I suspected she took no small amount of joy in her efforts.

"Just making sure you're staying alert," she countered with a smile. Then, more seriously, she added, "You're walking into a lion's den tomorrow. Anyone could be lurking around any corner at the Academy. Let your guard fall for a moment and someone will pull you into the shadows for no reason other than proving they can overpower you."

"First of all." I raised a finger. "That's eerie. Second of all, I'm ready. My guard is up, my focus is fixed, and my daggers are sharp. I'm prepared to take care of the pack."

"I know you are, but don't forget to take care of yourself too." She reached up to tug on one of the braids scattered amongst the waves of my hair. She lowered her voice and took a step closer. "But that's not why I'm here. There was an attempted breach at the Eastern border."

"When was it detected?" *And why didn't you lead with that tidbit of information?* I pivoted on my heel to head east.

"Ten minutes since I was notified, two more since something triggered the enchantment." Meaning if she'd told me immediately instead of following me, I would've been there by now. Instead, I'd spend ten more minutes backtracking across the entire compound. What a waste.

The disapproval must have been written across my face because she waved a hand through the air and said, "The

Enforcers who were on patrol already swarmed the area, or I would've told you right away."

I disagreed with her decision but kept my opinion to myself. She was the Luna of this pack, I was merely her Beta–for now. Unfortunately, a voice in the back of my mind assured me it would be my name, not hers, that was grumbled as cause for the delay.

"Have we confirmed the enchantment held?" I asked, falling into step at Ivy's side.

"It held," she said as we strode through the lantern-lined halls toward one of the side exits. "Whatever they tried using to penetrate it bounced back, but the team heading that way was instructed not to cross the border until one of us arrives on the scene. I need you to go meet them while I circle the perimeter and find Lucas. Do as you see fit once you arrive. They're awaiting your command."

"Understood." We were nearly to the door now.

"It's likely just a flock of rogues hoping to prey on whatever vulnerabilities they can find, but don't lower your guard. More than rogues infest these woods." I, more than most, knew what horrors could lurk in the darkness of trees and rustling leaves; my guard was never down.

"Be careful, and above all else—"

"Protect the pack," I finished for her and grinned as we exited the main lodge. Her slender shoulders fell as she exhaled deeply.

"Yes. Always."

"Until my last breath," I promised. "I'll see you soon."

"Goddess guide you."

"And you, Luna." I dipped my head in her direction

before turning on my heel toward the location she described. I saw her shift from the corner of my eye, and a streak of orange darted across the clearing as her tiger ran to join her mate.

My two legs may be chronically human, but they were fast–faster than many who had the benefit of four. They carried me past the school and into the woods in record time. The brisk air pierced my skin as I picked up speed, dodging branches and trees while I ran. The Eastern border was the closest to the compound, but it was still a solid two miles through trees, vines, and underbrush to reach it.

I loved the woods. I loved every inch of them, from the dew-dropped moss glistening in the morning to the rustles and growls it hid between its trunks under the blanket of night. The former was a lovely sight during a dawn run, and the latter wasn't nearly as frightening after you'd slept amongst them for weeks on end.

Ivy didn't specify which of the Enforcers waited for me at the border, but as I grew closer the hints of juniper in the air promised one of my favorite snow leopards was amongst them. Unfortunately, it was polluted by a distinct tinge of clove. *Goody for me.*

"Did you take a tour of the compound on the way here?" Logan groused from his pedestal atop a tree stump. The shadow of loss, of guilt, that hit me with every encounter reared its head in the back of my mind. I pretended it didn't. "Or did you simply not deem this matter urgent enough to warrant your presence?"

The other Enforcers left the areas along the border they were scouting to head in my direction. The eyes of the two younger members of the trio, Mia and Brody, flitted from Logan' still seated form to the elder snow leopard approaching to my right before landing on me. The animosity Logan felt toward me was no secret to the rest of the pack. He'd follow direct orders– eventually– but had no qualms about questioning each and every one before doing so.

I tried to give him grace. Loss and wounded pride had a special way of turning something sweet into something bitter, and his loss had been great. The position he spent his life preparing to fill was stolen by a friend ten years his junior. It was stolen by someone he mentored and trained.

It was stolen by me.

After the Pack Rite, I tried to mend our relationship–to restore some semblance of the relationship we'd once had– but I couldn't. He wouldn't let me. In truth,I'm not sure I could either, in his place. I'd publicly taken the Beta Luna position from him and defended it. *Twice.*

So I tried to be understanding, really I did, but it'd been a year and a half since I first became the Beta Luna. A year and a half of not-quite-whispered-insults. A year and a half of defiance and attempts at undermining my authority. My understanding was growing thin.

"Good evening, Enforcers," I greeted, ignoring my predecessor's questions completely. "Tell me what we know."

Fenrir stared pointedly at Logan before giving a slight shake of his head and turning to address me, "Evening, Beta. Thank you for coming."

"At such a leisurely pace."

I ignored that too.

"The enchantment was triggered approximately twenty-two minutes ago," Fenrir continued, "Logan was closest to the point of impact and arrived on scene. I joined him shortly after, along with Brody and Mia. We surveyed the perimeter from this side of the border and found a patch of disturbed brush about a half mile due north. No sign of lingering threats or tracks from this distance. No detectable scents."

I nodded, but my response was cut off by Logan's next comment.

"There may have been something detectable if we could've crossed the border to investigate twenty minutes ago instead of sitting around waiting for one of our *leaders* to arrive."

Fenrir scowled. Brody crossed and then uncrossed his arms before pulling at the hem of his shirt. Mia, as still as a boulder in the forest, looked as if she were hardly breathing.

"And yet you're still sitting," I said without looking at him. "We'll cross the border and see if there's anything deeper in the wood." Fenrir's eyes were still on Logan, now filled with more disappointment than anger, but he nodded his ascent.

"Mia, Brody you're with us. One of you keeps an eye to the north, the other to the south. Understood?"

Three confirmations rang through the night air. I turned north as the three Enforcers fell in around me. Then, and only then, did I address the still slouching, still sneering male flooding the space with his scent.

I used to be so fond of cloves.

"Logan?"

"Yes, *Beta*?" he spat the title, finally rising to his feet. He stretched his arms overhead and leaned his head toward one shoulder then the other. The movement exposed a strip of flat stomach marred by claw marks. My claw marks. "I presume you need me to check for tracks and report back to you before the Pack Leaders arrive? I'd hate for you to make a bad show of things and have nothing to report."

Logan took a step toward me, shoulders set, chin raised a fraction in the air. His eyes met and held mine.

"That won't be necessary," I deadpanned, feeling no pressure to drop his stare, "I need you to wait here for Ivy and Lucas. Bring them to meet us. Catch them up on the way."

He took a step back as his mouth fell open without words to accompany it. I didn't wait for his reply. I started north toward the area Fenrir described. Someone should have stayed to monitor the location until I arrived, but there was no use pointing it out now.

I shook off the fragment of guilt sitting on my chest as I walked past Logan. Someone truly did need to stay and wait for Ivy and Lucas, but if not for his poor attitude I would have given the task to one of the less experienced Enforcers. There were pressing matters to attend to and his defiance would only slow our progress.

He should be grateful that rather than strip him of the pride he'd managed to hold on to during his descent into self-destruction the past year and a half, I chose to leave him there to stew instead. Or at least that had been my plan.

A plan that went awry the moment Logan made a choice I could not ignore: he grabbed my arm.

"You are *not* leaving me behind like some messenger boy at your beck and call. I'm the best damn tracker in this pack and you know it." Decidedly not true. "Why don't *you* stay behind and wait for your wannabe mommy and daddy while I do what I should've been doing from the second I arrived–finding and eliminating this threat."

I pushed back the flames roiling beneath my skin that longed to flood to where he grasped my skin.

"I suggest you let go of my arm, *Enforcer*," I commanded. "Now."

Then Logan made his second mistake in as many minutes: he laughed.

The final thread of patience I'd clung to throughout the day snapped.

THE ROSE

"**P**rincess, I'd love to see you try to make—" The gurgling sound that escaped his mouth as my hand locked around his throat brought a small grin to my face even as a weight settled in my gut. No matter how many times we did this dance, he still chose the wrong steps. He insisted on forcing me to prove that, between the two of us, only one could control the other. It wasn't him.

It shouldn't have had to be this way.

I didn't regret taking the Beta Luna position from him. I was stronger than him, faster than him, and I *needed* to prove that even if I couldn't fully shift, I was not a liability to this pack. At least, not for that reason. My stomach dropped as I considered the one secret that could put me–us–at risk, but it would stay buried where I left it–in the ashes of a town long forgotten.

I wished it didn't have to be that way, but it did. I didn't revel in putting Logan of all people in his place, but I'd be lying if the smallest spark of satisfaction didn't flare inside me each time I proved I was anything but weak. Maybe *he* hadn't thought so before he'd left, but I'd proven it a thousand times over in his absence.

Each dig, each snide remark, each chuckle in the corridors grated against my nerves. I grinned and bore it all, and the knowledge that I was the stronger shifter was my reward. Maybe it came from the demon in me.

"It would seem," I said slowly, "that the night air has muddled your mind, Logan, or maybe it's too many shifts on patrol." His hands batted at my forearm, but I didn't release him. Instead, I descended my claws and let them dig into the stubble-studded skin of his neck. I didn't draw blood—yet.

"Maybe you need to take a break from guard duties and spend some time in the stable clearing your head, or perhaps the kitchen."

His eyes narrowed. His face grew redder until the shade bordered violet, and yet he refused to submit. I could have let him struggle. I could have tightened my grip and taken his breath until he slipped into unconsciousness.

Letting him struggle would only lead to more time being lost than had already been wasted. Rendering him unconscious would mean tasking a second Enforcer with staying behind. I did neither. To him, what I did instead was likely much worse.

I forced him to fall in line.

"Stop struggling, Enforcer," I commanded. I infused each syllable with the power my rank held over the other members of the pack. It left him no choice but to obey. "You will sit on this stump until the Alpha and Luna arrive. You will bring them to us, and you will do so swiftly. Do you understand?"

I watched him struggle to fight the order, but even if I hadn't earned the Beta Luna title, my level of dominance would always outrank his. It always had, I'd simply let him believe otherwise. I'd let everyone believe otherwise.

I loosened my grip on his throat to allow him to answer. I sent a quick prayer to whatever goddess was listening that he would fall in line. It'd barely been six months since his last challenge, and I didn't relish defeating him again.

"Do you understand me?" I repeated slowly.

"Yes," he gritted out between his grinding teeth.

"Yes, what?"

"Yes, Beta."

"Good." I let my claws score his neck as I released his throat. I moved past his hunched-over, coughing form. Any marks would heal by the night's end—they weren't nearly deep enough to scar—but they'd sting for at least the next hour. Sometimes pain delivered a clearer message than words.

I'd tried words. They weren't enough.

"I wish you'd never come to this pack."

And sometimes there was a pain that only words could inflict.

I should have kept walking. I should have pretended not to hear the half-whispered wish. I definitely shouldn't have turned back to kneel by his side, but I did.

"We cannot go on like this, Logan," I said low enough only the two of us would hear. "I won this position from you fairly and through the customs of our people. You have to let it go, both for the sake of the pack and yourself."

He said nothing in response, but lifted his gaze to meet mine. I thought I saw a flash of something akin to regret in them, but it disappeared as quickly as it came.

"It was luck," he said in a voice just as low. "You were lucky to beat me. I know I'm the stronger fighter–the stronger leader."

I knew my next words were cruel. For a moment I considered keeping them to myself, but if clarity only came with a tinge of cruelty, it was a price I'd have to pay.

I paused, then said in as gentle of a tone as I could manage, "You may believe that to be true for the first Pack Rite, but I didn't simply win the first battle between us. I also won the second, and then the third."

I shifted my weight to block him from the other Enforcers' view. Logan deserved to be put in his place when he stepped out of line. He didn't deserve for the others to see his expression crumble.

"You're still a leader in this pack. Its members look up to you–trust you," I continued, "so be better for them."

There were only twelve Enforcers appointed amongst nearly two hundred pack members. To be selected for the role was an honor in any pack, but to be selected in the Othniel Pack–the largest, strongest on the continent–bordered on prestige.

When he offered no response, I rose to my feet and left him where he knelt in the grass.

"They'll never fully accept you, you know. Not with what you are." My back tensed at the half-taunted truth. He had no idea what traits made me what I was. Latent was the least concerning among them. "*He* will never claim you as his mate. No self-respecting shifter will."

"And yet I'll still outrank you without one," I called without turning back. I kept my eyes fixed north as I strode past the waiting Enforcers toward the border.

If my lack of prospects for a mate was the only insult he could think grasp onto in a moment of desperation, I chose to consider it a compliment. At the very least it was a change from the usual, "She can't even shift," though I suppose he'd used a variation of that too.

Disappointingly unoriginal.

I didn't need the Alpha heir to claim me as his mate. The days of a female taking her rank from a male mate had long passed. Despite what *some* chose to believe, a Luna rose to her position the same way an Alpha rose to his–by earning it.

Before she and Lucas were anything more than friends, Ivy challenged her predecessor for her position and won. One day, when it was time, I'd do the same.

A Luna and an Alpha didn't need to be a mated pair to lead together, but most–really, all–chose to become one. The nature of their roles nearly forced it into existence. What else could be expected when two people worked together day in and day out? Each had an equal voice to the other. No decision, ruling, or plan could move forward if they were at odds. Beyond the requirements of their position, it was only natural they'd be drawn to one another. Power attracts power. Strength attracts strength.

"It's just ahead." Fenrir's deep tenor pulled me out of my head and back to the scene in front of me.

At first glance the woods were as usual: a compilation of

bushes and trees accompanied by the smell of dirt and freshly crinkled leaves. But then there were the finer details, like the half-snapped branch hanging by its bark, the leaves clustered around a small patch of dirt, and the faintest hint of something else—something wrong infesting the usually fresh air.

"Can you catch a scent?" I asked. Brody's sense of smell was unmatched in the pack, courtesy of his wolverine. It made him an invaluable tracker, and having him around made hiding my own heightened senses easier.

"It's faint but it's there," he confirmed, walking between where we stood and the border. "It's stronger in the brush than by the border. Whatever they did to try breaking through, they did it quickly."

He crouched down to the patch of dirt, picking the soil up and lifting it to his nose. His eyes closed as he sniffed it, and a crease began to form between his brows.

"It's strange," he said as he opened his icy blue eyes, "the scent is sour, putrid almost, like a gutted carcass left in the sun, but there's a hint of something earthy underneath."

Fenrir's face turned to stone.

My breath was stolen from me as panic's inky tendrils wrapped themselves around me from my head to my toes. It wasn't possible, I reminded myself. They were gone. There were hundreds of other explanations for the odor to be here. I was being paranoid—on edge for tomorrow's impending journey.

"Great imagery," Mia grumbled under her breath. "Next you'll be smelling vomit left on the ground." Hers and mine both, though admittedly for different reasons.

"Any sign we're dealing with more than one intruder?" I asked.

"Hard to say. The smell of rot is overpowering. It could be covering the scent of one or many."

"Can you follow it?" If he couldn't, I'd have to think of a reason to suggest heading northeast myself. The longer we waited the less likely we were to find anything of note. We were already losing time.

Brody stood, and the dirt fell between his fingers to rejoin the earth below. He turned to look east, deeper into the woods before saying, "The trail is faint, but it's there."

He looked at me, awaiting the order.

"Go," I told him. I nodded my head at Mia. "Go with him. If it's a rogue, they've likely fled from the area by now, but I'd rather we stayed in pairs beyond the border. The threat we know isn't always the only threat amongst us. We'll canvas this area once more, then meet you."

"Yes, Beta." They departed. Then it was just Fenrir and I, alone in the woods.

"You handled Logan well today," he praised, one corner of his bearded mouth raising. "We've let him rebel for quite long enough. He needs to fall in line or fall from the ranks. He's behaving like a petulant child."

"I think I recall it was your idea," I reminded him, "to make that petulant child an Enforcer, was it not?"

I'd planned to offer him the position myself before Fenrir approached me. As the pack's Head Enforcer, he was entitled to nominate which shifters filled the ranks. Everyone was confirmed by the Alpha and Luna, but a dispute was rare — if not entirely unheard of. I was happy to let him think it was solely his idea to appoint Logan, especially given the man's recent behavior.

"I prefer not to relive follies of my youth."

"Your youth?" I scoffed, "It's been less than two years' time!"

His eyebrows drew in as his eyes narrowed as he said, "Yes, my youth. I hadn't reached my fourth decade yet. A man learns a lot when he reaches that kind of milestone. I'll thank you to leave my mistakes in the past where they belong, unless you'd like to revisit a few of your own. I seem to recall an incident at Summer Solstice with an ancient urn you thought would make the perfect—"

"Alright," I cut him off, "Message received. No more trips to the past."

I refrained from pointing out I'd been nine when I tried to use that urn to heat the cider in the fire. He'd been thirty years older when he appointed Logan.

He chuckled, but the sound died as he scanned our surroundings. Concern was etched in each line drawn by his down-turned lips.

"You know where these signs may lead." He leaned and kept his voice low. Brody and Mia may be out of earshot but there was no guarantee Ivy and Lucas wouldn't arrive at the most inopportune time. If they overheard something they shouldn't, it would spell disaster for us both.

"That the rogues have begun basking in the blood of their prey to cover their scent?" I quipped, ignoring the sinking feeling in my chest. "Yes, and I find it a bit disturbing. It's at the very least unsanitary. Imagine how many pots of water they have to boil for their baths. I doubt they've discovered the joys of a water system yet."

I would forever thank any god or goddess who listened for the day they discovered how to distribute a vat of water heated by the fire throughout the compound. I'd choose a steaming bath over the wash basin every day if I could.

"This isn't a joke," Fenrir's words bordered a growl. His hand came down atop my shoulders, and I let him pull me toward him until our faces were less than a foot apart. "If you're discovered, I won't be able to save you this time. I won't even be able to save myself."

"It's not them." But it could be. "You know it's not. The demons were pushed to the Wastes. The elemental shifters are extinct."

I prayed my words held more confidence than my heart. The word *demon* had been plaguing the back of my mind since the putrid odor entered my senses. It could be something else–something foul, but not as foul as them, or they'd returned. I didn't know which was true. I only knew that if demons had surfaced among the Hidden realms testing borders, I'd be delusional not to think they could be coming for me. I'd spent a decade wondering if they would, but what good would it do to send Fenrir into a panic alongside me?

I was leaving tomorrow. If they knew I was here–if they were watching me, then any immediate danger would leave with me.

"Even if they weren't extinct," I continued more seriously, "you wouldn't need to save yourself. I would never reveal you know what I am. Ever. They'd have no reason to suspect otherwise. If the Alpha and Luna haven't discovered me over the years, no one would think you would have observed what they did not."

I'd never seen a grin full of sorrow until one appeared on his lips.

"And I'd never watch them execute you in silence. Ever," he promised solemnly. "So your secrecy would be for naught."

"You would have to. You'd lose your life, Fenrir. You'd lose Isaac. You'd lose the respect of every member in this pack and beyond."

As the heads of the realm's strongest pack, Ivy and Lucas sat on the Hidden Council amongst the leaders of the other courts. Treachery discovered under their rule would not go unnoticed.

"I'd lose the respect I have for myself by doing nothing, and Isaac would know in his heart what I did was right."

Stupidly stubborn, honorable man.

"Or we'd be forever immortalized. Me as an abomination, and you as a traitor. Isaac would live a life under scrutiny and be executed if he gave any indicator he knew the truth. Which could easily happen because he *does*."

"Or that." He dipped his head in a slow nod.

The thought of Fenrir and Isaac had my world tilting on its axis. I'd conjure a pillar of open fire with a hundred witnesses, expose myself a thousand times over, if it would mean saving them.

It would doom them instead.

When I first came to the pack, I had far less control over my power. I was more emotional, more volatile then. I tried so hard to suppress it, but I was terrified of being caught.

That fear only amplified the fire inside me. One day, one of the other children had made a particularly hateful comment about my inability to shift while we were running the obstacle courses. He'd hinted that maybe I'd been cast into the woods by my parents from the shame of having a latent child. So I did what any kid who felt like they could never belong did, I ran away.

They thought it cowardice, but I saw it as saving his miserable little life. I'd already woken to the destruction of one community. I would not be responsible for another.

Fenrir found me in the woods shortly after. I'd been sobbing, struggling to quiet the flames rolling up and down my arms. No matter what I tried—burning piles of leaves, shooting fire into the stream, plunging my ever-scorching hand into the mud—I couldn't stop. I was terrified. Terrified of being discovered and exiled, or worse. Terrified of hurting someone.

And then I saw him.

He stood maybe ten yards away, bracing himself on a nearby tree as his mouth hung open in shock. Looking back, it was miraculous really, that he didn't recoil in disgust at seeing me for what I had to be: demon born.

He didn't report me to the Alpha and Luna as protocol demanded, didn't attempt to drown me in the stream or tell me to leave pack lands and never return. Instead, he soothed and comforted me until the flames fell dormant.

And every day since, he risked his life by helping me keep mine.

"It's good then," I said, ignoring the tremor in my voice, "that they're extinct." And if they'd returned, I'd put them back in the ash-trodden graves from which they'd risen.

Fenrir looked at me from head to toe before his eyes landed on my hands. They were dotted with embers I hadn't felt come to the surface.

"Except they're not."

A knife to the heart would have been less painful.

"Extinct," I amended as I closed my hands into fists, quelling the fire on their surface, "with the exception of one, lone, elemental who means no harm."

"That we know of."

"We'd know if there were more."

"How?" Fenrir scoffed, "As easily as someone would know about you? If you've stayed hidden, do you think others would not be just as capable?"

Because if any had remained in the decade since I'd survived, after what I did, they would have come for me. Not that I could tell him that. Asking someone to keep one deadly secret was selfish. Asking them to keep a second would be unforgivable, and I had enough sins marring my soul without adding another.

"We just would." He opened his mouth, but I was quicker to speak. "It's not them. Our secrets are safe. Our biggest issue right now is figuring out why the rogues keep returning. It could all be unrelated, but that feels too coincidental to be true."

Maybe one or two attempts could be attributed to rogues looking to ransack an unsuspecting pack, but this was the third attempted breach in as many months. Previously, the intruders had left nothing behind; no broken branches, no trampled leaves, and certainly the scent of death to follow. Even thinking of the smell set me on edge.

But why break the pattern?

"They're trying to make us uneasy," I realized.

I straightened and looked around the scene again, my gaze lingering where Brody and Mia had disappeared only minutes before.

Damnit.

"Fenrir," I said with more force, "They're trying to make us uneasy. Uneasy enough to make a mistake."

"Mistakes like separating outside of the border." The blood drained from his face, his usual olive complexion turning pale.

I pulled my knife from its sheath, and then we were running.

THE ROSE

I cut through the trees, following their trail as quickly as I could.

Stupid.

I'd been stupid to think pairs were numbers enough to protect against a threat. I pushed my legs to go faster, Fenrir following a breath behind me. My fingers grew warmer as my heart rate grew more rapid, and I willed the fire threatening to spill from them to stay beneath my skin. Careless. Unacceptable. I was better than this. I had to be better than this.

They could've been surrounded. They could've been captured. They could've been—

They could've been crouched over a dead deer looking at me in alarm.

I ground to a halt, Fenrir's forty-plus years of honing his instincts the only thing preventing me from being flattened as he stopped behind me a few moments later. The two Enforcers shot to their feet, weapons drawn, and looked beyond our panting forms for what I'm sure was whatever threat they imagined we must have been fleeing. They'd find nothing in the darkness other than our own paranoid conclusions.

"Oh thank the goddess," Fenrir muttered with a sigh. From the corner of my eye, I saw him lace his fingers atop his head and look up at the star-speckled sky.

So," I began, my heart still beating violently against my rib cage. "Dead deer?"

Mia's eyebrows squished together as she watched me catch my breath. Thankfully, she didn't question our abrupt arrival aloud. The likelihood of me coming up with a reasonable explanation at that moment was about as likely as a block of ice holding its shape over a fire.

She returned her sword to its place across her back and confirmed, "Dead deer. It explains the smell. This thing is putrid."

That it was. It took a conscious effort not to gag standing this close to the body. Brody had kneeled down beside the animal to examine it more closely. He had a stomach of steel.

"She's large enough that if she wandered into the border she'd trigger the enchantment," Fenrir said with a tinge of relief coloring his voice. I wanted to join him in the feeling, but I couldn't.

He was right. The beast was surely large enough to trigger the enchantment but that explanation left too many unanswered questions in its wake. Did it die in the time it took us to reach its side? A smell this overpowering would surely take days to develop, would it not?

"Cause of death?" I asked.

"Looks like an infection in her rear leg." Brody beckoned

me closer, and I reluctantly kneeled by his side. His finger circled the air above the gaping wound. I would *not* let myself vomit.

"I can't make out the exact shape under all the puss." Nasty. "But I'd wager it's an animal bite. Maybe one of the wolves in the area got ahold of it. You know they love running the border. It makes them feel closer to Lucas."

I snorted and immediately regretted inhaling through my nose. I had a theory the local wolf pack stayed close to our border because they considered Lucas' wolf to be their Alpha. A theory he did not find amusing when I shared it over breakfast last year. Ivy, on the other hand, laughed so hard she fell off her stool.

"It makes sense," I said even though it didn't–not fully. "We should take her back to the healer to see if we can confirm it."

"Briar," Mia started, "I'm not trying to question you, but why are we worried about a deer and a wolf? I don't see the threat here. It got away, was injured, and stumbled into the border and sounded the alarm. Why do we care about the infection?"

"We might not," I acknowledged and returned to my feet. "But we can't deem it irrelevant without a proper investigation. Just because something appears harmless doesn't mean it can't do harm." Just look at me.

"So we're going to start conducting medical exams on any injured wildlife we find?" she asked skeptically. "It just seems like a lot of time and energy for a wolf bite."

"What if we're wrong and it's not a wolf bite? What if the rogues are testing a new poison? What if they lace their

27

swords and arrow with it, and the healers haven't concocted an antidote because we failed to investigate?"

She said nothing in response.

I continued, "And it's not just the infection. Look at the angle of her neck. Feel the lack of warmth emitting from her hide. Maybe this is nature taking its course, but I'd rather spend a few hours investigating an animal carcass than risk harm to the pack. Wouldn't you?"

"Yes, Beta," she said sheepishly and nodded her head, then muttered under her breath, "I still think we're likely worrying about a wolf."

I'd love to be worried about wolves. Wolves I could handle. They may not understand our words, but they understand our place in the dominance hierarchy–above them. This felt like something more, like an unknown enemy waiting to take us by surprise the second our guard was lowered.

My gaze darted around the surrounding area, looking for any sign another predator had been there, or may still be there, lurking in the shadows. I saw nothing. The forest was eerily still. Eerily silent.

"I don't like this, Briar," Fenrir said, drawing to my side. His keen eyes were narrowed and bore directly into mine. I didn't like it either, but lingering in the woods wasn't likely to improve the situation.

"We'll take her to the healers."

Brody took the animal in his arms, careful not to touch the wound, and began the trek back to the compound. Fenrir and Mia fell into step behind him with Mia keeping an exceptionally wide berth between her and the animal. I didn't blame her.

I didn't want to linger so long as to be left behind. If they encountered a threat on the way back to our borders, I needed to be with them. I moved swiftly, looking up through the treetops. No one was ready to pounce from their canopies.

After pacing a few meters from where the body had been found, I looked behind the thick tree trunks and wrestled through the bushes. That was when I saw it: a small pool of water at the base of a shrub.

It hadn't rained in two weeks.

"Bri?" Mia called from up ahead. "Are you all right?"

"Fine!" I called back.

I abandoned the small pool and broke into a jog to catch up to them. Fenrir's questioning gaze found me. I gave him a brief, easy-going grin that seemed to placate him enough to nod his head and look forward once more.

I could lie to myself that there was nothing to be concerned about, that there were a million reasons for the water to be there that had nothing to do with elemental magic. A hunter could've spilled their water flask. The area could've been flooded during the last storm, and that small puddle was all that remained. Even a rogue could be staging the scene to play mind games with us.

The last thought was a stretch, but it could have a smidge of truth to it. The rogues grew more restless with each passing year. It was obvious to anyone paying attention that the packless cast-aways and rebels had begun to form their own kind of hierarchy away from society's eye. They were angry. They were rejected. History had shown time and time again that angry, rejected people became one of two things: cutthroat or cunning.

The more I considered it, the more likely it felt to be true. The rogues would know that smell, eerily reminiscent of demons, would set off those of us who remembered the atrocities from a decade prior. The water was just the second step and their fabrication. But why? What was the end goal? What did they gain by drawing us out of the territory? They didn't use it as a chance to attack. So, what purpose did it serve?

My frustration only grew the longer I thought of it. The walk back to the border was silent. As we approached, I moved to the front of our group and lifted my hand to the shimmering air. It was solid against my skin. Before the enchantment opened, our territory would appear to be an open glen, surrounded by the wood. An intruder would run against the border but would be unable to see any details or the layout of a compound. It was an invaluable charm a mage gifted to our pack when we came to her coven's aid against an ogre a few years back. Magic was a gift, unless you gained it by consorting with demons.

Then it was a death sentence.

We crossed into the safety of our territory just as Ivy and Lucas came jogging into view with Logan a few strides behind. The Luna's ivory hair glinted in the moonlight. Both were in their human form and fully clothed. Another delay, but at least this one was a better use of time than a game of cat and mouse through pack grounds. Shifters were no strangers to nudity, but that didn't mean we didn't prefer to be covered by *something*–whether that something was clothing, feather, fur, or scales was less of a concern.

"What have you found?" Lucas's deep tenor boomed across the distance.

Fenrir looked to me, awaiting my go-ahead before recapping the events of our investigation. The Alpha and Luna were both experts at masking their reactions, but I'd spent years cataloging the minute changes in their expressions and body language. When Fenrir described finding the deer, already dead after following the scent trail left for us, Lucas' lip twitched. Ivy shifted her weight to her left foot.

They were nervous.

As Fenrir's recount came to a close, Ivy turned her attention to me. "Working theory?"

"A wolf–" Mia started.

"Someone orchestrated it."

All three Enforcers at my side looked at me with various degrees of shock. From where he still stood near the Pack Leaders, I expected to see derision on Logan's face. I wouldn't have been surprised had he scoffed at my conclusion or rolled his eyes, but he didn't. He waited for me to continue with keen eyes, and a slight tilt to his head.

"What brought you to that conclusion?" Ivy asked.

I pointed out the same facts I'd told Mia in the forest and added my theory about the rogues without mentioning the demons or the pool of water. For them to draw their own conclusions about the scent was one thing. Me putting the idea of demons resurfacing in their mind, raising suspicions that could draw more attention to my own secrets was another.

"I just can't see the rogues organizing well enough to come at us this strategically." Lucas rubbed his jaw as he considered the possibility. "Ambush a carriage full of supplies or try to break into one of the smaller pack's territory? Sure. But to come to *our* border and try to lay a trap? It's difficult to imagine."

"I have to agree with Lucas," Ivy said. "I acknowledge the circumstances are strange, but I'm struggling with what motive someone would have to do this."

She and Lucas started thinking through other possibilities like an angry pack or the deer falling, breaking its neck, and a predator feasting on it. Brody, Fenrir, and Mia occasionally interjected, but I only half paid attention to what they said. My focus was fixed on Logan instead. I could see it in his eyes, he agreed with me.

Say something. I silently urged him. *Pretend it wasn't me who suggested it, and say something because you know I could be right.*

Even if it wasn't the rogues, it had to be someone. The more intricate the design, the more likely there's a designer. There were too many oddities to be inconsequential. *Say something.*

"I agree with Briar."

All conversation stopped.

"What did you just say?" Mia asked with a nervous laugh. "I don't think I heard you correctly."

"I'd rather not," Logan deadpanned, but added, "The rogues have every motive to do something like this."

Fenrir's elbow dug into my side. I didn't turn to him. If I stopped focusing on the Pack Leaders and Logan, I may snap out of whatever dreamscape we'd entered for him to side with me

"Go on," Ivy said, her eyebrows nearly reaching her hairline.

"Many of them may be disorganized but it would only take one powerful leader to bring them—even a few of them—back into order." He lowered his head in thought for a moment then directed his next words directly to Lucas, "And I can think of at least one rogue capable of positioning himself as their Alpha who has a grudge against this pack. Can't you?"

Logan's father, Malcolm Grey, and Lucas' best friend. At least, he was at one time. Attempted murder did tend to put a strain on a relationship. Driven by jealousy and greed, Malcolm had challenged Lucas for his position as Alpha and lost, but he couldn't accept his fate. Instead, he tried to poison him. He failed.

Lucas was within his rights to have him executed, but chose to send him into exile to spare his family the grief. I wish he could have spared them the shame.

"You think this is Malcolm?" the Alpha asked gravely.

"I don't know." Logan cracked his knuckles and rolled his head from one shoulder to another. "I'm not saying he's the only person who could do something like this or who'd have motive to attack the pack, but he proves Briar's theory is possible. It's not like we've never cast out a strong shifter, let alone those banished from another pack. We may not be easy prey, but we are the most attractive prize for someone ambitious enough to try taking it."

Ivy and Lucas lowered their voices to discuss the added

perspective Logan shared. I caught his eye from where I still stood on the other side of the Pack Leaders and gave him a small nod of thanks. His lips turned into a sneer, but it was a small one. My own turned into the tiniest of grins when he nodded back.

"Have we entered the afterlife?" Fenrir leaned in and asked under his breath.

"If we have, I'm disappointed. I really hoped there'd be hot springs and cake," I whispered back and glancing at Brody added, "And preferably no animal carcasses."

Poor Brody would probably have this smell clinging to him for a week.

"Why don't you go ahead and take that to the healer's apothecary," I suggested. "Regardless what theory we align on, we'll still need their examination to confirm it."

He took two steps in that direction before he was stopped.

"You really are arrogant, aren't you?" Logan asked. I sighed. For a moment there, things were going so well. "Who are you to give orders when the Alpha and Luna are present?"

His interjection stopped the two leaders' conversation and drew their attention to us. Lucas wore a pinched expression. Ivy bit her lip.

"I'd hardly call that an order," I said. "And even if it were, I'd have every right to give it."

"What if we'd had more questions after you'd sent him inside?" Was he serious?

"Unless there's a secret portal that whisks him away to a far off land, I think we'd be able to find him," I observed dryly. "He's been holding a dead animal for the past twenty minutes, in case your nose missed its presence."

Insulting his senses wasn't my most mature moment, but he'd been immature first. I was merely meeting him where he was at. How very kind of me.

"If holding it is part of fulfilling his duty then it's one he should happily bear," Logan spat. A quick glance at Brody's expressionless face assured me he was unfazed by the former Beta's outburst.

"And he bore it without complaint." I drew on whatever scrap of patience the suns and moon would grant me. I planned to let it go. Truly, I did. But then Logan rolled his eyes, and I simply could not. "Why don't you take it from him then?"

"I'm not doing that." His laugh of derision set me teeth on edge.

"And why is that, Enforcer?" Lucas asked.

Mia and Fenrir had less success hiding their grins than me.

"I—," he stumbled over his words as he searched for a viable explanation for defying an order from his Beta, "I wouldn't want to further contaminate the body. We've probably already altered it more than we should. It would've been better for us to leave it where it was found and return with a healer to examine it."

"If we left it in the woods, any other predator could've stumbled upon it and claimed it for their next meal. I doubt adding your scent to her skin will have any influence on our findings, unless you intend to hold it so tightly you break bones or burst organs." I dismissed his excuse with a wave of my hand.

He still didn't reach to take it from Brody.

"Take the deer, Logan, and bring it inside," I ordered. "Now."

He didn't move.

"Is there a problem, Enforcer?" Lucas asked in a deceptively calm voice. Ivy remained silent at his side. Logan sent a scathing look at me before responding.

"Of course not, Alpha."

He strode off toward the main lodge, rotting carcass in hand. I hope the smell ruined his clothes or even stuck in his hair. It'd serve him right to have folks grimacing when he drew too near for weeks to come. Maybe I could pay a witch to make it stick forever.

Ivy turned to the remaining Enforcers. "Excellent work tonight. The rest of your shift on patrol has been filled. Head home and rest up. We'll plan the next steps once we hear from the healers."

Fenrir, Brody, and Mia left after being dismissed, leaving me alone with the Alpha and the Luna. I closed the distance between us until I stood between them both, a foot or so of space separating us. Lucas smiled down at me, dimples appearing on his often unyielding face.

"So, Little Warrior." He draped an arm over my shoulder and pulled me into his side before dropping a kiss on the top of my head. "Logan is still having trouble letting go, I see."

At least he'd never tried to poison me.

"And that brings a smile to your face?" I asked, pulling away from his hold.

"Absolutely." He smiled wider. "I'm imagining the many ways you'd remind him why he has no choice if you weren't abandoning me tomorrow. What am I supposed to do with both you and Grayson away?"

"I'm sure the pack will keep you plenty occupied in our absence," I said dryly, then added, "You could always focus on keeping Logan from turning even more of my pack mates against me while I'm gone."

"He just needs time." Ivy's voice was as stiff as her shoulders. "Logan is a valued member of this pack. He's done so much for all of us, we can extend our grace to him."

Lucas sighed but didn't contradict her. They led the pack as one, but as her former Beta, Lucas would defer to Ivy's judgment on dealings with Logan. As her current Beta, I was forced to do the same.

"I suppose I can continue to bear it," I said with a teasing lilt, "but it's going to cost you." Lucas' chuckle vibrated through his chest to my shoulder as we began walking back to the house.

"I'll be sure to get your payment to you before you leave."

"It's hard to believe it's already time for you to enroll at the Academy," Ivy said, with a dreamy smile on her face. "Grayson will be so happy to have you there."

She sounded so certain, I didn't have the heart to tell her that was unlikely to be the case. I had heard her son's true feelings for me with my own ears, and they were far from affectionate.

Thinking about my past blindness toward him as we

walked, a phantom of my shame threatened to rise from the deep well I'd battled for years to force it into.

Once upon a time, I'd been Grayson Pierce's shadow. At age eight, I clung to his side and refused to let go. At age twelve, he was the first person I called a friend at the compound, and he took me under his wing while I adjusted to the boisterousness of pack life—a drastic contrast to isolation in the woods.

In my adolescent eyes, he'd been perfect. Cunning, strong, and handsome, there was no hope that my young, damaged heart would resist him. Growing up, Ivy often hinted that I would be the perfect mate for him one day, and I had preened at the thought that I could be his match. For what pauper turned princess didn't long to find her prince? At least that's how the stories always went.

Then one day, I'd gone off to find him— probably planning to invite him to play at the creek or show him a new bauble or treasure I'd found— only to happen across a conversation with his father that reminded me of a crucial fact I'd forgotten while playing house with my newfound family: I was no princess.

"You and Briar have spent a lot of time together lately." I watched as the Alpha smiled. "Any developments you'd care to share?" I'd entered the library intending to call out and greet them both but froze at Lucas' words. Nothing good ever came from eavesdropping, but I couldn't tamp down the small thread of joy I felt at his question, and I surely couldn't interrupt before hearing Grayson's answer.

"I'm sure I don't understand your meaning," Grayson deadpanned.

"Don't be coy. There's nothing to be ashamed of—nothing you'd need to hide from me," Lucas continued, and I drew closer as he looped an arm around his son's shoulders. "If you're concerned I wouldn't approve, don't be. I wholeheartedly do. She's growing into a beautiful girl, and she adores you. I can't think of a more amiable mate for you to pursue."

My heart soared at the compliment, but it quickly plummeted when Grayson shrugged off his father's arm and ran a hand over his inky hair as he paced a few steps before turning back.

"She's just another kid in the pack," he bit out, driving a knife into my heart with each word he spoke. "She trails after me, I don't call her to my side." I'd taken another step back into the shadows, moving more fully behind the curtain at the edge of the corridor.

"She's only three years your junior," Lucas dismissed with a wave of his hand. "And you've never seemed bothered by the attention she gives you."

"What would you have me do? Tell her to go away? When she came here, you asked me to watch over her—help her acclimate to the pack. I've done as you asked. I've indulged her every whim, every adventure, every request to tag along or stay by my side. I'll continue to do so, but you cannot ask me to give her more than I've already given."

"Look at you, your cheeks are heated and you're downright flustered." The Alpha laughed, but I'd found no humor in it. I still didn't. "If you're not interested in the girl, then so be it. I just thought there might be something there. My mistake, but have you considered how you'll feel when it's someone else at her side? Can you truly imagine someone other than her as your mate?"

"Someone like her will never be my mate," he declared in a tone so final, that it may as well have been written in stone. "A pack will crumble under weak leadership. She'd be a liability to us all, and I'll have no part in making us vulnerable."

I didn't stay to hear the rest of the conversation. Instead, I backed away slowly and escaped to my room, having gained a phantom knife lodged deep in my gut.

Looking at his parents now, all I could think to say was, "It's been a long time."

And I wasn't anyone's shadow anymore.

4

THE ROSE

"Concentrate!" As if I had a choice.

I'd like to see Fenrir juggle spheres of fires before sunrise in a field, surrounded by rain-deprived grass and trees, to see how well he concentrated. Maybe I'd be the one yelling orders and tossing things for him to dodge and see if he fared any better than I had my first time.

"Is this really necessary?" I asked, side stepping from the path of a thrown dagger. The blade had been dulled, but the impact would still leave a nasty bruise. "We've been doing this five mornings a week for seven years, and I haven't lost control of the spheres for half of that."

An occasional spark or two? Sure. But a complete loss of control? Never.

"It's necessary now more than ever," he implored. "You risk more than just discovery at the Academy. Inter-realm relations are strenuous at best these days. And you don't just represent the pack, you represent—"

"I know, I know," I said exasperatedly, "I represent the

entire shifter community in the new age." As if I needed another reminder that my every movement, every choice could be watched, noted, and used against me by the other realms or even my own pack mates.

Every child of the Hidden Realms' elite had entered the Iolite Academy when they came of age for more than two hundred years. It was founded to educate the next generation of leaders and bolster inter-realm relations, but an opportunity to create an alliance is also an opportunity to create an enemy. I was no one's child, but I confirmed my place at the Academy when I challenged Logan and won.

"You can't show weakness," he continued to lecture and began to pace. I took that as my cue that we were done for the day. I walked over to my water skein as he continued, "No matter what's thrown at you, no matter how you feel or what you have to do, you are impenetrable. Nothing can get beneath your skin."

His hands were a frenzy of movement in the air now, and I half expected a sheen of sweat to coat his skin as though he'd been the one training for the past hour.

"Fenrir." I waited until he stopped pacing and looked at me, the fear in his heart reflecting in every line of his face. "If you keep fixating on the many ways I can screw this up, you're going to give yourself more gray hair than you're already sporting, and while you look very distinguished with a tinge of gray, I don't think you're ready to look like a grandfather before you're fifty."

His eye roll confirmed I'd successfully distracted him from his doom spiral of what-ifs. Good. There was only space for one of us to be anxious today and considering he got to stay here while I trekked across the continent to unseat a Luna in her pack, it didn't get to be him.

"Fine." He came up behind me and rested a hand on each of my shoulders. "I do believe you can do this, you know."

I snorted.

"It sounded like it," I said dryly, but I smiled as I spoke. His worry was his care. His fear was his way of shielding me from harm.

"I do," he said more emphatically. "It's my job to give you counsel, but that doesn't mean I think you're incapable of making your own decisions."

"If you say so," I said with a chuckle. "I'll try to use sound judgment while we're apart, though I'd wager your quill will stay plenty busy keeping tabs on me through your son while I'm away."

"I've been thinking about that." He didn't bother denying my observation. "I would never presume to tell you what to do–"

"Oh, of course not."

"But I really think you should appoint Isaac as your Beta," he instructed and began to pace. "No one will question a Luna and her Beta disappearing together. They'll assume you're training or seeing to pack business not suited for the ears of others. Furthermore, he–"

"Okay," I agreed, but he didn't hear me.

"– has exceptional attention to detail and intuition which will–"

"I said, okay, Fenrir."

"– be paramount in navigating pack politics and relations with the other realms. Now I know you may have already–"

"Fenrir!" He halted his back and forth to look up at me in alarm.

"I was already planning to offer him the Beta Luna position." He pursed his lips before nodding more to himself than to me.

"Right," he drew out, "of course you were. He's the natural choice."

"He'll make an excellent Beta," I agreed, and he would. Not just because he knew my secret, but because he was as steady as a rock in a storm. If the world turned to chaos, it was Isaac I'd want facing it beside me.

"I know he will," Fenrir said, a proud smile stretching across his lips that reminded me so much of his son's expression after setting a new record in the obstacle course–a record I broke not half a year later.

"You're quite a confident family."

"Better to be confident in the face of a threat than uncertain. A cunning opponent will sense both but only benefit from one."

"I'll keep that in mind." I raised my hands to begin braiding the front half of my hair away from my face.

"You need to," he said gravely. "We were lucky Isaac didn't report you while he came to terms with what he discovered. If someone else realizes who–realizes *what*–you are, we may not be so lucky a second time."

Isaac learned my secret just days after Grayson had left for the Academy. He'd been too observant. He noticed Fenrir sneaking off into the woods occasionally and decided to follow him on a day we were training in this very meadow—a typical curious cat if I'd ever met one. He'd stepped out in front of us, just as I was conjuring a ball of fire in my palm for target practice against a nearby boulder.

Once he stopped screaming about demons, death, and damnation—you know, the usual topics surrounding my kind—his dad lectured him about putting his nose where it didn't belong, and tried to frighten him with the threat of what would happen if he breathed a word of it to anyone. He'd been begrudgingly sworn to secrecy.

His horror had cut me deeper than any blade ever could. I understood the reaction—I even expected it—but watching someone I considered a friend look at me in revulsion and fear was a blow that flattened me, even though I saw it coming. I wanted to be strong and unyielding in the face of adversity, but as he and his father argued over the morality of my very existence, I failed to stop the tears dripping down my face.

Were years of sharing secrets, playing in the halls, and training together so meaningless, one revelation could transform it all to dust? Was I so inherently repulsive—so unworthy—as to deserve instant vilification without trial, testimony, or trust?

I stood there, not five yards from the quarreling pair. I had an epiphany: I was weak. Weak to be so dependent on the affection and approval of others. I didn't need them. I only needed myself. The rest would be ancillary.

After what felt like hours of watching them in silence, Isaac finally looked at me. He ceased his protests. He just stared at me, drinking in whatever he found looming in the pits of my eyes. I didn't look away. I met his gaze and steeled myself against whatever ignorance-born venom would spew from his mouth even as tears continued to leak from my eyes. I kept waiting, but the words never came. Instead, he dipped his chin to his chest.

"Fine," he'd said on a breath. "I'll say nothing of this." Then he'd left.

I'd spent the next week with my breath half-held, waiting for him to break his word and the Enforcers to come drag me from my bed in the middle of the night, but he never did and they never came.

Our once lighthearted friendship had morphed first into an ocean of silence, but then, after months of tepid tiptoeing, we evolved. It started with Isaac sitting next to me in the dining hall each meal. Not conversing, just coexisting. A week later, he would nod at me in the halls as our paths crossed. Another week and he lingered on the outskirts of my sessions with Fenrir. Eventually, he reclaimed the roles of sparring partner, confidante, and friend.

In many ways, we'd grown closer from the time he'd discovered me until he left to join Grayson at the Academy last year, but I'd never forget the revulsion on his face when he'd first seen me. It ran through my mind every time I even fleetingly considered confiding in Ivy. If she ever looked at me that way, I don't know how I'd bear it.

I shook my head at the thought and refocused on the man behind me now, in the present.

His hands fell from my shoulders as I turned to face him.

"Do whatever it takes," he said in a deadly serious tone.

"No matter what you have to do or whoever you may need to do it to. Do you understand?"

My blood turned to ice as I took in his meaning. I'd killed before, and I would kill again, but to take the life of an innocent? Of that even I was incapable. I already had the blood of too many on my hands. One more would stain them red for eternity.

"It won't come to that," I promised.

"I hope it doesn't." Then with a tight smile, he took his hands off of me and said, "I should let you head back to get ready. I'll see you at the send-off."

I moved to collect the dagger, stones, and other weapons from the training session, but Fenrir waved me off. He'd gather the training supplies and bring them back to the compound. It'd give me time to take a much needed bath, he'd said. A quick self-sniff proved he was right, but I made a gesture in the air as I walked away all the same. His laugh echoed against the surrounding trees.

I SHOULD HAVE GONE STRAIGHT to my bedchamber to wash this morning's grime from my skin, but my feet carried me in the opposite direction instead. The hallways were dimly lit as I made my way to the apothecary, and the first stirrings of life reached me from behind closed doors as I passed. Soon my pack mates would be flooding the halls as they set about their daily tasks and responsibilities. I wanted to be back in my bedchamber readying for the day's journey before that happened.

Someone seeing me pay a visit to the healers would have more than one tongue asking questions. I'd once gone to have a cut stitched and by the time I left the apothecary, not twenty minutes later, there were already rumors I'd been poisoned, was gravely ill, or covertly collecting a treatment for one of the Pack Leaders. I gave a final glance around the halls before taking the three shallow steps down to the apothecary's entrance and pushing the iron laden door open.

The only light in the near-windowless room came from the three half-melted candles on the High Healer's desk. Her head rose from the documents scattered across it at my arrival, a mug of steaming liquid cradled in her hands.

"Good morning, Helena." The bird-shifter looked at me over the glasses perched along the bridge of her nose and leaned back in her chair.

"Beta Briar. I take it that it's you I have to thank for that monstrosity contaminating my clinic." She nodded her head to where the doe splayed across one of the sick beds. It was difficult to see in the low lighting, but the stench was even more repugnant than it had been the night before.

As Helena raised her mug to her lips, I had to ask, "How can you keep anything down with that smell in the air?"

She swallowed and said, "Thirty years of death, decay, and infection tends to steel one's stomach."

Or maybe her sense of smell had been destroyed from the ever-present burn of antiseptic.

"Have you had a chance to examine the body?" I approached the side of her desk and leaned against it, only to straighten at her scowl. Best not to anger those with the skills to kill you without leaving a trace of foul play.

"In the five minutes I've been here?" She reached to straighten a paper I'd inadvertently crinkled on the edge of her desk. "No, I haven't. I'll take a look after the morning clinic, but I'll remind you I'm a healer not an expert in the anatomy of fauna."

"Oh come on, Helena," I said with a cheeky grin. "Don't tell me you've never treated a deer shifter over the years. You're far too experienced for me to believe it."

"I, in fact, have not." She sniffed and raised her nose in the air slightly. "Though I suppose I have seen to an elk or two. There may be some overlap."

My smile grew.

"I have no doubt you'll be able to find us some answers. I'll leave you to it." I knocked my knuckles on her desk as I turned to go, earning a final disapproving glance.

"I'll have Fenrir send a copy of the report sent to the Academy when it's ready. It's a nasty wound, but I do suspect we'll find the natural food chain to be the source of it," she grumbled as I walked away.

"You may be right." I suspected she was wrong. "But I'd like it confirmed all the same. We can't be too careful when it comes to the safety of our borders." And the pack mates residing within them.

She grunted before calling, "Goddess guide you on your journey, Beta. The Academy is no tranquil place."

So everyone continued to warn me.

"Then it's a good thing I'm no tranquil woman."

5

THE ROSE

I hadn't had time for a bath, and I was more than a little
cranky to have missed the luxury.

The trip to see Helena, however brief and ultimately
unproductive, cost me precious minutes I could've spent
basking in a warm tub. Instead, I made due with the wash
basin and a pitcher. It'd taken longer than I'd like to comb
through the damp tangles of my hair, but I'd made quick
work of braiding the front of it away from my face. I left the
rest to hang down my back before dressing in my black
leathers and pulling on my boots. I considered it a perk I'd
failed to remove my knives from them the night before.

By the time I grabbed my bags and closed the door
behind me, I headed toward the sound of laughter ringing
from the front hall. I was cutting it close. Surely there were
less than ten minutes to spare before the portal was due to be
opened. When I turned the final corner, a little body ran into
me from the side, wrapping its arms snugly around my torso.

A flushed, smiling face peered up at me under a mass of brown curls. "I caught you, Beta Briar!"

I laughed and dropped my bags to pick her up and spin her around, loving the high-pitched giggles that echoed across the stone walls of the corridor. "You certainly did!"

I perched the still giggling girl on my hip and bopped her nose with a finger.

"When did you grow so big?" I teased her, "I feel like I just spun a bag of stones around. Are you planning to join our ranks sometime soon, and you forgot to tell me?"

"No!" she exclaimed through her laughter. "I'm only four, silly! I can't rank anything yet."

"Oh my mistake," I said in a faux serious tone, "I thought maybe you'd turned sixteen and forgotten to invite me to all your birthday parties. I was going to be sad I missed all the treats."

"I'd never forget to invite you, Bri Bri," she promised with a sweet grin, lifting her hand to run over the braids on my head. "You're my best friend, but don't tell Ollie. It'd hurt his feelings and he might not play with me anymore."

"I'll keep it between us," I promised and placed the hand not securing her to me to my heart.

"Thanks," she exhaled dramatically. "That would've been a dis-bastard."

"I think you mean disaster, dear one," I gently corrected, holding in the bout of laughter threatening to burst from my lips.

"Nuh-uh, it's definitely dis-bastard," she said, shaking her little head at me. "I heard my daddy say it." Of course she had.

"Adeline!" His voice boomed from down the hall, and she gave me a sheepish look as she turned to face him.

Logan stopped short at the sight of his daughter in my arms, back stiffening, chin lifting.

"Hello, Enforcer," I greeted cordially, setting Adeline on her feet and running a hand over her hair as she looped an arm around one of my legs and leaned against it.

"Beta." He inclined his head toward me, behaving far more civilly in front of his daughter than in front of the other Enforcers.

"Daddy," she said exasperatedly, "where have you been? I've been waiting for you for ages!"

"I've been trying to catch up to you calling your name," he spoke in a stern voice, but I saw the corners of his mouth raise ever so slightly as he gazed at his little girl.

"You were too slow." She shrugged. "I had to catch my Bri Bri before she left for her adventure without my hugs."

"I'm glad you caught me, Adeline," I said, glancing at Logan quickly before settling back on her, "But you need to listen to your father and wait for him before running through the compound alone, okay?"

Surprise flashed through Logan's eyes, and I fought the urge to roll my own. I hadn't undermined him in front of Adeline before I'd won the Beta position from him, I certainly wasn't going to do it now. Our frustrations with each other didn't change the fact he was an excellent father, nor did it change that I adored his daughter.

"Fine." She drew out the word and tilted her head up at me.

"Do you really have to go?" she asked, her bottom lip

quivering ever so slightly, eyes shining. I dropped to one knee so we were nearly eye level and took her soft, little hands in mine.

"I really do," I told her. Her chin dropped to her chest, but I used one crooked finger to tilt it up until she was looking at me again. "I'll be back though."

"Promise?'

"Promise."

"Fine," she agreed, then narrowed her eyes and added, "And when you're back we'll do our Saturdays again?"

"I'm not sure I can do that, dear one." Though I wished I could. The likelihood of Logan welcoming me into his home for a Saturday meal was about as likely as a kelpie drowning. "But seeing you and getting one of your hugs will be my top priority, okay?"

"Okay," she agreed sadly before wrapping her arms around my neck and squeezed tightly. She put her face to my ear and said in what I think was meant to be a whisper, "You're my very favorite person in the whole wide world, Bri Bri. I'm going to be just like you when I grow up."

I cleared my throat against the ball of emotion her words caused. "That's one of the best compliments anyone could ever give me. Thank you."

I dropped a quick kiss on the top of her head and returned to my feet, sniffling a bit to hide my reaction to her. I didn't need Logan adding 'too emotional' to his list of reasons I was unfit to be Beta.

Adeline gave me one final, watery look, and rushed into her father's arms. He held her tightly to him with one hand cupping the back of her head that she hid in the crook of his neck. I didn't want to draw out the goodbye longer than necessary. Hopefully, once I was gone, she'd return to playing with Oliver or find a treat to lift her spirits.

I gathered my bags back into my arms and started to pivot back in the direction I'd been heading when Adeline had found me, but froze when Logan called my name. I looked over my shoulder to meet his eyes. To my surprise, he lowered them after only a few moments.

"Have a safe journey," he said through a mild grimace. "Maybe when you get back we could do breakfast or something. Maybe."

He turned on his heel and quickly exited the way he came, Adeline waving her hand at me over his shoulder as they went. After I picked my jaw up from the floor I continued my journey to the front hall. When I reached it, it was filled with people passing through or chatting in clusters.

"Afternoon, Beta!"

"Safe travels today. Keep an eye out for any ruffians on the road."

"Beta, we're going to miss you so much! Have a safe trip!"

At least half of my pack mates who had shown up to send us on our way. My path was blocked every few feet by hugs, well-wishes, and handshakes. I thanked and nodded my way through the crowd until I reached the Alpha and Luna standing hand in hand by the doorway.

"You look ready for battle, Briar," Lucas observed dryly, only the glint in his eye letting onto his teasing. "Are you expecting a fight today?"

"A wise old man once told me I should always be ready

for a fight." I mimicked his dry tone and said, "You never know if a rustle in the woods is a bunny or a chimera." Ivy snorted beside him.

"An old man, now am I?" His laugh echoed through the room. "I guess I deserve that."

"At least I called you wise."

He cupped my face briefly before letting his hand fall back to his side. Truthfully, Lucas had yet to reach his forty-second year and looked every bit as youthful. The faint whisper of lines beginning to form around his eyes was the only indicator of his age.

"I'm going to miss you, little warrior," he said more softly. "I would tell you to take care of everyone at the Academy for me, but I already know you will. Oh, I almost forgot."

Behind him, the bags were being loaded into the carriage and the horses were being saddled for our journey. He walked over to one of the rucksacks and pulled out two wrapped parcels.

"I have something for you." He held them out to me and dropped them into my open hands.

"What are they?" I couldn't exactly open them with both hands occupied. I brought one up to my nose and breathed in the lovely aroma of vanilla.

"You packed me a piece of cake?" My smile stretched from one side of my face to another at the thought.

"I packed you *two* pieces of cake," he said proudly. "I was thinking you could give one of them to Grayson." I froze, willing my smile to stay in place.

"Oh." Not one of my most intelligent responses. "Thank you. I'll make sure he gets it and let him know it's from you."

"I thought maybe you two could eat them together," Lucas rushed to say. "As I remember it, slices of cake often went missing with only a trail of crumbs left in their place. Maybe you could share a few pieces again and reconnect?"

"Leading is difficult," Ivy interjected softly, "but it's easier with a partner you can lean on."

Do not ask me to give more than I have already given.

I pushed the memory away.

"We think you'll make an exceptional pair." The hope in Lucas' eyes filled me with guilt.

"We'll do our best, both to serve the Iolite pack and to represent the Othniel pack well." And I believed we would, but we weren't going the kind of pair they hoped we'd become. I lifted the cakes in thanks, and walked past the couple to place them back in one of the bags for our journey. I'd decide if I was sharing with Grayson after I got there.

Lucas remembered our childhood antics correctly, though at the time I'd thought him unaware. Making friends as the new kid who was found wandering alone in the woods wasn't easy. I hardly spoke to anyone, but I'd speak to Grayson. He'd sneak into the kitchen and steal us treats to eat hidden in a corner of the library. He could've been doing anything else with anyone else, but instead, he stayed with me. I loved him for it, and that's when I knew: I'd always be by his side.

Until I wasn't.

Cake securely packed in my rucksack, I looked back to his parents.

"I hate goodbyes," Ivy lamented as she took my hand in hers, "but I'm so excited for you. I hope you know how proud we are to have you as a leader in this pack, and a member of this family."

My throat tightened as silver pools gathered in the bottom of her eyes. I wanted to throw my arms around her neck and tell her how much I'd miss her, but I settled for giving her hand a gentle squeeze instead. She leaned closer and whispered, "Remember, no matter what happens when you arrive, show no weakness. You are the rightful Luna of that pack and you will demand their respect. To disrespect you is to disrespect the pack, and to disrespect the pack..." She trailed off but her meaning was clear. To disrespect the pack would be a grave mistake.

"I understand."

"I know you do. Give Grayson this for me." She leaned in and pecked my cheek. "And tell him to write more often." I would pass on the request to write but nothing else.

"Right then," Lucas sighed. "We'd better get you saddled up. The portal will be opening soon."

Naomi and Marcus, the twins who'd just come of age with me, had already climbed onto the bench of the carriage and were now—to no one's surprise—bickering over who would hold the reins.

"Will you two pack it in already?" The serpents' mother groaned, "You'll be lucky if Briar doesn't leave you behind in the forest."

"She—He— started it!" they exclaimed in unison.

I walked over to my horse, Isis, and took the reins from a

waiting Fenrir. He patted my arm and said, "Be safe, Briar," before stepping back.

"I will," I promised. His answering smile looked forced, but it was a smile all the same. I mounted my horse and took my place ahead of the carriage.

The attending pack members gathered around us, all calling out farewells and promises we'd be missed. I'd miss them too. I'd miss waking up to the sun rising over the mountains. I'd miss dancing around the bonfires in the evenings. I'd miss it all, but I'd be back, I reminded myself. Ivy approached and rested a hand on my knee as Lucas ran his fingers through Isis' mane.

"Portals can't be opened on Academy grounds so it'll drop you just outside the Sorrowood. Just take the eastern path and you should arrive before nightfall. Grayson and the rest of the pack will be there to welcome you."

"I'll write to you both soon," I promised as the air began to ripple twenty yards ahead.

I gave the crowd a final wave and gestured to my travel companions. "Let's go."

THE ROSE

"I swear to the moon, stars, and sun if you don't silence yourselves in the next three seconds, my daggers will do it for you."

"Oh come on, Briar," Marcus groaned, letting his copper-covered head fall back in boredom. "What are we supposed to do? Just ride along listening to the frogs croak and the birds sing?"

"Better the birds than you two." At least the birds sang on pitch. "Keep the melodies in your heads so I can keep what small shred of sanity I have left today."

I should've been grateful they'd stopped bickering, unlike the first five hours—five long hours—of our journey, but I wasn't. Their off-tune screeching was so ear-splitting, that every creature in a ten-mile radius probably scattered for cover as we approached. If I couldn't have silence or civil conversation, I'd choose the bickering instead.

The journey had not gone as expected, to put it mildly. We'd walked through the portal and entered a meadow full of bright green grass and flowers. It stood in stark contrast to the dim, murky Sorrowood we needed to cross to reach our destination. The longer we walked the more I expected someone to pop out from behind a tree and reveal we'd fallen prey to a cruel enchantment, cursed to wander a never-ending path for the remainder of our days—or something equally dramatic.

It'd been hours since we began winding through the swamp, and as we continued east per Lucas' instructions, I saw nothing but more trees, vines, moss, and marsh ahead. I could only hope we were heading in the right direction. Giving this new pack a reason to doubt me before I'd even arrived was not what I'd consider a positive start.

"You should be happy we're here to keep you company," Naomi said with her nose tilted slightly up in the air. "If they hadn't moved up the cut-off date, we'd have to wait until next year, and then you would be traveling through this hell hole alone."

"Oh, no. The horror. How would I have survived without your aid?"

She rolled her eyes at my monotone reply, but she didn't comment further. Marcus, on the other hand, wasn't ready to end the conversation.

"Do you think that just because you, Isaac, and Grayson have always been the three chords in a power braid, the rest of us aren't just as capable? We're your pack mates too, and a Beta should know better than to treat her pack like a burden."

I pulled Isis's reins and brought her to a halt. He didn't

notice at first, he was looking off into the trees until Naomi elbowed him in the side to get his attention.

"A burden?" I asked. "Tell me, Marcus, other than wishing the goddess had blessed you with an ounce of self-awareness to know your gifts, or rather lack thereof, what have I done to make you feel burdensome?"

His pale cheeks flooded with color, and he tripped over his reply. "I mean, maybe the burden was a bit harsh. I chose the wrong word."

I tilted my head to one side. "Then what is the right one?"

"Let's just forget it, Bri," Naomi said nervously. "Marcus is just irritable from the long ride. We all are."

"No. Let's not forget it. Your brother claims my behavior is unbefitting of a Beta. I'd like to better understand his complaint so I can remedy it in the future."

"You know what I was trying to say." His eyes shifted between his sister and me. Mine stayed fixed solely on him.

"I don't, so why don't you explain it to me."

"Look, I just meant that when the three of you are together, it's like the rest of us don't even exist. It's always Grayson, the golden heir leading the way with you trailing after him, and Isaac hovering close behind you like you're the little sister he has to watch over in case she gets too close to the fire."

More like he was afraid I'd conjure, and play with it.

"So by being close before they left, we treated the rest of you as a burden? Have I ever ignored a request from you?"

"Well, no," Marcus said.

"Have I ever put your safety at risk?"

"Of course not." He shook his head at the thought.

"And who was it that met with you at dawn to train for three months straight when you were falling behind in hand-to-hand combat?"

"You, but —"

"And who spent hours scouring the woods around the compound with you to find Naomi's pet hedgehog when you accidentally let it out?"

"You almost lost my —" We both ignored her.

"It was you, Briar."

"That's right. It was me. So what exactly have I or have I not done to make you feel like a burden?"

He said nothing.

"Nothing? Then is the problem truly how I treat my pack mates or is it your own jealousy?"

He huffed and reeled his head back. "I am not jealous."

His sister looked him up and down. "Yeah, sure you're not."

"Oh, like you're one to talk. Your face turns green every time you look at Briar next to Grayson."

"That's not true!"

"You are dying for him to pay attention to you the way he pays attention to her."

"Well, he certainly hasn't paid attention to her lately, has he? So what could I possibly be jealous about?"

"Oh, I don't know, how about —"

"We should keep moving." I cut them off before they could say more. Both serpents looked at me. One's face grew more flushed, and the other's drained of all color.

"Briar, I —"

"Just leave it, Naomi, and let's get a move on. I'd like to make it there while we still have daylight to travel by." I squeezed Isis between my heels and continued down the path. The twins muttered accusations at each other for a few moments longer before falling into utter silence. It wasn't as blissful as I imagined it would be. The air was tense with things unsaid.

Grayson had only been home a handful of times since starting at the Academy. The first was for the winter solstice. I'd barely been able to eat the week leading up to his return. I'd had to make up a story about picking some bad berries in the forest to keep Isaac from asking too many questions about my behavior. I did my very best not to fixate on his impending arrival, but all I could hear when I thought of him were the words he spoke to Lucas in the breezeway before he'd left. The words I'd give anything to go back and avoid overhearing.

But there was no going back.

I stood beside his parents with a smile painted on my lips and tried not to flinch when he walked through the portal. The first thing he did after greeting Ivy and Lucas was to sweep me into a hug and spin me around with such force my feet hovered above the ground.

He acted the way he always had during that visit, but I noticed things I'd been blind to before. Things like the way his smile lost a fraction of its brilliance when I walked in a room, or the twitch of his lips when we were sent on an assignment together. The signs were obvious once I started looking for them.

I'd kept what distance I could without calling attention

to the change. I stopped seeking him out in my free time. I didn't take the seat next to him at meals, or ask him to spar with me during training. A tiny part of me had hoped I had misheard him before and that, when I stopped looking for him, he'd come to find me instead.

He hadn't.

"Do you smell that?" Naomi's question drew me out of my retrospection. I looked over to see her nose, scrunched in disgust. Her brother's head tilted up and he sniffed the air before grimacing. It took the scent a few moments longer to find me, but once it did, it sent a chill racing down my spine.

"Is there an animal carcass nearby?"

"There has to be. What else could smell like that?"

It smelled of death: tar, with the subtlest hint of brimstone, and I felt no small amount of ill ease at encountering the second for the second time in as many days. I knew that smell. I'd once woken surrounded by it in a field of ash. A second death was too coincidental, but like I assured Fenrir, it couldn't be what I thought it was. They were gone—I knew they were gone. It wasn't possible, but what else could it be?

Were they watching us? Have they finally found me? I scanned our surroundings for the glint of orange eyes watching behind brush and through leaves of the trees, but saw no trace of them. No. I was safe. The water by the deer and Fenrir's paranoia were getting to my head after a poor night's sleep.

They were dead.

No one was looking for me.

I was safe.

"Just keep moving," I instructed. "The odor will pass."

They continued grumbling about the smell and speculating. What kind of rot could cause it as we moved forward? It grew more pungent with each step.

We rounded the bend in the path, and that was when we saw it: a wolf, or at least, what was left of one. It was nearly torn in half, its entrails strong between its torso and flank.

"I think I'm going to be sick." Naomi jumped from the carriage bench and retched into the bulrush plants surrounding the bog. Marcus gagged but remained seated, and I was just doing my best to look disgusted rather than relieved. I'd been wrong; a carcass could cause that type of smell after all.

"What could've done something like that to a wolf? Naomi asked when she returned to her seat. "They don't make for easy prey."

"Yeah, but they're usually in a pack," Marcus pointed out. "Even the strongest predator is vulnerable alone."

"Exactly. There's always another threat," I said, as we passed, its mangled body. "Sadly, it seems he found one bigger than him."

"Well, I hope we get to the Academy before we meet ours," Marcus said under his breath.

"There isn't going to be—"

A roar interrupted Naomi's reassurance as a chimera landed on the path not twenty feet ahead of us. I groaned and unsheathed my sword.

"You just had to say it, didn't you?"

THE ROSE

"It wasn't my fault."

"Then whose fault was it?"

"Goddess, Naomi, a chimera drops from the sky and you believe it has to be someone's fault? How does that make any sense?"

"Words have power, Marcus, and you spoke the possibility into existence!"

I ignored the twins' squabbling as best I could and sent up a prayer thanking the goddess we were almost there. I blamed Lucas for our poor luck with the chimera. It could only be the world's way of reprimanding us for mocking his sage advice at our departure.

We'd passed through the iron gates of the Iolite Academy grounds a few hours after we – or rather, I – had dispatched with the chimera, and in that time I'd wished the chimera had slain me no less than ten times. It would've been a small mercy to save me from listening to my blathering travel companions a moment longer.

I was tired, I was covered in blood, and I wanted a bath, a meal, and a bed – in that order. The one bright spot in my otherwise stormy mood was seeing the spires of the stone campus peeking over the next hill.

Well, that and the change in scenery from the dreary swampland we'd been traveling in. The cobblestone road we were on had lanterns, just beginning to glow, floating on either side of it. Behind them was a plush forest of burgundy-topped trees; I had never seen anything like it. It was stunning, but its full beauty would be lost to me until I'd eaten and bathed, or at least when I had less frustrating company.

Finally, we were passing under a stone archway that led to a grand courtyard. Vines grew along the walls and extended up beyond my sight toward the towers above us. At the center stood an ornate fountain and I ignored the memories of the mist falling onto my skin, threatening to pull me in. I pretended not to smell the phantom ash flooding my nose. I didn't think of charred bodies or guilty consciences from events unknown. Instead, I smiled.

I smiled because beyond the fountain, reclined on stone steps, leading to a pair of wooden doors, was a familiar man with golden hair and honey-brown eyes smiling up at me. He gave a languid stretch as he rose and crossed the courtyard to meet us. He lifted a hand to stroke Isis' mane.

"Isaac."

"A man could die of starvation and thirst, waiting for you, Briar Lennox, but I must say, the view when you arrive is always worth the wait."

"It's the blood, isn't it? It really brings out the color of my eyes. It makes for a striking sight, I'm told."

The corners of his mouth rose.

"More like it brings out the violence in them, but yes, it's a striking sight all the same."

He held out his hand to me, and I took it while dismounting my horse. As soon as my feet were on the ground, he pulled me into him for a tight embrace.

"I missed you," I said into his ear.

"I missed you too, Bri." I reveled in the comfort of his scent—burnt sugar and rum—before I addressed the obvious problem before us.

"He's not here." Isaac's arms held me tighter.

"No. He's not here." I pretended that that didn't hurt. Instead, I dug my face deeper into the crook of his neck for a moment longer.

"You think they'll remember we exist anytime soon?"

"Unlikely."

Isaac's chest shook against me, and he stepped back to wave at the nonplussed twins. The three of them spent a moment exchanging greetings and inquiring about each other's well-being, but this simply wasn't the time for idle chatter.

"Isaac." He turned back to me. "Where is Grayson?"

He rubbed a hand along the back of his neck, and looked at the ground, saying nothing.

"Isaac."

"He sent me instead."

"Yes, I noticed that. What I want to know is why. Stop stalling and tell me what's going on." He exhaled deeply and finally looked up at me, something came to pity shining in his eyes.

"He wants you to abdicate your position as Luna."

The world went silent.

She'd be a liability to us all.

I knew Grayson Pierce didn't believe in me. I knew that even with everything I'd done, everything I'd *proven* in his absence, it wouldn't be enough. I knew all of that. So why did I feel like someone pulled the ground from under me?

Then the silence was broken by the twins' curses.

"That fu –"

"How could he –"

"Disloyal bastard."

"When I get my hands on him, I swear I'm gonna–"

"Enough." I raised a hand in the air.

They stopped talking.

"Explain." So Isaac did, and my blood heated with each new word he spoke.

"He thinks I'm going to lose?" I chuckled, but the sound held no humor. "What must Grayson think of Logan if he knows I can win against the Beta of our pack but believes I don't stand a chance against a teenager at school?"

"Isn't Briar technically a teenager at a–" Marcus whispered to his sister, but Isaac spoke over him.

"Kenna is strong – very strong. He just doesn't want you to look weak in front of the pack if you lose the challenge, and no one wants a Pack Rite "

"You mean he thinks I'll make him look weak, right? She may be strong, but we both know I'm stronger than her." I was stronger than all of them.

"He's trying to protect you."

"And yet he sent you to do the dirty work on his behalf, instead of coming himself." Isaac didn't contradict me.

"And you?" I asked him, praying that I already knew his answer "Do you want me to step down?"

"Never." There was no hesitation in his response. No waver in his voice. No break from his gaze to mine. Grayson's opinion meant nothing. *He* meant nothing. Isaac saw me. He believed in me. He mattered, and he was with me.

I swallowed the ball of emotion building in my throat, squared my shoulders, and commanded, "Then take me to him."

THE FUNNY THING about confronting someone who's wronged you is that sometimes practicality forces you to wait. Horses needed to be stabled, watered, and fed. Belongings needed to be unloaded–though I'd kept my knapsack with me when we handed the rest of our bags to the attendants. Washrooms needed to be visited. In my hurry to get the inevitable confrontation over with, I'd chosen to forego scrubbing the remnants of my fight with the chimera from my skin. Other things simply couldn't have waited.

A choice that, unfortunately, resulted in more than one stare as we strode through the halls searching for Grayson. Apparently in the hour Isaac had been waiting for my arrival, the Alpha had relocated from the study hall where he'd bade Isaac to do his bidding.

"Are you planning to explain the blood at some point?" Isaac leaned in and asked as we passed a small alcove with a spiral staircase. It was equal parts eerie and intriguing. I was definitely exploring it later. "I'm all for experimenting with your style, but I do draw the line at poor hygiene. At least use dye instead of actual bodily fluids."

"Chimera," I answered with a wave of my hand. "You know they pour blood like a fountain when you cut off one of the heads."

"And somehow you are the only one bathing in it? What, are the twins more careful than you?"

I snorted as we turned a corner into a window-lined hall. "Yeah, they were more careful. Careful not to leave the carriage."

Marcus and Naomi immediately gave their excuses and explanations for why hanging back was the only logical choice they could've made. Isaac's uninhibited laugh rang through the corridor, and a wave of warmth washed over me. Despite the unease that grew with each step that brought me closer to finding Grayson, I smiled.

I'd missed this.

Isaac's departure had broadened an already gaping hole from learning the truth about Grayson the year before. On the rare occasions the twins weren't driving me to the edge of my sanity with their bickering they were decent company. One on one I may have gone so far as to say they were *fun*, but they weren't family. They weren't home.

I wrapped my arm around Isaac's side and rested my head on his shoulder.

"I'm glad to be here with you, my friend." Even if it meant seeing Grayson and pretending a pang didn't still shoot through my chest when I pictured his dimpled smile.

Stupid dimples. "Just think of all the quality time we'll have now that we're roomies. Will you braid my hair in the mornings? You know it never looks as good when I do it myself."

I didn't know why but someone else doing your hair felt a million times better than doing your own. It was a fact of life. Even if the Luna suite hadn't been rudely occupied at my arrival I would have trekked to Isaac's room to ask him to do it for me.

"Are you sure that I'm the best person for you to stay with?" Isaac asked hesitantly.

"I haven't even seen the room yet and you're already trying to kick me out of it?" I huffed, picking my head up from its resting place. "I'll have you know I am a *fantastic* roommate. You don't actually have to braid my hair every day. Maybe on special occasions it would be—"

"No, that's not what I mean. Wouldn't it be wiser if you were staying with someone like, I don't know, Naomi?" he asked and rubbed at the back of his neck.

"You bite your tongue." I glanced over my shoulder to make sure she hadn't heard the suggestion from where she and Marcus followed a few feet behind us.

I cared about Naomi. I'd lay down my life to protect hers like I would anyone else in the pack, but I best appreciated her in small doses. Sharing a room was not a small dose. Thankfully her attention was focused on a passing fae male. I suppose he was attractive enough, but the female walking next to him was the more interesting of the pair. I'd never seen someone with hair the color of a sunset.

"I just think," Isaac started, pulling my attention back to him, "that some people will find it inappropriate." I laughed, but it trailed off when his expression remained perfectly serious, if not a little exasperated.

"You're serious?" He nodded, and I asked, "Isaac, do you feel uncomfortable with me staying with you?"

"No, of course not," he said easily.

"Then who cares what anyone else thinks?" I paused, then added, "And given I'm about to unseat a Luna from her pack–without the support of its Alpha–I doubt people will be talking about much else."

He hummed in agreement, and we fell into a comfortable silence as we wound through the stone halls. I should've been mapping out the labyrinth of buildings as we went, but was too distracted by my impending reunion with Grayson. The main campus grounds couldn't have been more than a few square miles, but we'd surely explored every inch of it by the time we pushed through a glass-paneled door into an outdoor common area. My breath caught in my throat as I took my first step over the threshold. Don't be a coward, Briar, I told myself, he's just a man. He has no hold on you.

I saw him before he saw me.

Grayson was smiling. Broadly. It was a bright, uninhibited smile, that boasted of joy and a clear conscience. He sat at the head of one of the stone tables scattered throughout the quad surrounded by a group of people–my new pack mates. I didn't spare them more than a glance. I kept my focus on Grayson. He still hadn't noticed me, but the woman next to him twirling a dagger between her fingers was watching me with an impassive face and a calculated gaze.

I held her stare. If she expected me to look away first,

she'd be disappointed. A corner of her mouth drew up, and she turned to Grayson to gesture my way with her blade.

His smile fell when he saw me. I told myself it didn't hurt.

But it did.

The stares of the students gathered around him bore into my skin, but I didn't drop his gaze as we approached. I kept my pace unhurried and steady even as the rate of my heart pounding against the walls of my chest was anything but. I hated myself for noticing that he looked good—really good.

At home, I'd managed to avoid him after his first return by volunteering for out-of-territory assignments or faking an illness. I'd mastered giving shame-driven excuses disguised as honorable coincidences. In the three years since he left, he'd only grown more handsome. His jawline seemed sharper, his body more muscular. His inky hair was slightly tousled like he'd run his hands through it a few too many times.

"You have nothing to prove to him." Isaac spoke the words so low, no one else would be able to hear his muttered reassurance. "You outrank her, and you're the rightful Luna of this pack."

I was the rightful Luna. I had nothing to prove—to Grayson or anyone else—but I would prove it anyway. I'd prove it a hundred times over if necessary.

We stopped less than five feet from Grayson, and he still hadn't spoken a word to any of us. I tilted my head and let my eyes rake over him from head to toe.

On the surface, he looked comfortable, unbothered by our arrival, a picture of complete control. The only tell he couldn't hide from me, was the vein, pulsing rapidly against the skin of his neck. If he wanted to play the dismissive silent leader, I'd let him. My first order of business wasn't with him, anyway.

It was with her.

The woman who'd alerted Grayson to my presence was no longer smirking, but beaming as she looked between us.

I turned from him to the now-beaming woman beside him whose gaze alternated between us. "I've been informed you'd like to issue a challenge." She inclined her head. "Go ahead. I will hear it."

Naomi protested behind me, but I didn't address her. If she thought I planned to abdicate my position with so small a fight, she was even dimmer than I'd thought. Thankfully, Isaac shushed her before she could continue.

"I'll need your full name and rank to issue it." Her voice was almost lyrical. Between that, her near ethereal beauty, and her propensity for dagger twirling I would be tempted to befriend her. At least I would if she hadn't been trying to usurp me.

"Briar Lennox, Beta of the Othniel pack." Her head drew back an infinitesimal amount, and a few gasps rang from the pack members around us. I looked to Isaac and gave him what I hoped was a 'what the Hades is going on' look. He grinned sheepishly at me. I pointedly avoided looking at Grayson, whose stare was still burning the side of my face.

"Lennox," she drawled, "Not Pierce?"

"No. Not Pierce."

"And you are the Beta of the Othniel Pack?"

"Were my name and rank unclear? Do you need me to repeat them for you?"

Her smile only grew as she looked at Grayson, who was clenching his teeth. I hoped they cracked.

"No, what you said was quite clear. I'm afraid it's someone else who's caused the confusion."

Grayson narrowed his eyes at her but still said nothing. Maybe he'd lost his tongue in the years since we parted. "Oh well. It doesn't matter if you're the Beta or a Pack Princess, my challenge stands." I'd ask Isaac about that princess comment later.

"Then say the words." She didn't bristle at my command.

"I, Makenna Lenoir, Enforcer of the Hallewell Pack, challenge you, Briar Lennox, Beta of the Othniel Pack, for the honor of Luna of the Iolite Academy. Do you abdicate this position to me, or do you accept my challenge and invoke the Pack Rite as our customs demand?"

"I accept your challenge." And pandemonium broke out around us as Grayson finally found his voice.

8

THE ROSE

"**H**ave you lost all sense?" Grayson sounded more wolf than man as his roar echoed through the square. His chair fell back against the ground and he rose from his seat.

"I could ask you the same. Is there something you'd like to discuss?" It took every ounce of willpower to keep my voice level, but the urge to scream at the top of my lungs was growing stronger with each moment that passed.

"Do you not understand what invoking a Pack Rite means? People die in these challenges!" His stupidly broad chest heaved with every breath he took.

I laughed humorlessly. We both knew that between the two of us, I was the only to have actually competed in it. For him to act otherwise was one more insult added to an already open wound.

"Oh, do they?" I asked. "Funny, I thought it was a tea party. I was really looking forward to those little sandwiches." Makenna snickered but rolled her lips between her teeth at the Alpha's glare.

"This isn't a joke, Briar." He stepped closer to me, hands balling into fists at his hips.

"I'm not laughing, Grayson." I looked him dead in the eye and cursed his tall height when I had to tilt my head up to do it. I used to love how tall he was–how small, safe I felt next to him. The follies of youth. "Makenna issued a challenge, and I accepted it. Which part of that involves you?"

"I do like her, and it's Kenna. Please gods never call me Makenna again." She came up to stand beside Grayson and said pleasantly, "Briar, after I win the Rite, I'd love to make you one of my Enforcers."

She sounded utterly sincere. Who was this woman, and wasn't she the one Grayson should worry about losing her senses?

"Kenna, will you please stay out of this?" Grayson's reluctant tone told me he already knew her answer.

"Not a chance, wolf boy." My head jerked back at the nickname, and Grayson's glower grew fiercer as the corners of my mouth rose. *Wolf boy?* "She's right. Which part of this involves you?"

"The part where I don't want to see my pack mate turned into a living dummy you use as target practice or a scratching post for your lion."

So. Little. Faith.

"I think you underestimate her." She turned her emerald eyes on me. "I'm going to win, make no mistake, but something tells me it won't be a simple fight. I'm looking forward to it."

Kenna patted Grayson's shoulder before walking, or

more like skipping, out of the quad and into one of the nearby buildings.

I looked at Isaac and asked, "Is she always that peculiar?"

"That was actually a more normal, pleasant interaction with her. If I'm honest, it was a little unnerving to see her smile." Isaac stared, dumbfounded, at the door she'd disappeared through.

"I don't know if that makes me like her less or more." Striking fear into your enemies with a smile was an admirable quality in my book.

"Well, I'm pretty sure she plans to be your new best friend, so I'm not sure it matters either way." We'd see how she felt after I won the Pack Rite. She wouldn't be the first person to turn against me for doing so.

Grayson was right when he said people died in these challenges. There were three ways the battle could end: yielding, being knocked unconscious, or death. When the time came, I hoped she'd yield. I didn't relish the thought of adding another soul's passing to my already murky conscience, but this wasn't the time to get lost in memories of sins past. There was an angry Alpha to handle.

The brooding wolf was back to staring me down, arms folded across his chest, raised brow, down-turned mouth in a frown. He was the picture of a disapproving older brother, and I wasn't in the mood to argue with him further.

I didn't trust myself to keep my temper under control. The flames simmering under my skin begged louder and louder to be released the longer I stood there frozen in his gaze. It only worsened as his scent assaulted my senses. *Pomegranate and leather*. He'd barely come of age before he left, but those few short days were enough for the smell to haunt me in his absence.

I'd missed the boy who made me feel like I belonged. I'd grieved for the man I believed he'd turn into, even when I knew neither had existed at all. Not really. But staring up into the face of the mirage who'd played him, I longed for him anyway.

The fire drained from my veins, and I released a sigh. I didn't want to fight. Not then.

Being the extremely mature woman I was, I ignored his glare and took off my rucksack to reach inside. I removed one of the two packages Lucas had given me and shoved one into his stupidly broad chest.

"Your father sent us these. He hoped we could share them to start our partnership leading the pack. Forgive me if I prefer to eat mine alone. Something here is rotten. It's made me lose my appetite."

His flinch was small, but it was there. Good. I hoped it hurt to know he was betraying his father's wishes even if he cared nothing about betraying mine. I looked at the gobsmacked pack members still sitting around the table, and said, "Lovely to meet you all. I'll see you in class."

One of the females gave a shy grin and waved at me, but both fell when the male next to her nudged her side.

I walked back the way we'd come, and kept my head high as I went. A ball of emotion rose in my throat when I realized Isaac was not the only one following me. Naomi and Marcus were close behind. I wouldn't have blamed them if they'd stayed with Grayson, but I was grateful for their loyalty.

Just as we reached the door, I heard Grayson call my

name. I turned back and waited to hear what he could possibly want, but he rolled his lips between his teeth and said nothing.

Did nothing.

I gave a small shake of my head, straightened my back, and turned away. *How disappointing.*

I crossed the hall to rest my forehead against the cool stone of the wall as soon as I passed through the door. Two minutes. I just needed two minutes to let myself feel this and then I'd move on.

"Do you think this is a good time to point out that once again, we were completely ignored? I mean, Grayson didn't even look at me." Naomi was likely trying to whisper, but as usual, her attempt was unsuccessful.

"Probably not." Isaac's tone left no room for discussion on the matter.

One more minute.

"Why would he be looking at you, anyway? Did you not notice the stare-down he was having with Briar? I doubt you crossed his mind. Maybe if you were the one covered in blood, he'd have said something to you, but you chose to stay in the carriage," Marcus pointed out helpfully.

"You didn't leave the carriage either, you hypocrite!"

"Yeah, but I also didn't complain about Grayson ignoring me."

"You were the one who complained about being left out in the first place!"

I was going to intervene before their bickering escalated to the point of no return, but just as I opened my mouth to reply, the wolf in question burst through the door. The small parcel of cake I'd given him was still clutched in his hand.

I was surprised he hadn't tossed it in the waste bin alongside his loyalty. He noticed my stare and quickly put the small parcel in his pocket.

I wished I had cake-sized pockets.

"Sure," Marcus mumbled, "Now he comes to find us."

Grayson's gaze skimmed over the others before fixing on me. I refused to acknowledge the flicker of hope I felt that he'd come after me.

"Would you all excuse us?" His tone was chilling. "Briar and I have much to discuss."

To their credit, none of my pack mates took a single step until I nodded my head for them to go.

"Come on," Isaac said, "I'll show you to your rooms." The three of them reluctantly made their way down the hall with a pace that would make a turtle feel like it was flying. Isaac's hand squeezed mine, and the twins sneered at Grayson as they passed.

As they rounded the corner, I heard Naomi comment, "That didn't count as a hello." She wasn't wrong.

I tore my eyes from where they'd disappeared and reluctantly looked back at Grayson. He was leaning against the wall I'd rested my head against moments prior, arms and ankles crossed.

"Well?" I asked, "You wanted to talk."

"Do you think you can drop the attitude long enough for us to do that?" he asked. One of his eyebrows raised as he awaited my answer like an expectant parent handling a petulant child.

"You don't think my attitude is justified given the choices you've made today?" I countered. "My gods, Grayson, even if you don't think much of me I thought you'd at least have enough respect for your home pack–not to mention your other pack mates arriving today–to face me yourself instead of sending Isaac to deliver a message in your place."

"Oh, I'm sorry." He splayed his hands in front of him and looked around in mock confusion. "Did you not enjoy arriving somewhere and the person you were hoping to see was nowhere to be found? I wonder what that must feel like."

I narrowed my eyes and took a step closer to him. Had he always been this infuriating?

I refused to be enchanted by the dimple that appeared as one corner of his mouth raised in an arrogant grin. I hated that dimple.

"Is something bothering you?" I crossed my arms over my chest. "Because the last time I checked, you weren't the one whose position was undermined by their own pack mate."

His head drew back as he asked, "That's what you're upset about?" His forest green eyes flicked between mine. "You should've been thanking me for arranging that. Instead you let a few hurt feelings drive you into accepting a challenge you have no standing to take."

"No standing?" I growled. "I am the highest ranking female in this pack–in *any* pack–with the exception of your mother. I have every right to defend my title against anyone who would question it, and I will do that with or without you at my back."

"Just because my mother gave you the Beta Luna position at home–"

"*Excuse* me?"

" –doesn't mean you can just be handed the Luna position here at the Academy. Kenna's claws would slice you to shreds in seconds. Goddess, Briar, I thought you were smarter than this."

"And I thought you were *better* than this," I said, "so I guess we're both disappointed."

The silence between us was louder than any scream I could have mustered.

Grayson's face held the same expression it held when he was preparing to hunt a rogue or defend the pack against intruders—I'd seen it countless times in our youth. It motivated me to take up my sword by his side and cut down our enemies—together.

I just never thought the enemy would be me.

He opened his mouth to, I could only assume, continue airing his disappointment in me. I straightened my back and took a step closer to him, steeling myself against whatever venom would spew from his mouth. I refused to lower my gaze no matter how much it hurt to see the coldness in them where warmth used to radiate.

Instead of the barrage of insults or condescending lecture I expected, he exhaled deeply, releasing some of his body's rigidity with his breath..

"I hate that it feels like we're on opposing sides," he said and dropped his head to the wall behind him. "This isn't what I wanted. The first time we saw each other again in years wasn't supposed to be filled with animosity."

"Well, it's definitely not what I wanted." I snorted. "What did you expect to happen? That I'd just listen to Isaac's message and fall in line."

He nodded and said, "Yes. That's exactly what I thought would happen. I expected there to be some slight frustration that I didn't come to see you, but nothing we wouldn't get past quickly." To be fair, not that I'd *ever* admit it aloud, in the past I might have, if only to stay in his good graces.

"Then that's your own fault for making asinine assumptions."

"There was never a shadow of a chance that Kenna would accept a new Luna. Issuing the challenge was inevitable, but we have the chance to control what happens next. I'm trying to do what's best for the pack–for both packs."

"And you decided that what was best for the packs couldn't possibly be me, right?" The cuts just kept coming.

"You have to see where I'm coming from, Bri."

"Don't call me that," I snapped at him, "We aren't friends right now, and only friends get to call me that."

He turned toward me then, eyes full of torment I'd wanted to see from him in the quad. Torment that begged me to understand, to fall in line before something was broken that we couldn't repair. He couldn't have known, but we'd never get it back.

We'd never had it at all.

"What else would you have had me do?" he asked. "You can't win against her. Even if she never shifts, she's too strong for you to defeat. I'm not just trying to protect the pack, I'm trying to protect *you*. Don't you get that?"

"What I get," I said, slowly, "is you have so little faith in me that you made a choice all on your own with a ripple of consequences. People are maimed in the Pack Rite, Grayson. People die, and not just the first challengers to fight. This puts the entire pack at risk!"

"That's why I wanted you to abdicate without accepting the challenge. If you'd just stood down, we wouldn't be in this mess."

"We wouldn't be in this mess if you had shown me a shred of trust, or given me a modicum of respect. If you had waited for me—if you'd come to talk to me—maybe we could have avoided this entire thing, but instead, you went behind my back and sent our friend to deliver the news in your place."

"I sent Isaac to save you the embarrassment."

"You sent Isaac because you were being a coward!" His nostrils were flaring now, but I didn't stop. "Something in you knew this was wrong or you would've been there, on the front steps, waiting for me. If not that, then you would've at least said something to me the second I entered the quad. Instead, you acted as if I didn't exist even as I stood right in front of you."

"Well you'd know best when it comes to pretending like someone didn't exist, wouldn't you?" I chose to ignore that as he raked his hands through his hair and pulled at its roots. "Don't you get it? I'm trying to protect you! Catering to you would only put a bigger target on your back."

"I don't need your protection! I wanted your support, but even that I can manage without. The only target on my back is the blood you drew stabbing me in it. "

Before I even fully realized it, he was moving. A second later, I was caged against the window with him leaning over me, trapping me with a hand on my waist and a forearm above my head.

"You can't win this challenge, and I can't watch you get hurt. I can't watch you die."

He moved even closer, only inches separating us now. My chest rose and fell faster, and I tried to look anywhere but at him.

"Do you think I didn't want to run to you the moment you walked through that door?" he asked. "Could you not hear my heart drop at the sight of the blood marring your skin? Could you not see that I would cut down every person, every creature who'd hurt you?"

"No." I admitted in an equally hushed tone, "I couldn't. I didn't think you thought of me at all because if you had, you couldn't have done this to me. The only one who hurt me today was you."

"Back out of the challenge." It was more of a command than a request, but I noticed the hint of desperation in his voice.

"No."

"Then what am I supposed to do?" he asked. "What is it you want from me?" I was torn between crying for him and strangling him. I wanted him to know what I wanted. I wanted him to want it too.

"I won't ask you to give anything more than what you've already given." The skin framing his eyes creased. "I don't need you to watch over me or help me acclimate. I don't need you to indulge my whims, take me on adventures, or have me at your side. I don't need you to do anything except stay out of my way while I prove to this pack I am the Luna they deserve, whether you believe that to be true or not."

The blood drained from his face with each new word I spoke. "Briar, don't let pride prevent self-preservation. You don't have to go through with this."

"You aren't listening to me." I stood taller, bringing my eyes a few inches closer to his. "I will be the victor left standing at the end of this challenge. Arguing amongst ourselves isn't going to solve this. What's done is done and can no longer be undone. The longer we talk, the more this hurts, and the more I fantasize about beating your head in with the shovel I'd later use to dig your grave."

His eyebrows shot toward his hairline, and, if I didn't know better, I'd say his lips were pressed together to fight a grin.

"Did you just threaten to kill me?"

"Of course not." I rolled my eyes. "I was merely fantasizing about gutting you and hiding your body where only maggots and rot could find it. That's completely different than a death threat."

"Is it now?" He did smile then, a bit of, dare I believe it, warmth entering his eyes.

"Obviously. I'd never be so careless as to warn my prey of their impending demise, let alone provide a step-by-step plan for them to counter. It's fun to dream though, isn't it?"

He chuckled and paused for a minute before he next spoke.

"It is fun to dream," he said, "But as fun as it is, we eventually have to wake up. We have to face reality."

"And who said our dreams can't shape our reality?"

Grayson shifted a fraction closer.

"Were you hiding this side of you from me, or have you always been this bloodthirsty?"

"Don't blame me for your own poor observations." I threw back, "I am who I've always been." *You've just never seen what I look like when I'm not trailing after you.*

The longer we stood there, his face so close, his breath mingled with mine, the hotter the blood coursing through my veins grew.

For once, my magic had nothing to do with it.

"Sorry, Pierce," a warm, teasing voice called from the end of the hall, "Do you need us to take another route and give you two a moment? I rather expected you had said everything you needed to say outside. Clearly, I was wrong. Or maybe it isn't talking that's on your mind."

Grayson sighed and pushed away from the window, giving me a chance to see the man behind the voice. There were three of them, two men with a woman walking between them.

The man I presumed had called out to us was smiling with a jovial saunter as they made their approach. His amber eyes seemed to radiate contentment, while the lilt of his mouth promised nothing but mischief. As far as first impressions went, I'd wager he was the man you'd lounge with in the sun in between having a picnic and plotting a treasure heist. The other man was his opposite.

If it was death incarnate who approached me, the last thing I'd see before entering the afterlife was a pair of deep blue, nearly black, eyes that sent chills rippling down my spine.

I knew I wasn't breathing—my inhale frozen somewhere in the back of my throat as I stood trapped in his expression. Deep in my mind, where thoughts were still capable of forming, I recognized that underneath the promises of cold violence that came off of him in waves, he was striking — maybe even more so because of his palpable lethality.

"Fabian," Grayson greeted the first man, drawing my eyes away from the death god, "Allow me to introduce my pack mate, Briar."

I inclined my head at the man. In truth, Grayson should have introduced me as his fellow Beta if he wasn't going to do me the courtesy of acknowledging my right to the Luna title. I'd add it to the list of today's transgressions.

"Yes, I heard." I grimaced at how fast word traveled on this campus. Fabian's grin was ever-widening. "Beta of the Othniel Pack and soon to face Kenna in a battle to the death, defending her place as Luna of the Iolite Pack. I must admit, I'm very much looking forward to the show."

He gestured to the woman beside him whom I'd overlooked in my fascination with the cold man on her other side. Her eyes were kind, and her face was oddly akin to a cherub. "This is my sister, Eris. It's her first year joining the Academy as well. I suspect you'll share a few of the same classes."

"It's a pleasure to meet you, Luna Briar." Oh, I liked her already. "I wish you the best of luck in the challenge."

I mustered my most confident smile and gave her a quick wink. "Thank you, but luck will have little to do with it. If you'll excuse me, I should clean up and get some rest. It's been an eventful day." I turned in the direction Isaac had left earlier when a question from Fabian stopped me.

"What's the blood from?" he asked. "It's not often someone arrives bathed in red, and I can't help but wonder."

"It's from a chimera who found me in the Sorrowood." I smiled sweetly and looked at Grayson when I added, "Thank you for asking." Someone else certainly hadn't.

For a man who claimed he wanted to cut down anyone who'd cause me harm, he wasn't very good at knowing who to add to his list. From the corner of my eye, I saw Eris conceal a giggle behind her hand.

"I'll show you to your room," Grayson said it as a fact rather than an offer, but I waved him off.

"My room is still occupied, I'm afraid." He narrowed his eyes, and his face turned a new shade of red when I said, "I'll be staying with Isaac until that's rectified."

I gave him no time to protest. I wouldn't feign compliance by accepting lodging other than the Luna suite that was rightfully mine.

I pivoted on my heel and left, grinning when I heard Fabian mutter, "I think I just fell in love." Followed by a thud and a grunt.

9

THE ROSE

As much as I'd have liked to say I found Isaac and the others right away, it took me at least half an hour of walking the Academy grounds before I finally came across them in the dining hall. I could have asked for someone to point me to the shifter wing, but my pride had taken enough of a beating for one day. I'd at least had the chance to explore the creepy stairwell I'd seen earlier. It led to a broom closet.

And there I was: lying in Isaac's bed, blood-free and full of good food, yet unable to find rest. Isaac and I had spent a few minutes debriefing before turning in, but I dodged his subtle inquiries about my conversation with Grayson. Instead, we'd started planning for the Pack Rite.

It would be held in an outdoor amphitheater on the new moon when shifters were thought to be at our weakest; if you can't defend your pack at your weakest, you don't deserve to lead it at your strongest. Unlike the others of my kind, I loved the new moon. Maybe my inability to shift lessened the moon's effect on me, or maybe it was the demon blood, but I felt most alive when the night sky was at its darkest.

The ache in my chest grew more intense the longer I lay in bed, fiddling with my necklace and staring at the ceiling. What if Grayson was right, and I wasn't strong enough to win? Yes, my magic fueled my strength, but that didn't make me invincible. What if the bloodstone didn't work? What if it worked too well? How would I face them if I lost? What would I tell Lucas and Ivy in my letter home? Between the questions racing through my head and Isaac's bed-shaking snores beside me—he should really get checked by a healer—I was spiraling into a vat of disastrous possibilities.

No. Fixating on the what-ifs for the next fortnight wouldn't help me. I would not lose. I couldn't. Lying there any longer wouldn't stop my racing thoughts. I tucked my necklace back in my top, carefully extricated myself from beside my sleeping friend, and quietly left the room. Maybe the fresh air would quiet my mind.

I found myself walking back along the road we'd taken through the gate that afternoon. The lanterns were fully lit now, casting a warm glow across both the stones in the road and the vibrant trees beyond it.

I could love it here. If I could get through the next fourteen days–the next fourteen hours–then I could love my life here.

"Peaceful, isn't it?"

I halted and looked around, but saw no one. Surely, she wasn't... I looked up toward the top of the trees and there was Kenna, lounging on a branch, spinning a dagger on the point of her finger before placing it back in the sheath at her hip.

"It's surprising how few students venture this way. Most prefer to keep to the main campus or the fields and forests to the south, but I love it here the most." She stretched her lithe arms above her head and arched her back in a stretch before dropping them to her sides, letting them hang on either side of her branch. "There's something magical about being surrounded by nature that people have yet to taint."

"It's beautiful." I agreed. I'd never seen plants and trees like these.

"The view is even better from above. Care to join me?"

The invitation sounded innocent enough, but the sincerity in her voice didn't put me at ease. The mischievous glint in her eyes set my teeth on edge and made me want to find out what she was thinking at the same time. I could have made an excuse to keep walking or go back inside, but I didn't. I climbed the tree. I chose a branch near hers and let my legs hang over one side. I looked around and the forest that stretched for miles in every direction and said, "You're right. The view is better up here, though I was content on the ground."

"You can see more from here, and I always prefer to be closer to the stars, don't you?" Kenna looked up at the sky and a softer, less cunning smile crossed her face. I followed suit and my breath caught in my throat. I had never seen so many stars swirling in the sky, encased in a web of burgundy leaves.

"I meant what I said you know."

"About what?"

"I'm looking forward to our duel." She turned a blinding smile my way and I had to chuckle.

"You're not the least bit concerned you could lose, are you?"

"Not even a little," she spoke with such confidence like she was stating a fact rather than her opinion. "Please don't take offense. I don't mean it as an insult. I'd like to believe you'll be a worthy opponent. It's obvious from the moment you walked through that door in the way you carried yourself, and the way your pack mates are loyal to you that you're a strong leader. It's just that however strong you may be, I know I'm stronger. That's why Grayson wanted you to abdicate, idiotic as his methods may have been. Truthfully I would have done the exact same thing if I were you."

"We'll see who's left standing in the end. No matter the outcome, I hope you know this isn't personal. I know you've been an exceptional Luna to the pack these last few years."

She waved her hand dismissively. "I'd take it personally if you didn't care enough about the pack to ensure it has the strongest leaders. If I had a drink, I'd toast to leaders who care, but alas, I'm drink-less."

"I'll accept the gesture all the same." I was smiling despite myself. I didn't want to like this woman, yet I felt completely at ease lounging in a tree beside her, only weeks away from a battle that would likely result in injury and could escalate to death. As odd as she was, her presence felt calming–familiar even.

"Very gracious of you." She raised a cupped hand, mimicking a raised glass, before dropping it, "And speaking of being gracious I'm thoroughly impressed you didn't ream into Grayson in the middle of the quad. I don't think I'd have been as kind. Tell me the truth, on a scale of mushroom soup to a chocolate cake, how close were you to killing him?"

Was that meant to be a scale I knew how to use?

"He was just doing what he thought was best for the pack, "I said, "I can't be furious with him for that."

I very well could be, and I was, but speaking poorly of him to someone who'd lead beside him, who would be in our pack after this was resolved felt like a betrayal. He may choose to turn his back on me, but it felt wrong for me to turn mine on him.

"Right," she drew out the word slowly, "For the pack. And when he made us think you were his sister, that was for the pack too?" And the mystery of why she asked if my last name was Pierce was solved. I paused before responding. The part was a bit more puzzling to me.

"I think that was for me." She turned to face me more fully. "In Grayson's mind, it would be easier for me to step down as the Pack Leaders' daughter than a ranked shifter."

"We would have found out eventually. One second of him looking at you, and it was obvious to anyone watching."

"Well, I never said it was a good plan." We both chuckled before falling back into silence. I rested my head against the tree trunk behind me and basked in the subtle sounds of the breeze brushing against the leaves surrounding us. In the distance flickers of light from fireflies dotted the air.

I wasn't sure how much time had passed when I pulled my feet up and stood on the branch. "I should head back and get some sleep."

"Answer one more question before you go?" I nodded. "What happened to the two of you?"

"I'm not sure what you mean," I drew out slowly.

"I've known Grayson for two years now, and in that time I've never seen his eyes light up the way they do when he's talking about you." I held my breath as she went on to say, "I thought he was just an adoring older brother, but now I'm thinking something else."

"I'm not sure what you're thinking," I said, "But I can assure you Grayson's opinion of me is anything but adoring."

"If you say so." She closed her eyes, laid down fully along her own tree limb, and folded her hands behind her head. "See you tomorrow, Briar."

I wanted to probe further into her question—to ask what Grayson had said about me in my absence, but I didn't. Instead, I looked at the treetops surrounding us as I dropped back to the ground to study them again once I was steadily on my feet. It really was stunning here.

A moment later, I was making my way back to the campus, and a shiver raked down my spine. Two spots on my back burned like eyes were boring into them. I searched the tree line for any signs of life but saw nothing. I was alone.

IO

THE MOON

S he wasn't mine. I knew it was impossible, that she couldn't be, but goddess help me if she didn't look like she was.

When she strode across the quad this afternoon and I glimpsed those lilac eyes, I was transported back to days of dancing in the woods with flower crowns I hadn't wanted to wear atop my head. I'd let her put them there for a chance to see her smile. That smile was worth any amount of teasing the other children had thrown at me.

Those eyes spoke of nights spent sneaking away from my parents and watching the stars across the sky with a small, soft hand encased in mine—of shared secrets and whispered promises from another life. But this wasn't the past.

I was no longer a child, and if I was sure of nothing else, I was sure that Briar Lennox was not destined to take the place beside mine.

Yet there I was, hiding behind a tree, hoping she

wouldn't see me watching her from the shadows like some kind of trained guard hound.

I hadn't planned to see her tonight, but sleep eluded me no matter how long I'd searched for it. I was heading to the training room to burn off some energy when a flash of wine-colored hair crossing the front courtyard caught my eye through the window. I felt her pull like a moth drawn to a flame. I had no other choice; I followed her.

The Academy grounds were safer than the lands surrounding it, but something in me rebelled at the thought of her trekking through the darkness alone. I'd been surprised when she'd headed to the entry road instead of the forest to the south, and even more so when she'd joined Kenna of all people in the trees.

The woman challenging her for her place in the pack was the last person I thought she would befriend. I expected bitterness, anger—goddess knew Briar had plenty of both earlier in the day—but instead, I saw smiles, contentment. The two of them had lay there dangling from the branches like long-forgotten friends who were grateful to be reunited.

I should've left them there; there was little danger traveling in pairs, but I lingered. I was transfixed by the soft smile that stretched across Briar's lips when she looked at the stars —captivated by the ring of her laugh in the otherwise silent trees. Yet my chest ached at the beautiful sound. Her perfection changed nothing.

I stepped out from behind the tree I'd used to conceal my presence a few minutes after she'd re-entered the main building. The risk of her seeing me then was next to nonexistent. I moved toward the stone building then stilled, listening more closely.

Murmurs echoed from within the wood.

It could be nothing—a couple sneaking away to be alone, a professor collecting samples for their next class—or it could be a threat, and Kenna would be facing it alone. I turned and silently crept back through the trees. I'd confirm she was fine and then leave. If the sounds were nothing she wouldn't even need to know I'd been there.

The murmurs were a whisper on the wind but grew the slightest bit louder with each step I took. Two voices, male, from what I could make of them. I slowly drew my blade from its sheath and then—

"It's not nice to linger in the dark," a cheery voice chimed behind me, "You could at least say hello to a girl before you follow her around. Didn't anyone teach you common courtesy growing up? It's like you were raised by wolves or something."

I put a finger to her lips and shushed her, listening for the voices I'd been tracking, but only silence remained. I dropped my sword.

"I thought I heard voices," I said. "Was someone out here with you? Did you notice anyone?"

Kenna rolled her eyes and shoved her hands into the pockets of her brown linen pants. "The only someone who was out here with me is the someone you were following. What? Were you worried the new girl would meet an unfortunate end before the Pack Rite could even begin?"

"Can't be too careful at this school. People have a penchant for getting what they want by whatever means necessary. I can't say I'd be shocked if I woke up to learn she had a tragic accident in the night."

"I need neither trickery nor subterfuge to claim what's mine. Besides, I like her." She smiled wide like a feral cat, which, I suppose, is more or less what she was. "It seems like someone else does too, which surprises me, and I'm rarely surprised. Are you planning to actually talk to her or just stare at her from afar, silently pining away?"

I shook my head and looked back into the trees. "Are you sure you didn't see anyone?"

"Only you." She linked her arm with mine and pouted when I pulled away. "Be a gentleman and walk me back to my room, would you? I hear there are suspicious noises about, and I'd hate to meet my own untimely demise." I glared at her but her smile only grew. She turned back toward the campus, nearly skipping.

"Come on stalker in the night," she called over the shoulder, "If we're being honest, you and I both know I'm the most dangerous thing in these woods. We have plenty of real threats, let's not waste time focusing on the ones that don't exist."

THE ROSE

"If one more person stares at me and whispers, I won't be held accountable for the blood running through the halls."

I made no effort to lower my voice, and a small zing of satisfaction raced through me when a nearby siren went pale and darted into the closest classroom. She reappeared moments later. I guess she entered the wrong one. Isaac watched her scatter down the hall with a positively wicked smirk as we cut through the waves of students leaving the assembly hall. The entire student body had been gathered to kick off the school year with speeches and presentations I'm sure were meant to be inspirational. The only things they managed to inspire were a handful of students to nod off in their seats.

Orientation beforehand had been even worse, although anything held at the crack of dawn that didn't involve weapons had little chance of being pleasant. The Headmaster hadn't bothered to show up, sending a timid admin in his stead whose voice barely carried to the middle of the room the first years gathered in. I'd pretended to look as confused as all the other students in the back as I listened to her prattle on about the core classes we'd all be taking this year. We wouldn't decide which area of study to specialize in until the year following. The only worthwhile time was the five minutes it took to pick up our class schedules. Everything else could have been published in a notice.

"I pity the creature who sparks your wrath," Isaac said with a smile, then added more quietly, "As long as there are no actual sparks."

"You ruin all my fun." I shoved him away and rolled my eyes. He couldn't even tease me without adding a word of caution.

"On the contrary, I think I add to your fun rather nicely, especially when it's wrathful and bloody." A fair truth. "And you know I have to ask, any plans to turn that wrath onto a certain wolf with a newfound penchant for poor choices?"

Infuriating bastard.

Any shred of hope I felt that Grayson would come to his senses after yesterday's conversation died the second I saw him sitting in the assembly hall, Kenna sitting at his side. Their Betas were perched next to them, both tracking each step Isaac and I took toward their seats. The Enforcers took up the remainder of their row, and the rest of the pack filled the two rows behind them. Marcus and Naomi were among them. Neither looked up from their laps. Kenna simply smiled and waved.

As we approached, Grayson gestured over his shoulder for us to take the only two seats remaining–at the very back of the pack. I'd laughed and chosen a spot for us across the aisle from them a few rows up. If Grayson or I had to spend the next two hours staring at the back of the other's head, he could look at mine. Let him enjoy the braids Isaac had woven through my hair that morning.

Unfortunately, his eyes weren't the only pair I felt drilling into me at the scene. The attention we'd garnered only increased when Marcus rose from his seat and took the seat to my left. My eyes burned at the show of solidarity, but I kept my face neutral. That didn't stop me from reaching over and giving his leg a quick squeeze of thanks.

"I won't kill him in his sleep if that's what you're worried about," I said, "Ivy and Lucas would never forgive me. He may benefit from a new scar or two though."

"A more intimidating look for him and a release for you." Isaac nodded. "I like it. Maybe looking at the marks will remind him of what–and who–really matters."

"Because the giant wolf shifter with arms like a boulder looks pretty timid without them." Stupid arms.

"Exactly. People snicker at him in the halls. You'd basically be doing him a favor," Isaac quipped with a chuckle that fell flat as he exhaled and shook his head. "I'd happily rake my claws over his skin too if I could."

A familiar pang of guilt hit me at his dejected expression. They used to be so close, yet the wall that formed between them the moment Isaac learned my secret grew taller by the day. It's difficult to stay close to friends when your secrets could get them killed.

"You know, just because Grayson and I are at odds, doesn't mean you and Grayson have to be at odds too." I rocked into him with my shoulder and said, "He's your best friend."

Isaac shook his head and smiled as he wrapped an arm around my shoulders. "I'm going to try not to be offended that you think I'd consider my best friend to be anyone but you. Grayson chose to go against his pack. Any fallout between us is on him, not you. If you say there shouldn't be any fallout on your behalf, I may have to throw a tantrum in this hallway. I have no qualms about drawing even more attention than you've already garnered, and prompting more rumors."

I'd opened my mouth to say just that but promptly closed it at his threat. "Fine."

"Fine," he echoed and gave my shoulder a squeeze.

"And just to be clear," I said, "I do consider you my best friend. I just wouldn't begrudge you claiming Grayson as yours."

"You're ridiculous," he said fondly, "and this is your next class."

"Just try with him." I held on to his forearm to draw him near. "Okay? Don't throw away twenty years of friendship over him being an idiot for twenty hours. Let the issues between him and I be between him and I." Even if a selfish part of me reveled in his choice to shun Grayson on my half.

I blamed the demon blood.

Isaac didn't respond to me, but I didn't need him to. The set of his jaw was indication enough that he'd consider my advice.

We said our goodbyes next to the open doorway with Isaac promising to meet me here after class and walk me to my next. I didn't need an escort, but I wouldn't reject it either.

I ducked inside the room where Naomi was already seated at a desk in the middle row. She smiled and eagerly waved me over and gestured to the chair next to her. I guess she was still happy to sit next to me as long as the pack wasn't around to see it.

I would not roll my eyes. Our kind craved the connection of the pack, it would take someone with a strong will to risk angering its Alpha. I believe Naomi's intentions were mostly good, but her will was—well, less than strong.

"Oh my goddess I'm so glad we have this class together." She clapped her hands and shook with excitement. "I was dreading it. Some of the other pack members told me it's dreadfully boring."

"I don't think I'd classify inter-realm studies as boring," I said off-handedly. I'd considered specializing in it as Isaac and Grayson had, though I loathed the idea of having any classes with the latter. Maybe alchemy instead. "Learning about the other realms is half the reason we're here. How else will we create alliances? Avoid wars?"

"That sounds like a you and Grayson problem to solve." At least she hadn't said a Kenna and Grayson problem to solve.

"And when your thoughtlessness offends the wrong person and *you* become our problem to solve?"

She wrinkled her nose and looked down at her desk, but said nothing more on the matter. I took out my journal and pencil, and stared pointedly at her empty desk until she did the same.

"Did you see him?" A trio of females entered the room and took the seats behind us. "I swear he was looking at me when we walked by."

"Only in your dreams." Another countered. "Asher was obviously looking at me." I fought the urge to roll my eyes. Whoever Asher was, he certainly wasn't worth competing over with friends.

"I think both of you are dreaming," the third said in a much more level tone. "Asher doesn't look at anyone. He looks through them. Why you'd expect to be the exception is beyond me." Naomi snickered beside me as the trio continued to argue about the likely insignificant, two-second encounter.

"They're talking about the Moon Fox Crown Prince. It seems like everyone always is," Naomi leaned in and whispered, "Apparently he's as cold as ice but everyone who looks at him feels pretty warm if you know what I mean."

I really wish I didn't.

"And why would that matter to me?" I asked.

"I know you're this amazing warrior who can cut any man down where he stands, Briar." I smiled. That may have been the nicest thing she'd ever said to me. She rolled her eyes and went on to say, "But you're also a person. Surely you can appreciate the draw of an attractive, powerful male."

My response was cut off when she exclaimed, "Oh look! It's his cousin!"

I grabbed her pointed finger and pushed her hand down before the female entering the room noticed. Surprise ran through me when I saw she was the fox I'd met in the hall yesterday, Eris.

"Don't point. It's rude, and I'd rather not offend one of the other realms within twenty-four hours of our arrival." Naomi pouted and mumbled her apologies. Goddess grant me patience.

Asher, I realized, had to be the death god accompanying her and her brother. Just the memory of his stare sent shivers down my spine. If the females behind me thought they could break through the man's icy exterior, I bet they'd be chipping away at it for an eternity.

Eris briefly glanced around the room and cut through the desks in our direction when she spotted me. The now ever-present whispers grew louder when she stopped at the desk beside mine and asked, "Do you mind?"

Her voice was every bit as sweet as her face led me to expect.

"Not at all." I reached over and pulled back the chair for her. "Please, have a seat."

Eris' smile emitted the same warmth as basking in the sun. I briefly wondered if she was truly a moon fox. If not for her silver and rose hair, I'd be certain she came from a solar court. Maybe the warmth in her bloodline had missed her cousin and entered her instead.

"Thank you. It's lovely to see you again, Luna Briar." Naomi's jaw dropped as Eris sat and began to unpack her belongings. I'd forgotten she and the others had already left when the foxes had interrupted Grayson and me.

"You don't need to use my title," I assured her, "But thank you for the show of respect. You're welcome to call me Briar."

"Alright, Briar. Then you are welcome to call me Eris." I

was happy to hear it as I had no clue what title I'd use to address her. A duchess? Countess? Lady fox?

"You didn't tell me you met the Viscountess," Naomi whispered in my ear. Mystery solved. Did that make Fabian a viscount? The distinction between royal titles gave me a headache. Life would be simpler if everyone were in a pack.

"I wasn't aware I needed to report my introductions to you," I replied. I didn't bother to look at her as she sputtered that, of course, I didn't need to report anything to her. By the time she'd moved on to another topic, I managed to block out her voice entirely.

Unfortunately, she was not the only person prone to jabbering.

"Did Asher's cousin just sit with those shifter girls?"

"Isn't that the one Grayson rejected?"

"Oh my goddess, do you think Asher's dating one of them?"

"Why would his cousin sitting with them mean he's—"

"Sorry," Eris said, not bothering to keep her voice down, "It seems even a simple conversation can inspire quite the scandal these days. I have to say, I'm shocked no one has more interesting topics to discuss. Their lives must be rather dull." The contrast of her bright smile and cutting words had me mirroring her grin.

"Rather dull, indeed," I agreed, chuckling at the now outraged whispers that continued around us.

The professor, a Fae judging by his pointed ears and haughty demeanor, introduced himself as Professor Cornelius J. Richards with an addendum that we were to call him Professor Richards.

"Why not just introduce himself as that, then?" Naomi grumbled, and I covered my laugh with a cough. Professor Cornelius J. Richards was too preoccupied with spouting his accomplishments for us all to notice.

When he finished listing his accolades, he picked up stacks of booklets from his desk and began distributing them to the first person in each row to pass back.

"This is your syllabus. Treat it like a precious gem because if you lose it, I'm not giving you another." He continued to be such a pleasant male. "Each lesson we'll cover this semester is outlined for you to review, along with a list of assignments and their due dates. I will provide neither reminders nor extensions if you fail to set your own. Questions?"

The classroom was silent as Professor Richards looked at us with his upturned nose and lifted chin. He abruptly clapped his hands together and smirked when a pixie in the first row jumped in her seat. "Great. Let's begin."

I leaned back in my seat and flipped through the pages of the syllabus. At a glance, it seemed we'd cover a vast range of topics, from court hierarchies and battle histories to cultural differences and enchanted bonds. I closed my book and gave the male parading at the front my full attention.

"—And that conflict is how the Hidden split into two courts: Solar and Lunar."

Well damn, how long had I been staring at the syllabus that I'd already missed the entire split? I looked at Naomi to see if she'd written anything down, but she was gazing out the window, twirling a lock of hair between her fingers. How helpful.

"Some of the Hidden realms aligned with a single court." He flicked—actually flicked—his shoulder-length hair back and said, "The Fae, of course, were one of the first to fully declare allegiance to the Solar Court."

As he paced, his eyes landed on mine and Naomi's table and his lip curled. I smiled back–that smile only grew when he shuddered.

"Other realms favored the more, well, let's say rustic Lunar Court and a few split between the Courts." Good goddess, were all members of the Solar Court this superior? I'd never been to a Solar realm, but I'd rather be back wandering alone in the woods than surrounded by people like him with their noses in the air.

"The tension between the two courts has ebbed and flowed throughout the centuries, but never fully diminished. We'll start by taking a look at the Kallistar dynasty."

Professor Richards spent the next hour prattling off the many reasons the first Solar Court was the cornerstone of life as we knew it. His subtle jabs at the Lunar Court didn't go unnoticed; more than one student stiffened in their seats. I was more annoyed than offended.

He had to have been the student constantly starting unfounded rumors when he was in school–the one everyone rolls their eyes at when they open their mouths but whose words still seem to spread like wildfire. He'd probably been locked in his share of cupboards and broom closets by his peers.

The way he spoke made it sound like the Courts were on the brink of war, yet there we sat beside one another in the classroom, Lunar and Solar, without issue. The only incident I'd heard of in the past half-century was between the Sun and Moon Foxes a decade or so back, but the details of the dispute hadn't spread beyond their realms. If Eris and I became friends, maybe I'd ask her about it one day.

A chime rang, and my classmates immediately began packing their belongings and rising from their seats. Professor Richards loudly clapped his hands together and every person who'd risen froze—my blood froze along with them.

"Class is dismissed when I say it's dismissed," he said. He propped his hands on his hips and shifted his weight back on one leg. A spiteful smile spread across his face. We waited in silence. Some of us had no other option.

He waited a full minute more before he said "Those of you who can leave, leave. The rest of you, well, I think you'll make excellent additions to my next class."

My mouth went dry, my knuckles turned white as I collected my belongings and rose with my rucksack in hand. Eris and Naomi rose beside me, Naomi's face turned ashen, and Eris' warm demeanor had chilled. Over half the class stood still as statues including the females who'd been gossiping behind us.

Every inch of them was still as stone except one, well, two: their eyes which frantically darted from around the room. There were few things worse than someone holding power joyfully choosing to abuse it for their own ego.

Disgusting excuse of a male.

I knew men like him. No good would come from my interference. If confronted, he'd inevitably grow more

117

extreme in an effort to prove he was in control. As much as I'd like to challenge him, I couldn't. Not then.

I could, however, pay back his malice if only a little. Passing his desk as I strode to the door, I spotted a mug of brown liquid on his desk. I didn't break my stride as I gave the smallest twitch of my fingers in its direction just as he reached for it.

A shout followed by the sound of ceramic shattering rang out behind me as I crossed through the door into the hall. I ducked my head to hide my smile and looked down at the floor until I could wipe it away. I hoped the scalding liquid drenched him.

When I looked up, the death god was in front of me, dressed in black and sporting an expression that without my magic would've surely chilled me to the bone.

"That professor is such a jerk," Naomi grumbled. I didn't disagree.

"Bye, Briar." Eris waved at me and joined her cousin's side. "Thanks for sitting with me." His stare lingered on me but said nothing as he fell into step beside her and disappeared down the hallway.

"Hey!" I turned as Isaac jogged toward me from the opposite direction. "Sorry, I'm late. I got held up talking to someone." He offered no other explanation, but I caught a flash of forest-green eyes as they disappeared around the corner behind him. Good. Let their reconciliation be my kind deed of the day.

"Don't worry about it," I forced a smile, "We just got released anyway. Now show me to this potions lab I'm supposed to be in. I think I'll be a master brewer in no time, don't you?"

"Let's take it one step at a time." He wrapped his arm around my shoulder and we started across campus. "I'm pretty sure the last potion you made, made half the enforcers go bald from the vapors alone."

"I was ten."

"Exactly." He shuddered. "Think of how much more dangerous you have to be at eighteen."

12

THE ROSE

Classes finally ended for the day, and what little tolerance I'd had for the stares, snickers, and whispers had disappeared completely. The other students took to calling me the rejected princess under their breath after I'd run into Grayson in the hallway between afternoon classes. For my part, I'd tried to keep things civil, but he brushed me off before a greeting could even pass my lips.

For a few seconds, our eyes met, and I was almost certain warmth–or something like it–flashed across his face. That annoying speck of hope I'd squashed at the assembly hall reared its head at the possibility. He'd looked at me that way a hundred times growing up.

It was the way he looked at me the first time I'd spoken after his parents brought me home and shot my first bullseye with an arrow. It was the way he looked at me when he came home from his first mission as Beta and told me every detail over hot cider. It was the way he looked at me that made me feel like I was the only person in the world who mattered.

That same look was gone a moment later and he'd continued walking as though he hadn't seen me in the first place. It was as if he was two different men: one of them promised me solace and the other stole it from me. I didn't know which was real. It didn't matter anyway; whoever the real Grayson was, I didn't have the time or patience to wait for him to reveal himself.

"She's that Briar girl who challenged Kenna in the quad. I heard she can't even shift. She must be delusional to think she could unseat a lion shifter just because she comes from some great pack or whatever."

I moved before I'd consciously decided to do so. My dagger landed a hairsbreadth from the gossiping selkie.

The girl froze, all color draining from her face. Beside her, her friend jumped more than a foot backward, knocking into the group of students behind her. They fell to the ground like a house with a glass foundation.

The commotion drew even more eyes and the hallway seemed to stop altogether, everyone stood like my classmates had been when under Professor Richards' spell. Now they were under mine.

The selkie managed to take a single step back and turn to look at me. I twirled a second dagger between my fingers and studied her, taking care to keep my face impassive. Her loose tongue wasn't worth losing control, but this couldn't continue to go on. Someone had to be the example of what happened to someone who disrespected the Othniel Pack, and she'd all but offered herself on a platter to me.

"Was there something you cared to say to me?" I asked. She shook her head frantically back and forth, denying it.

"You seemed to have quite a bit to say about me–about my *pack*– to your friend, why don't you tell me your concerns instead? I'm sure they're riveting."

She stammered, presumably searching for an explanation or excuse, but no legible words passed her lips. How quickly the bold turned timid when faced with consequences of their own making.

"Nothing to say now?" I taunted, stepping closer to her and letting the tip of my favorite dagger glide across her cheek. I didn't break the skin. "Why are you shaking? Didn't you already decide I don't pose a threat? I mean, I can't even shift."

On the last word, I sank the tip of my blade into her soft, obviously pampered, flesh until the smallest rivulet of blood formed. I smiled as it dripped down her neck.

"I—I'm so— sorry!" Her chest rose and fell faster than a hummingbird's wings.

"Don't worry, little fish," I said, "I'm not going to hurt you–at least not too much."

"Playing with your prey, Luna?" Marcus asked from behind me and joined me at my side. He looked the girl up and down and snickered. "She's not exactly a worthy opponent for the Beta of the Othniel Pack, is she? Did *she* really challenge *you*?"

Marcus was far from the most intimidating male in the Othniel Pack but he was still from the Othniel Pack—the most powerful pack on the continent. That alone would give anyone with a partial brain pause. I didn't need him to back me up, but sometimes we can want things we don't need. I took comfort in the reminder I wasn't alone.

"No, she isn't." I dragged the dagger under her chin to the other side of her cheek. Sometimes violence was the only universal language in the realm. The dance of dominance was understood by all, and it was time for me to clear up any miscommunications. "She must be delusional, but challenge me she did."

"I did—I didn't." If she shook her head any harder it was liable to fall free of her neck.

"Oh, but you did," I reminded her, "The second my name crossed your lips as you spewed your nonsense as though it was truth sent down from the gods."

"She isn't worth the time it will take to wash the blood from your blade." Marcus propped his hand beneath his chin and tilted his head as his eyes studied her. "I have a better idea, if you'll permit me?"

I nodded my consent, and his grin was vicious as his human form shrank toward the floor, disappearing into a pile of his clothes. The bunched-up fabric moved this way and that until a black snake slithered from its confinement toward the female.

She shrieked and moved to jump away, but my blade beneath her chin halted her progress. Now I was the one grinning.

Marcus' snake wound his way up her legs and abdomen until he was coiled around her torso, flicking his tongue against her neck. A wet spot grew against her linen pants. Gross. The snake pulled his tail away from the area and hissed in her ear. I'd be nonplussed if my lower half was covered in selkie urine too. He grazed her skin with his fangs but didn't pierce it, mimicking the motion of my dagger.

"Should I order him off you?" I asked in a whisper, drawing my face near her ear. "Or maybe I should let him feast on your flesh. I assure you the venom coursing through your veins will be a once-in-a-lifetime memory. You'd never forget it. You'd never forget *me*."

I drew back and the snake lifted his head to watch me, waiting. Marcus was a brat, but he was a loyal brat. He'd follow whichever command I chose. I could show strength or show mercy–both had their benefits, and both had their consequences.

"Briar, what the hell?"

Interfering wolf. I turned my eyes from my prey but left the dagger against her skin. From the corner of my eye, I saw that Marcus hadn't turned to look at the Alpha stomping toward us. His eyes were still fixed firmly on me. I'd remember this the next time I contemplated cutting out his and his sister's tongues.

"Can I help you, Alpha?" I asked dryly. Grayson's head drew back an inch at the title. If he wanted to act like we were strangers, I'd address him as one. He walked to my side and looked between the growing crowd, the snake-ensnared selkie, and me.

"Let her go." He spoke the words quietly between clenched teeth, but it still couldn't be mistaken for anything but a command.

"It's cute that you think you can tell me what to do." I smiled and said, "Now if you don't mind, the little fish and I were in the middle of something."

"I'm serious," he said, stepping closer until he towered over me, "You're causing a scene."

"I'm causing a scene?" I could have laughed. "What would you call the past twenty-four hours?"

"This isn't you," he hissed, "you're better than this. I know you're acting out right now, but–"

"This is me being better." I straightened until my face was but a few inches from where his leaned over me. "I'm defending myself, and I'm defending my pack. Can you say the same?"

"Who are you to question my commitment to this pack?" he snapped, "You have no idea what I've given up on its behalf."

"And yet the whispers and slander prevail as you walk through the halls with your head held high as though the words hold no meaning," I accused, "Or am I no longer part of that pack you're committed to? I believe this seal on my arm says otherwise." I raised the wrist that bore my Beta mark between us, but he didn't spare it a glance.

"You're experiencing the consequences of your own missteps."

"And now she's getting hers." I gestured to the still trembling selkie with a tip of my head. "So if you'll excuse me, I have matters to attend to."

He growled under his breath, and added another offense to the many he'd committed since I'd arrived. He grabbed my arm and tried to pull me away from my prey.

Three things happened in tandem next: Marcus' snake lunged, the selkie screamed, and I sank the claws up my dagger-free hand into Grayson's forearm to pry his hand from mine.

"Did you seriously just draw blood from your Alpha?"

"Did you seriously just try to put your hands on me? I know you seem to keep forgetting, but you don't outrank me, Grayson Pierce." I withdrew my claws. I was not going to think about the rush of satisfaction I felt at seeing my marks on his skin. "And you're welcome, by the way. I promise you my claws are better than Marcus' fangs, or do you enjoy paralysis, fever, and unending agony?"

The selkie whimpered as the snake flicked her cheek with his tongue. I think he may have been enjoying this a little too much. I can't say I blamed him. I felt immense satisfaction seeing the small drops of blood on Grayson's skin. I may not be able to shift into my animal, but I could descend its claws and fangs when needed. As Fenrir liked to remind me as a child, a partial shift was still more useful than no shift at all.

"We'll address Marcus' disrespect later." He glared at the snake.

"Are you joking?" I looked at him incredulously. "You think you have any place to lecture anyone on respect?"

"He attacked his Alpha."

"He defended his Luna." I dropped my dagger from the selkie's throat and turned to face Grayson fully. "No matter what you tell yourself to sleep soundly at night, Grayson Pierce, we both know that I outrank Kenna and am the Luna of this pack until something proves otherwise."

"That doesn't matter he—"

"Stop whining like a petulant child." Gasps sounded around us. I knew I should hold back, do the right thing, save him the embarrassment; humiliating him meant humiliating the pack—both the Iolite and Othniel—but dammit he'd embarrassed me first and I was beyond tired of being the better person. I didn't want to be a better person. I wanted him to grovel on his knees and beg my forgiveness after experiencing a fraction of what this felt like.

"Watch your words, Briar," he said between clenched teeth and closed the distance between us until I was staring up into his eyes, our noses almost but not quite touching.

"Why?" I asked, and said more quietly, "You certainly haven't watched yours. Did you expect me to take this in silence? That I'd walk through the halls amongst sneers and whispers that derived directly from your words and actions without lifting a finger in retaliation? To disrespect me is to disrespect the pack, and to disrespect the pack is a grave mistake. You used to know that."

His throat bobbed as he swallowed but said nothing. His eyes darted between mine and down before landing on them again.

"You seem to have mistaken the deference I showed you at home as blind obedience. It wasn't." I reached a hand up to trace the line of his face, contemplating if this would be the last time I'd let it cause me any pain. "I listened to you before because more than anyone else, I believed in you."

Something akin to devastation flashed in his eyes.

"I don't anymore."

I took one step back from him, then two. He looked at me in silence for a beat. Both of us stood there, saying nothing, eyes locked, and pretending we didn't have half the school circling around us, watching for what would happen next.

He looked down first.

"Now little fish," I said, turning to the selkie, "Let's not do this again. The next time my name leaves your mouth, remember that this is what happens when you cross a predator bigger than you."

I lifted my arm and she flinched. Pathetic. If she wanted to spew words of contempt, she could at least face a challenge head on without flinching.

"Marcus," I commanded, "Leave her."

He gave her a final hiss and flick of his tongue against her ear before languidly slithering over her shoulder onto my outstretched arm. Once he was wrapped securely around me, I grabbed his clothes where they'd fallen from the floor and stood.

"By the way," I told her with a smirk, "You may want to switch from linen to leather. I find it hides fluids much better. Though it's usually the blood of my victims staining mine, and not, well, other things."

Her lip curled, and I turned to leave with every intention of ramming my shoulder into Grayson's on my way out. I'd only taken two steps when I heard her curse under her breath, "Latent bitch."

I stopped walking.

Grayson's entire body stiffened at the whispered insult, but still, he said nothing. Did nothing. I raised a single brow and examined him from head to toe and back. I hoped he saw the judgment in my eyes. I hoped he saw the blame. He caused this mess, and I was left dealing with the clean up.

Slowly, I pivoted back to look at the selkie. She hadn't even noticed I'd heard her grumbled words. She was hunched over wiping at the legs of her pants like that would magically make the liquid disappear.

Though, I suppose that could be possible—I hadn't read much on selkies, to be honest. I didn't consider them much of a threat. Maybe they held power over the water they preferred to bask in. The friend she'd spoken to earlier had returned to her side and was fussing over her. Neither of their heads rose as I approached them again until my boots came into view.

"You're a slow learner," I observed. Both females turned pallid as their eyes grew as wide as saucers. "Marcus."

He struck.

One bite wouldn't kill her, but she may wish she were dying when the venom set in. The pain would start slowly and then build until it felt like her blood was burning her alive from the inside.

The snake looked at me, the unspoken question lingering in his eyes. I shook my head. A second would likely send her into shock, and that seemed a bit unfair, even to me. I doubted she had much if any training against torture tactics. What a pity for her.

"Maybe this will make a longer impression," I said, keeping the emotion out of my voice. "You should probably head to your room unless you want an audience when the screaming kicks in."

The whimpering had already amplified into groans. Her friend kept her head down but wrapped an arm around the girl's shoulder to guide her away.

"You're embarrassing yourself," her friend seethed so low, I was surely the only one to hear it, "I told you the shifters are all insane. You could've at least tried to fight back."

I didn't disagree, but I wondered if the second selkie

would defend herself if she'd been the object of my ire. She certainly hadn't stepped forward to defend her friend.

"Wait," I commanded. They obeyed. Good. Maybe they were capable of having sense after all.

I stood in front of the girl's friend and lifted her chin with my finger until her fear-filled eyes met mine.

"Did you want to say anything?" I asked. She frantically shook her head. I sighed. How disappointing.

"Marcus." He struck, sinking his fangs into the second female's neck. She cringed but didn't cry out. She was stronger than her friend. Somehow that filled me with even more rage.

"I didn't—" She flinched. "I didn't say anything!"

"Exactly," I growled at her, clutching a handful of her shirt and drawing her head up to be just under mine. "You said nothing."

I shoved her away. She dropped to the floor, the first selkie dropping beside her without her support.

"You did nothing," I sneered. I looked around the crowd in disgust. I spotted a pair of midnight blue eyes but ignored the death god's gaze in search of my target. One alpha male at a time.

I stared directly into Grayson's forest green eyes when I said, "Someone who sees their friend under attack and does nothing is the very worst kind of person. If the threat of defeat or failure stops you from taking action in service of the people you care about, you're nothing but a coward."

I looked back at the cowering females. "And I have no tolerance or time for cowards."

I strode past the still-silent wolf. I didn't knock into him with my shoulder like I'd planned. I didn't meet the gaze I felt burning into my head. I cut through the crowd of students who parted as I passed, kept my head high, snake-clad shoulders high, and let them see the message written on my face: I was done being treated like easy prey.

THE ROSE

I didn't stop walking until we'd left the building and entered one of the outdoor breezeways. It was partially to put as much distance between myself and Grayson as I could and partially because I hadn't actually known where I wanted to storm off to when I'd stormed off. Ducking into an alcove that seemed as good a place as any, I dropped Marcus's clothes onto the edge of the open-air window.

"Change and get dressed," I said, "You know I adore you and your vicious little fangs, but I need to speak to the man now."

The snake nuzzled his coffin-shaped head against my cheek once then slithered off my arm to the ground. I stepped back into the breezeway and turned my back while he changed. Shifters weren't shy about nudity—our very nature made that impossible—but it was polite to offer privacy when we could. Given I'd spent years in a pack as the only person to never shift, I'd grown used to being fully clothed while others were, well, less than.

"So, that was fun." Marcus pulled his shirt into place as he joined me in the breezeway. His mouth was set in a mischievous smile and his eyes were brighter than I'd seen them since we'd arrived.

"That's your definition of fun?" I asked. "You know Grayson won't forget you lunging for him today, right? The wolf is an expert at holding a grudge."

He shrugged, unfazed.

"I hope he does remember," he said, "I hope it's a reminder that our allegiance isn't something he's owed, it's something he earns. I hope that when he thinks of today he thinks about that while he hasn't earned it, you have. Maybe then he'll ask himself why and start acting like someone we can respect again."

For the first time, maybe ever, Marcus had rendered me speechless. I wasn't used to his words ringing with wisdom instead of immaturity.

"Plus think of how cool I'll be when word gets around I challenged an Alpha and lived to tell the tale. The females will be lining up to fawn over me."

And with that, the moment was ruined, and the world was back on its rightful axis.

"I'm going to pretend I didn't hear that last part and just say thank you." I reached over to ruffle his copper hair. "Thanks for having my back."

"Pack mates have to stick together," he said, "I may not be as powerful as Isaac or Grayson, but I won't turn my back on you. Like you said, someone who sees their friend under attack and does nothing is a coward, and I'm a lot of things, but not a coward."

Unless of course, it's a chimera. In that case, he'll be too scared to leave the carriage, but I chose not to bring that up. He'd done well today. I'd let him keep his pride.

"I'm going to meet Naomi for dinner," he said, "Want to come with? Or should I escort you somewhere?"

"Escort me?" I bit my tongue to keep from laughing. His attempt to be sweet was very thoughtful, but the idea of needing an escort made me want to giggle. "No, I'm okay, but it's sweet of you to offer. Have fun with your sister. Maybe I'll see you at dinner."

"Okay, I'll catch you later then. If I see Isaac, should I let him know where you are?"

"No need." I smiled conspiratorially and channeled my inner Fenrir when I said. "Let him track me down if he wants to. It'll give him a chance to sharpen his tracking skills."

When he heard about the events in the hallway he surely would. He may be horrified at my choices, but I felt good—proud. Not only had I shut down the rumors of my fragility, I hadn't felt my fire surface a single time during the confrontation, not even when that hateful fish called me a latent bitch and Grayson, again, stood by and did nothing. If that wasn't the epitome of self-control, I'm not sure what was.

Marcus gave me a half wave as a goodbye and strode to the other breezeway to find his sister. I sighed and let my shoulders relax, giving myself a minute to lean against the stone pillar and breathe.

It had been necessary, I reminded myself. The rumors and whispers couldn't be allowed to continue. They'd only spread and grow. I'd done what I needed to do, and I'd be lying if I said I hadn't taken some pleasure in it at the moment, but now? After it was done? The smallest tendrils of guilt invaded the perimeter of my mind.

What was wrong with me that I found joy in the ruin of others? Was it justice? Vengeance? Or was it simply part of my nature to be fueled by the pain of those weaker than me? I shook the thoughts from my mind and pushed off the wall. My minute was up.

I started walking aimlessly as I pondered where to go. I definitely wasn't in the mood to go back into the crowded hallways or face off with Grayson in the dining hall. I had no interest in being the evening's entertainment for the pack and the rest of the student body—I'd given them enough of myself for one day.

I stopped.

That was my fault—not theirs.

I let them put me in this position. Their behavior is unacceptable yes, but hadn't I all but accepted it? I didn't force my way into the pack. I didn't submit, but I didn't take what was owed to me either, did I? With the exception of the little fish in the hall today, I hadn't even brought the gossips and naysayers to their knees.

I'd been tolerant—too tolerant.

That ended now.

I straightened my back, raised my head, and turned toward the dining hall, meeting the eye of each student who crossed my path, and every time they were the first to look away a piece of me fell back into place. By the time I pushed through the double doors of the dining hall, I was feeling more like myself than I had since stepping foot on Academy grounds.

The stained glass encased room was unsurprisingly crowded with some students lining up to get their dinners as others huddled around the rectangular tables scattered throughout the room. I recognized a few faces from the day's classes and a few more from the incident in the hall. More than one selkie sent glares my way, but I didn't spare them a second of consideration as I scanned the room.

The only group that did capture my attention for a half second longer than it took to glance over was the table of foxes, but not even the death god's icy stare could distract me from my target. Why did he always have to be staring?

I kept walking through the room, noting who was—or rather wasn't—at each table I passed, and then I saw him.

Grayson sat at the head of the table, and a wave of familiarity hit me as I moved in that direction. Once again, I saw him before he saw me, but he wasn't smiling in my absence this time. He paid attention to each of the pack mates who spoke to him in turn, but the joy–the light–he'd had in his eyes before my arrival had disappeared.

Maybe I'd stolen it from him.

Another twinge of guilt hit me when I saw Isaac, Naomi, and Marcus easily conversing with the other pack members. They shouldn't have to choose between their loyalty and their desire to integrate into their new pack. No doubt, what I did next and how Grayson chose to respond would make it that much harder for them to accomplish both.

It wasn't Kenna sitting at the head of the table opposite Grayson, so I could only assume the petite brunette was her

Beta. She didn't notice me as I drew closer, no one did. Well, no one other than Isaac. I was pretty sure Isaac would find me in the middle of a white-out snowstorm if he sensed I was nearby—which he inevitably would.

Sometimes I wondered if he and his father hired a witch to enchant my bloodstone with a tracking spell. I wouldn't be shocked if they had and it would explain how any attempts I made as a child to hide away from them had proven pointless.

"I think you're in my seat." My tone was kind by design. I was impressed with my amiability, all things considered. I stopped a step away from her, there was no need to loom over her shoulder, at least not yet.

The girl looked up at me, and I knew the second she fully processed who was speaking to her when her spine stiffened. Her eyes darted to the pack mates sitting on either side of her and visibly stiffened when she turned her attention back to me.

The longer I stared at her, the more obvious it became she didn't want this fight. The mark of a great Beta was being ambitious enough to lead but not so ambitious they threaten their Alpha or Luna, and her Beta instincts must be screaming at her to yield to me.

As much as I craved a fight—a chance to prove I was done with allowing others to push me aside—she didn't deserve to be dragged into one, especially not one she had no part in starting.

There was a fine line between leading with a healthy dose of respect-driven fear and leading with fear as the foundation of your control, and I was teetering on the edge of it. So, instead of grabbing her by the hair and forcing her to her knees, I channeled my inner Lucas and attempted to take a calming breath.

I relaxed my shoulders and said, "We haven't had a chance to meet yet. What's your name?"

"What are you—" I held up a hand to interrupt Grayson's interruption.

"I'm not talking to you right now, I'm meeting my new pack mate." I didn't spare him a glance as I spoke. Getting to know the pack would be easier if I pretended he didn't exist– you can't argue with someone that isn't there. I asked the female again, "What is your name?"

She cleared her throat and answered, "Ainsley."

"Hi, Ainsley. It's nice to meet you." I curled my mouth in a smile, but I don't think it helped put her at ease. "I'm Briar."

"Hi."

I waited for her to say more, but she must've been a woman of few words. I quirked my brow and gave Isaac a look meant to say 'Goddess I hope the rest of the pack communicates better than its Beta'. He shrugged.

Not an encouraging sign.

"Hi," I repeated, pausing again in case she wanted to interject. She didn't. "Ainsley, I know the situation between Kenna and me is probably confusing, but can you move seats please?"

More than one intake of breath sounded around the table, and I lost the internal battle not to roll my eyes. I knew it was exceedingly rare for a Pack Leader to make a request instead of giving a directive, but it wasn't completely unheard of—excuse me for attempting to be polite.

To my pleasant surprise, she grabbed her plate and slid to the seat next to her, around the corner of the table. The others gaped at her compliance but still shuffled to make room for her to sit.

I took her place in the chair and leaned back against it, one leg crossing over the other. Only when I was comfortably sat did I look up, expecting to see an ever-glowering wolf staring back at me.

Except when I did look up, it wasn't anger or disapproval shining in his eyes. It was approval — maybe even a shred of respect.

"I'll grab you a plate, Luna." Isaac winked at me as he rose and walked toward the array of food at the front of the room.

I ignored the shocked expressions at his use of the title and called a quick thank you after him before turning to address Ainsley once more.

"So tell me, what pack are you from?"

"The Hemlock Pack," she answered after a moment's hesitation. "My mother is the Beta there."

"To Alpha Frederic or Luna Mara?" I asked.

"Uh, Alpha Frederic," she answered, eyebrows drawn in.

"So you're Charlotte's daughter, then." Her shock drew a smile to my face. "I met her during my visit last spring. She's one of the fiercest warriors I've fought beside. You must be very proud."

Ainsley crossed her forearms on the table, nearly dunking

her sleeve in the mashed potatoes on the edge of her plate, and leaned closer, studying me.

"You're the Beta who drove the kelpies from the lake?" she asked, a hint of awe warming her voice.

"Well, it was a group effort, but I certainly helped."

It really hadn't been. I'd been the one to dive in the lake and drive them away, but it was rude to brag.

"You captured their king and cut off his head!"

Forks clanged along plates in what became an otherwise silent room.

"And now the entire room knows it." I chuckled at the open-mouthed stares her exclamation garnered. "But yes, I did."

My chest felt lighter now that the tension at my arrival had been broken. At least it did until a deep voice rang from the other end of the table.

"You never told me about that." Grayson's accusation had me turning to him before I remembered my plan to ignore him completely. The tips of his fingers were white where he gripped the edge of the table. I wondered if he managed to snap it if we'd have to reimburse the school directly or if they baked the cost into the tuition.

"I must have skipped over it during our many heart-to-hearts and deep discussions about life the past few years." His eyes narrowed. My lips twitched as I realized I held the power to get under his skin. It was only fair—he'd spent years getting under mine even if the emotions driving it were opposite as fire and rain.

"Is that what you were off doing every time I came

home?" If he hadn't cared enough to ask where I was then, I saw no reason for him to care enough to ask now.

"The Hemlock Pack called for aid, and there was no need for your parents to miss seeing you when I had the matter well in hand."

He leaned so far forward, I suspected he'd left the seat of his chair entirely. It'd be a shame if someone knocked into him and he fell.

"I could've gone to help you," he said tersely, "If any of you had told me where you were or what you were doing, I would've gone to you."

"As I said," I deadpanned with a raised brow, "I had the matter well in hand. I didn't need your help then." I didn't need his help now. The unspoken words felt heavy in the air between us.

He lowered back into his seat. His posture said 'I'm at ease,' but the vein pulsing in his neck said 'I may throw a chair.'

"And every other time I came back?" he asked. He was either oblivious to the dozen faces watching us with rapt attention or he simply didn't care we had an audience. "Is that what you were doing without me? Risking your life battling creatures and making enemies rather than being there the two or three times I could make it home in a year?"

Now I was the one staring with an open mouth. This was neither the time nor the place for that conversation. I was quite certain there would never be a time or place for that conversation—not while I had a say in the matter.

"I didn't realize my absence was such a hardship for you," I admitted truthfully.

"Then you weren't paying attention." He sprawled back in his chair, his arms hanging along its sides like a king on his throne.

"On the contrary, I see and hear far more than you give me credit for," I said and mirrored his stance. "So let's not rewrite our history, okay?"

His jaw hardened and he pivoted the conversation back to my safety, when he said, "Kelpies are as loyal as they are vengeful. They will not forget you stole their King from them." As if I didn't already know that. What did he expect me to do? Only eliminate the threats who would never fight back?

"If being a bit more cautious when I swim in a lake is the price for keeping the shifter realm safe, I'll gladly pay it."

"And if it's more than that?" His voice dropped lower, but I still heard every word, "If the price was your life? What then? Will you still be so willing to give it?"

"In an instant," I answered without hesitation, "I will protect the shifters in my charge until my last breath and give even that if needed, just like I vowed to do. Just like you vowed to do. Would you truly expect any less of me?"

"No." A drop of relief hit me at his immediate answer. "But I wish you would stop choosing to face unnecessary dangers alone when there are people right there willing to help you."

"And I wish you'd trust that I know when to call for help and when help is not needed," I countered, "I guess we're both destined to be disappointed."

"Just because my mother made you her Beta—"

"And that's another wish of mine," I snapped, "stop

143

saying she made me her Beta as though she convinced Logan to throw the Pack Rite. I won that challenge fairly, and I've defended it proudly. Don't diminish my standing or your mother's integrity by implying otherwise."

You prick, I was tempted to add. For the sake of those around us, I bit my tongue and prayed for patience instead. After the Rite they'd acknowledge me as their Luna and a greater rift between their Pack Leaders would cause constant unrest.

I took a moment to study the ceiling while my blood cooled. I wouldn't admit it to him, but Fenrir was right. I needed the bloodstone to stay in control while I was here, but I doubted either of us expected my own pack mate to be the cause.

I braced myself for whatever quick retort or jab he'd throw me next, but it never came. The only sounds that reached my ears were the scraping of utensils on plates and the breathing of the people around me. One of them was breathing harder than they were before I'd spoken.

When the silence continued, and my neck began to twinge, I reluctantly looked away from the vaulted ceiling. I expected to see anger or maybe arrogance on Grayson's face. I hadn't expected to see awe.

"You challenged Logan?" His voice half broke on the last syllable. "You fought in the Rite? Against *him*?"

Was he joking?

It'd been nearly two years since I first challenged Logan, surely someone from the pack had told him, hadn't they? Staring into Grayson's shining eyes as his chest rose and fell more rapidly than it had before, I realized the answer was no. They hadn't.

It felt like my chest was caving in on itself without reason. I didn't trust myself to speak clearly enough to give him an answer. I simply nodded instead.

I'm not sure what I had expected from him, but the shaky laughter that left him as he rubbed a hand over his mouth certainly wasn't it. Judging by the widened eyes and slack-jawed faces of the others around the table, I wasn't the only one.

Looking back at Grayson, he wasn't laughing anymore, but had the smallest hint of his smile on his face. I didn't drop his gaze and he didn't drop mine, not when Isaac slid a plate in front of me, not when I muttered my thanks, not when someone coughed and cleared their throat, not even when footsteps signaled someone's approach behind me.

"Another staring contest, I see. I do wish you two would get over whatever issues you have and tear each other's clothes off already. If you have any regard for my sanity, you'll spare us all the longing stares while you pretend to loathe each other."

"We are perfectly amicable," Grayson assured her, not sparing her a glance but sounding more sincere than was trustworthy. What was he playing at?

"No different than any other pair of childhood pack mates," I added.

"Because that was super convincing." Kenna slid unceremoniously onto the bench opposite Ainsley and propped her chin up on her hands, elbows resting on the table. She then turned to me with a wistful sigh and said, "I heard about the scene with the selkies. Nicely handled, I wish I could've been there to see you get all dagger happy. I bet it was glorious. Is that what prompted this round of overly-charged eye contact between you and wolf boy? I totally get it, but maybe take it somewhere private, you know? Spare the rest of us."

"Kenna," Grayson chided half-heartedly, "Enough."

"Like you two aren't obvious to everyone sitting here." She rolled her eyes and grabbed a piece of bread from the plate of the male—I really should learn all of their names— sitting beside her. "You can ogle each other at the pack run tonight, but must you subject us all to it while we're trying to eat?"

Ice speared down my throat and settled in my chest.

"What pack run?" Naomi asked. "No one told me about a pack run. Did you know about a pack run?" So it wasn't just me who'd missed the announcement.

Naomi elbowed her brother who grunted, and said, "Can you not? I didn't know either, keep your pointy elbows to yourself."

My eyes cut to Isaac who shook his head. No one else at the table seemed surprised by Kenna's announcement, but more than one face turned sheepish. A willful deception then.

"It must have been an oversight." I put a smile on my face and said, "After all, the only alternative explanation would be someone intentionally excluding the Othniel Pack from an Iolite Pack event, well, at least some of us."

Not a single pack member met my gaze. Each of them stared at their food or looked down at the table, except Grayson.

Grayson didn't look away. He let me see the storm of emotions swimming in the green of his eyes: regret, determination, and affection? No, it couldn't be. I shook away the thought. No good would come from falling back into that trap.

"It had to be a mistake," I repeated, "unless someone is planning to have two packs at the Academy instead of one this year."

"That would be ridiculous," he said slowly, "and I'd never propose or support it."

"Right, ridiculous." I addressed Naomi next, "So you see? It was just an oversight. No one's perfect."

Kenna turned to me with a puzzled look on her face and said, "I take offense to that. I'm quite perfect, but I'll forgive you your mistake since you've only had a couple of days to take me all in."

"I'm sure that's the case." I reached over and patted her hand before picking up my fork and to stab a few green beans before stuffing them in my mouth to avoid further conversation.

"So you are coming tonight?" Ainsley asked. It seemed her voice had accompanied Kenna's arrival. "To the pack run, I mean."

I reached for the goblet Isaac thoughtfully brought me with my plate and took a drink before responding.

"Yes, of course." I asked, "Why wouldn't I?"

The question hung in the air without an answer. Ainsley's only reply was a nervous chuckle and a shake of her head before she became fully fixated on the food in front of her.

Isaac, bless his kind heart, took pity on us all and struck

up a conversation with the male next to him. They prattled on about the Myths and Legends class they shared this year and the professor's propensity for spitting as he spoke. *Gross.* A minute or two later everyone has returned to the conversations they'd been having before my arrival or started new ones.

By the time I finished eating Kenna had essentially stolen Christopher's plate—I'd finally learned his name—and spent the better part of the past twenty minutes explaining why she was so attached to her favorite dagger. She'd insisted on comparing it against the blades of everyone present to further prove its superiority.

The surrounding students looked utterly stupefied at my outburst of laughter when I presented my dagger and she'd been unable to find a flaw. Her entire face had closed off as she'd turned the blade over in her hands before glaring up at me and saying, "It's perfect. How can it be perfect? Do you even use it?"

She'd kept a firm grip on the handle, but I managed to pry it from her hand and slide it back into the sheath on my thigh.

"I truly don't know if this makes me want to be your friend more or accidentally kill you during the Rite so I can keep your blade as a trophy." She contemplated for a moment, her head cocked to one side as she thought it over.

"If you're planning an accidental death, it's not actually an accident," Naomi chimed. Kenna shot her a glare that had the blood fleeing from the serpent's face before she turned to her twin to ask about the weather.

Kenna returned her attention to me, and grumpily asked, "Where did you get this? I want one."

"I don't know, it was a gift." And the person who gave it was currently on my list of people to use it on. I'd rather not openly credit him for finding it even as he sat opposite me with a growing grin—the picture of smug satisfaction.

"That's still your favorite dagger, then?" Grayson asked. "You must not have forgotten me completely if that's still the first blade you reach for."

I knew he was baiting me—it was an obvious taunt in the same tone he'd used to rile me up as a child, and I cursed that it always worked. A wiser woman would ignore him, but I never claimed to be wise.

"The blade had no say in who purchased it," I quipped back, "I don't know why I should neglect it for factors beyond its control."

"So you admit you haven't really forgotten me?" His smile grew until it was borderline dazzling, how annoying.

"I haven't said or acted like I've forgotten you, Grayson I'm sitting right here speaking to you. I have been this entire time."

"Yeah, now you're speaking to me, but—"

"Stay on topic!" Kenna stalked toward Grayson and glared. "Where's my dagger, Grayson Pierce? If the two years we've led together mean so little to you that you've never thought to give me one then at least tell me the silversmith who made it."

I could hardly believe my eyes as pink tinged the top of his cheeks—in the entire decade I'd known him he'd never looked flushed—and he ran a hand through his hair before answering.

"He's not available anymore."

Kenna scoffed and flicked a hand through the air. "Don't be ridiculous. I'll make him available, just give me his name."

"Drop it, Kenna." Grayson's words were nearly a growl.

"I certainly will not. Now you tell me that silversmith's name or so help me I swear to the suns I will—"

"I made it, okay?" He cut off her rant and my breathing. "I made the damn thing, and I'm not making another so let it go already. You won't die if one person has a nicer blade than you."

Kenna began muttering the many reasons she surely would die, but it faded and the blood rushed to my ears and drowned out her words and the sounds of the dining hall.

"You made this for me?" He nodded hesitantly. "It must have taken days."

"Weeks, actually." His chuckle held no humor.

"You never told me." And I couldn't for the life of me understand why. I'd been ecstatic when he gave it to me thinking it was something he purchased. If he'd told me it was crafted by his own hands, back then I think I'd have fainted on the spot.

"It wasn't important," he dismissed, pushing back from the table and grabbing his now empty plate. "It was just a gift."

"Grayson," I said beseechingly, not sure what I planned to say next. I was spared from having to decide when he waved me off and turned to leave.

"I'll see you all tonight."

Then the man who'd spent weeks crafting me the perfect blade dropped his dishes at the wash station and left the room without a backward glance.

Kenna slid back into her seat and looked longingly at my thigh. I swore the sheathed blade there burned against my skin even through the leather.

She sighed and said decidedly, "If I accidentally kill you in the Pack Rite, I'm stealing that dagger."

Naomi looked at her in horror before whispering not so quietly to her twin, "Does she sound entirely too happy about that to you too?"

Kenna looked at her and smiled.

THE ROSE

"Staring at it isn't going to change who made it."

Isaac's grin was more than a little smug as we walked along the forest path that led to the clearing we'd gather in for the pack run. I briefly wondered if he'd be as smug if I reached a foot out to trip him.

"Who said I was even thinking about who made it?" I asked, keeping my voice light but still staring at the labradorite-encrusted blade. "Maybe I'm just admiring the glint of silver in the pre-dusk glow and contemplating the meaning of life."

"A decent evasion except I already know you consider the meaning of life to be enjoying its simple pleasures and protecting others from harm. You declared as much in the truth's circle at my going away party."

Sabotaged by a childish party game.

"Well, maybe I'm reevaluating." I wasn't. "I can't be expected to always feel the way I felt at fifteen, now can I?"

"I won't make you talk about it today." He threw his arm

around my shoulder and squeezed me to his side. "But I know you're thinking about him, and I just want you to know it's okay that you are. There's nothing wrong with it."

I shrugged off his arm and said sternly, "I'm not thinking about him."

Of course, I was thinking about him.

How could I be consumed by anything else after such a revelation? It went against everything I'd reminded myself to be true in the last three years. The unquestionable act of service by crafting my blade—my beautiful blade—was nothing short of infuriating.

I was not someone he would invest this much time, this much labor into pleasing. I was a nuisance, an obligation. I was a duty he upheld to please his parents and serve the Pack. I was unwanted.

I knew it was true. I'd heard it from his lips before he left, the words forever branded into the walls of my heart and mind, yet proof of the opposite lay perfectly balanced in my hand.

"It just doesn't make sense," I cursed under my breath. My hands gripped my hair, one still holding the dagger, and fell heavy at my side. I turned to my best friend and repeated, "It doesn't make any sense, Isaac."

"It makes perfect sense." He stared straight ahead, but I could still see the twinkle of amusement in his eyes.

"How?" I returned the dagger to its sheath and said, "Explain it to me, because I can't reconcile it with everything else I know for certain."

He said nothing for a moment, only looked at the dimming sky through the treetops and shook his head slowly.

"I can't explain what you won't allow yourself to understand. You and Grayson will figure it out together in time."

"I don't even know what we're figuring out," I grumbled, kicking a stone in my path against the trunk of a nearby tree.

"I know." He glanced down at my face and had the audacity to laugh. "Don't pout, Briar."

My mouth dropped open and I said, "I am not pouting! I would never pout."

His eyes stared pointedly where my arms were folded across my chest. I quickly dropped them to my side and unpursed my lips.

Maybe I was pouting just a little.

"It's chilly out, I have to cross my arms for warmth," I defended. Isaac's laugh echoed through the trees.

"You've never been cold a day in your life, and you know it!"

"Nonsense," I dismissed, "I'm quite sensitive to changes in temperature."

"It's summer." He stared pointedly at my neck. "And you're sweating."

I gasped and wiped at the liquid starting to pool there, "Rude! Don't you know better than to assume things? Maybe I'm not warm. Maybe I'm nervous or was poisoned!"

Isaac smiled and shook his head but played along.

"If you were poisoned would you want me to point out the symptoms so we can find the antidote?"

"No, I'd want you to let me die with my dignity intact and refrain from pointing out any bodily fluids that may appear."

"Yes, your highness," he swept in front of me and gave a

deep bow, "Whatever you wish." He lost his footing–potentially because of karma or potentially because I shoved him–and chuckled as he picked himself up from the forest floor.

"Speaking of highnesses," I said lightly a moment later, "Would you care to clue me in as to how the Pack Prince can be misinformed on his own pack's hierarchy?"

Isaac turned sheepish and winced.

"Seriously, Isaac," I said, catching him by the elbow and turning him to face me, "How could he not have heard about the Pack Rites? Even if you, Ivy, or Lucas didn't inform him directly–which I would find shocking in itself–the pack gossip had to have reached him. It wasn't exactly minor news."

"To tell someone something they have to be willing to hear it," he said with a grimace, "I don't know what happened between you two, and I'm not asking you to tell me, but whatever it was changed things. The first time Gray came home you became a ghost. He could barely find you when he went looking, and the second time you weren't even at the compound."

Except he *hadn't* looked for me.

"And then later on," Isaac continued, "You didn't want to hear anything about him, and he didn't want to hear anything about you. Goddess knows you both bit my head off enough times when I tried. If I had to guess, his parents sent him the minimum amount of information about you which is probably just your change in rank without all the nitty gritty details of the Rite."

I grunted noncommittally. Even if no one had told him the circumstances, he should've taken enough interest in his own pack to ask questions instead of making his own assumptions. I refused to believe his refusal to speak of me stemmed from anything other than annoyance–or maybe a bruised ego. I gave him what he'd always wanted: I freed him of his obligation to me. Isaac would understand if I confided in him, but what good would come of it? None, so I kept it to myself. Let him believe the best of his Alpha.

We walked without speaking for a while longer, the only sounds between us the distant rush of water and an occasional rustle of leaves from whatever creatures made their homes amidst the forest floor.

"I received an interesting letter from my father today," Isaac said, breaking the silence as we walked. "He asked me to pass along a message to you."

"Did he?" I asked. "I suppose I'll choose not to be offended that he didn't write to me himself. What did he say?"

"He wanted me to tell you the deer drowned," he said, studying my reaction as he spoke. "There was water in its lungs when Helena examined it. Does that mean something to you?"

There had been no water near the carcass, save the small pool—hardly even a puddle, really—I'd been able to find. That wasn't nearly enough for a rat to drown in, let alone a full-sized doe. Not for the first time, I questioned if I made the right choice hiding it from Fenrir. Would any good come from me telling him other than to raise unnecessary alarm? Was it selfish to keep that detail to myself?

No. I'd made the right choice.

The border hadn't been breached and they knew there

was a threat. That's what mattered. My paranoid suspicions would only lead to more questions—questions I couldn't afford to answer.

"We found a deer at the border before we left," I said without lying, "We weren't certain, but we thought it triggered the enchantment."

Two parallel lines appeared between Isaac's brows.

"If it drowned, how could it have triggered the enchantment?"

I shrugged.

"It had a nasty gash on its leg. Whatever predator found it was probably dragging it and got spooked by the border." Except there'd been no drag marks–no paw prints–and its neck had been snapped.

"That's pretty odd though, isn't it?" he asked, "Why wouldn't an animal take it back to its den, plus the wildlife would know the territory well enough to avoid the border, right?"

"I'm not sure." Not a lie. "I'm sure they're looking into everything just to be safe."

He didn't seem to be convinced so I forced a chuckle and added, "Besides, why would someone leave a rotting corpse at the border? If it'd been a trap they would've ambushed us, but no one else was there."

Suspect he would've argued further when a honeyed voice called from above, "Rotting corpses, huh? Sounds interesting. Are you covering up murders now in the Othniel Pack? That'd be quite a tidbit of information to spread amongst the realm."

Isaac's eyebrows hit his hairline when we spotted Kenna

standing on a branch leaning against the trunk of a tree to our right. Pressure built in my chest, and I pushed down the flare of heat rushing to the surface at the shock.

I hadn't heard her. I always heard everyone, so how had she gotten so close without attracting my notice? More importantly, how long had she been following us?

"If you've been lurking in the trees for more than a few seconds, Kenna, you know very well we're talking about an animal." Isaac eyed her from his place beside me and asked, "How long have you been tailing us?"

"Tailing makes it sound like I was spying on you," she said with a click of her tongue, "We're going to the same place. I simply chose a higher path than you."

"So the tree tops are both your bed and preferred method of travel?" I asked once the last kindling of heat disappeared from my veins.

Kenna stepped off the branch and landed lightly on her feet in front of us. She added a dramatic flick of her hair that had me grinning. The backdrop of the forest made the light green of her eyes even more striking than usual.

"They certainly serve more than one purpose." She grinned, and added, "Besides, travelers are less likely to look up than they are to look around."

"I take it you've been above us the entire journey," I stated rather than asked. She looked much too satisfied to have only just happened upon us.

"I don't know what would lead you to such an assumption," she said lightly. We began walking again. "But if you decide you want to get rid of that dagger because it was a gift from a certain surly wolf, I'll happily take it off your hands."

Her smile reminded me of a feral kitten, which, in many ways, she was.

"I'm not giving you the dagger Kenna."

"Fine." She drew out the word and sighed, taking a few steps in silence before turning her attention to Isaac. "Why do I feel like we've been in the same Pack for two years and have barely spoken? If I didn't know better I'd think you were avoiding me."

I stifled the giggle on my lips as Isaac stammered over his reply, assuring her that wasn't the case at all while eyeing her warily. The last few minutes of our journey were spent with Kenna playfully teasing—or possibly threatening—him about their lack of interaction.

She smiled the entire conversation and I felt my lips rise when I remembered Isaac's comment when I first arrived. It seems he still found it unnerving to see her smile.

"I think we're going to be good friends, Isaac Cadell." She leaned her head against his shoulder as we entered the clearing and his body physically jolted, ruining the self-control I'd managed to maintain. I couldn't help it, my laughter echoed throughout the field.

Which meant when we entered the clearing, every single eye turned to look at us.

Several of them looked surprised to see the three of us together, others looked nervous, but there was only one reaction I cared about—loath as I was to admit it—and he was smiling.

Grayson beckoned me over with a toss of his head, but I kept my feet planted. I looked at him expectantly, ready for his glare to return at my refusal, but his smile only grew. He said something to his Beta, Pax, and patted him on the arm before jogging in our direction.

"Is he coming over to us?" I asked Isaac under my breath.

"I wouldn't say he's coming over to us, but he's definitely coming over to you. He hasn't taken his eyes off you since we arrived."

I didn't have to look at him to know he was smirking. I could hear it in his voice. As if the wolf managing to focus on me for an entire two minutes was something to be smug about.

"Maybe he has a secret twin," I pondered out loud as Grayson drew nearer, "It'd explain the mood swings."

"Maybe he just figured out what he thought he had wouldn't always be there waiting for him. Some people don't realize what's important until it's taken away from them."

"Not likely." I gave it another moment's thought. "He's probably just worried I'll tell his parents. Ivy would have him on stable duty for a month for his behavior this week, and Lucas would make him run the training course from dusk 'til dawn."

Maybe he hadn't even made the blade. Maybe it was just a ploy to make me warm up to him after he–again–failed to have my back in the hallway with the selkies.

My two companions looked at me with varying expressions. Kenna stared at me the way I often stared at Naomi, and Isaac's gaze held an indulgent amount of pity as if he felt sorry for me.

I opened my mouth to ask them what their problem was, but Grayson arrived before the words could leave my lips. The joy I'd glimpsed across the field hadn't left his eyes but his smile was less prominent. It'd turned into something like a smug grin. I'd preferred it if he glared.

"Good evening, Luna." I narrowed my eyes but it only seemed to amuse him. What game was he playing? "Would you like to join me at the front of the Pack? Now that you're here I think we're ready to begin."

I looked at Kenna instead of answering, unsure what to expect. I wouldn't blame her if she wanted to challenge me for the right to lead the run leading up to the Pack Rite, but I preferred not to fight with her before it was unavoidable. The more turmoil we sowed in the Pack now, the more problems that would sprout later.

"The faster you go with him the sooner my lion can stretch her legs, maybe catch a rabbit or two." She said the last part a bit louder and smiled when a nearby female grew visibly pale.

"Rabbit shifter?" I leaned into Isaac and asked.

"Rabbit shifter."

"That's rough." He nodded in agreement. I returned my attention to the blonde lion still wearing her eerie smile—I bet she'd perfected it in a mirror at some point in her life to set others ill at ease.

"I'm a little surprised, Kenna. I thought you'd fight me for the Luna role." I paused and realized, "You didn't ask for my place at the table tonight either. What? Are you ready to relinquish the title to me after all?"

Goosebumps rose on not just Isaac's but Grayson's skin as well. She cackled and reached over to shove my shoulder with a surprising amount of force. Maybe the Rite would be a bit more interesting than I'd thought. Of course, no matter how strong she was, I knew I was stronger.

"Of course not. Goddess, you're the whole package, aren't you? Strength, beauty, and humor all wrapped up in one person." She wiped a stray tear from her eye as she caught her breath. "I have no problem stepping aside and letting you have this time while you still have some claim to it. I'll lead the next one."

"And the Luna suite?" I asked, knowing full well she hadn't packed a single possession.

"That's for the benefit of us both," She assured me. "Think of how much manual labor I'm saving us in the long run."

I shouldn't find her certainty that she'd win our challenge amusing, but I did. Even Isaac had a hint of humor in his eyes, though possibly at her expense knowing full well which of us would be left the victor once we entered the circle. If anything, I enjoyed her confidence and lack of animosity. It meant it wasn't personal and gave me hope that the pack could still stand as one after the leadership change.

I was enjoying the newfound lightness beginning to spread over me until I looked at Grayson. My joy was replaced with a pang of sadness.

His eyes were fixed on the forest beyond us. His clouded expression was a needed reminder of what he still thought of as my impending demise. The warmth he'd emitted when he'd met my eyes in the clearing was slowly disappearing from view.

Don't. Just stay with me even if it's only for a little longer. Believe in me.

"Looks like the other twin just joined us," I told Isaac under my breath. Grayson snapped out of whatever internal monologue he'd fallen prey to and refocused on us.

"The twins have been here for a while now."

"They're not who I was referring to." I forced a smile to my face and gestured to the front of the clearing. "Shall we?"

He nodded his assent and started moving forward. I took a step to join him when Isaac gently grabbed my elbow and said, "Give him time. When you win the Rite he'll have nothing to doubt, and he'll get over his hangups."

I watched as Grayson's back straightened, his next step taking a second longer than his previous, but he didn't turn. I chose my next words for him.

"If it takes until then for him to believe in me after all this time, it'll be too late. What good is a partner who has no faith in the other person?"

I hated him a little when he walked away from me.

I hated myself more for letting him.

I DROPPED down on the grassy bank beside the lake and leaned back on my elbows to take in the stars. Thousands were swirling overhead, and I soaked in the peace that seemed to emanate from their glow.

My first pack run was by all accounts, a success. There'd been a few grumblings from the odd person or two about how I could lead the run with Grayson if I couldn't even shift, but they'd been silenced. Surprisingly, it was Grayson's growl that had sounded in the air, not mine or Isaac's. I'd barely paid them any mind knowing their doubts would be put to rest soon enough.

Shifters were fast in their animal form. I was faster.

Whether it was a goddess-given gift to compensate for my stolen shift or it was a demon-driven perk of the elemental blood running through my veins, I could move faster on two legs than Grayson and the others could run on four.

Grayson and I had recited the words spoken to open every pack run. They rang of unity, companionship, and trust in one another, and they were more than just words. It felt like the incantation sent sparks of magic radiating through the entire pack, leaving us with feelings of warmth and comfort. I couldn't think of a time when a pack felt closer together except maybe a mating ceremony.

First Grayson, then others shifted and we'd taken off. I ran with Isaac's leopard for a while and even played with a few others in the pack I hadn't gotten to know yet. It was short lived. They'd quickly scattered when Kenna's lion came to pounce beside me. Eventually she'd left me to chase a small black and white rabbit, and I'd made my escape.

I knew I should still be with the others building bonds, making memories, and all that, but I needed a break from pretending the weight pressing down on my shoulders didn't exist. This was the perfect spot for forgetting.

The lake was completely still, not a single ripple to be seen. Its mirrored surface let the stars surround me from above and below. Streaks of light green and blue cut through the night sky and revealed a few clouds that had been hidden in the darkness.

What worries could remain here other than the

inevitability of leaving it? There were no pack politics, no challenges, no threats, and—other than me—no demons. I laid fully back against the plush grass and let my eyes fall closed.

This was peace.

I don't know how long I'd been lying there before I heard the soft pad of paws coming from behind me. I didn't bother to open my eyes or look up. The pomegranate and leather scent had reached me before he'd taken his first step out of the tree line.

"Don't think just because I have a soft spot for you I'm going to forget your other half betrayed me." I said, sinking further into the grass and sighing.

Grayson's wolf nuzzled the arm lying against my side until I lifted it. I felt more than heard him circle the spot a few times before lying beside me with his head on my stomach. I lowered my arm and stroked the soft fur covering his spine. It wasn't the wolf's fault the man showed poor judgment.

"He can't be very happy with you for pulling him away from the pack tonight."

The wolf huffed in answer.

"I take it you don't care, then," I said with a smile. "Just make sure you take accountability for your own choices. Let's not give him one more thing he can blame on me."

Then his whine reverberated against my torso. "Stop it," I said, "That tickles."

He whined again and I opened my eyes to see two green orbs looking back at me. I sighed and moved to scratch his head.

"What?" I asked. "Are you feeling ignored?"

This time the high-pitched sound made me smile as I trailed a finger down the bridge of his nose and back.

"You have my undivided attention," I promised.

He clamored to his feet until he stood over me with his face in mine to lick my cheek.

"Don't get your slobber on me, you know I hate that," I wiped at my face laughing. He moved to do it again, but I shoved him off of me and sat up.

The wolf pounced around, tail wagging in excitement. He crouched down and then leaped into a pounce that sent us rolling through the grass along the lake's edge.

"I win!" I had him on his back, shoulders pinned and neck bared. He showed no sign of caring with his head flung to one side and his tongue hanging to one side of his mouth. I rolled off of him, still smiling.

"I wish we were always like this," I admitted. At that moment, I didn't care that Grayson would understand my words alongside his wolf. Let him listen. Let him know that I knew the truth. Maybe then we could both stop pretending. "We used to be so close, but none of it was real, was it?"

The wolf pawed at my arm and huffed.

"Not you, buddy." I turned onto my side and scratched behind his ear. "I know you and I are bonded for life." He gave a happy yip and moved to snuggle in closer, but he froze halfway with a growl.

I'd heard the footsteps in the distance but hadn't been concerned enough to check who was walking by. From what I could tell they weren't headed in our direction, only passing through on whatever journey they were taking.

I flipped onto my stomach to see Eris, Fabian, and Asher a few meters beyond the tree line. Grayson's wolf was tense beside me and still growling.

I pushed him over.

"Don't be rude," I chastised. "They haven't done anything to you, and I like Eris a lot more than most of the people I've met at this school so far."

The moon fox waved at me as she passed, but didn't approach. Probably wise given the beast beside me had stopped growling but still looked ready to attack at the slightest hint of a threat. I returned her wave and dropped back to the ground, using my hands as a pillow.

"They're gone," I told him. "You can relax from the non-existent threat now."

The wolf harrumphed and stood to watch another few moments before lying alongside me again, this time nuzzling his head against mine, burrowing it into the crook of my neck. The soft mewling sound that left him as he settled in had a different note to it than before, but I understood its meaning all the same.

"I know," I acknowledged, leaning into him, "I missed you too."

15

THE MOON

S he was beautiful in the starlight. She was beautiful in any light.

I'd watched as she broke away from the pack and struck out on her own, ignoring my companions to trail after her instead. I didn't plan to approach, I just wanted to see what she would do after setting off alone.

Shifters were not solitary creatures. They craved the companionship of their pack, the closeness, the contact that it offered. A pack run was the opportune time to accomplish both.

It wasn't my place to be jealous—I knew that—but my blood had boiled at the thought another male would disturb her when she'd finally let herself shed her guard. It boiled even more she didn't seem to care. She'd hardly moved a muscle at the sound of footsteps she surely undoubtedly heard heading in her direction.

No, it wasn't my place to feel jealous—to feel anything— around her, but I did. I wanted to know her—really know her. I wanted to know what thoughts were hidden behind her carefully impassive face and false smiles. I wanted to know what made her shoulders tense when she walked down the halls. I wanted to see her smile at me the way she smiles at Isaac and hear her laugh ring out without restraint.

I wanted all of those things, if only they had been mine to take.

THE ROSE

Three days after the pack run I was beginning to wonder if we had a chance at harmony in the pack.

Grayson and I had managed to keep the silent truce we'd called the night he lay beside me on the bank in the days following. He'd taken to waiting for me at breakfast and walking me to class. When a pack member brought a concern to his attention—big or small—he invited me into the conversation. Both had taken me off guard the first day. By the second I expected it. On the third day I let myself look forward to it.

There were still moments when his face turned stony or his eyes clouded, but more often than not he found ways to break out of the thoughts that plagued him. He was trying, and trying was more than I had hoped to expect. Today I caught him looking at me the way I imagined the moon would look at the sun–with complete awe and affection.

I thought he would turn away or wipe the expression from his face when caught, but if anything, he only further softened. I didn't understand—didn't *trust* what it could mean. I only knew that the longer he looked at me that way, the more I wished I could forget everything that had happened since overhearing him speak to his father. I wished I could go back to the way we were when I still believed that I was someone he cared for—maybe even someone he most cared for. But wishes rarely led to the outcomes we expect, and I didn't have the luxury of risking uncertainties.

I had to get away from him. I couldn't trust myself to stay and not fall back into my role as his shadow, not when he looked at me like that.

So I fled—back to the woods where I'd found solace my first night at the Academy. I had considered taking the trails circling the lakes to the south—I'd yet to visit them and heard the water made for an enchanting sight—but remembered Kenna's warning they were well traveled. After a day filled with classes, pack squabbles, small-talk attempts from other students, and being flustered by a certain Alpha, the last thing I wanted was more interaction.

Grayson's approval was all it took for the same students who'd mocked me in the hallways to vie for a spot in my good graces. *Pathetic*. If those same people found me on the lakes' path I may be stuck listening to them for hours.

It was a simple choice to meander back into the burgundy forest instead. How the lantern-lined road wasn't a popular route, I'd never understand, but I was glad for the solitude. Even before night fully fell it was stunning. When I stepped beyond the road into the thick of the trees, I swear it felt like they were alive, calling to me to come and walk amongst them. I basked in the peace, in the quiet they provided as they blanketed me from the rest of the world.

But it wasn't just me they blanketed. Something was with me. It was in the subtle shift of the air, the softest sounds on the edge of the grass. Someone else may assume it was a harmless animal or leaves falling from the tops of the trees, but I knew better.

It was a predator stalking its prey.

I slowed my pace but didn't stop. Let them catch up to me, let them think they could prowl unnoticed. My hand hovered over my dagger and when the near silent padding against the grass paused, I turned just in time to see the sharp claws descending on me as the lion pounced.

She was lucky I caught her cinder toffee scent quickly enough to lower the dagger before it plunged into her gut. I let the lion pin my shoulders to the ground and lick my face before dropping my dagger to the ground and shoving her off of me. I stood and turned on her now shifting form.

"Goddess above Kenna, don't you know better than to sneak up on someone like that?" I pressed a hand against my sternum where my heart still thundered against my chest.

"Uh, no actually," she said. "How would I take someone off guard if I wasn't sneaking? That would ruin, like, half of my fun."

I chuckled on an exhale and said, "I can't argue with that, but I also can't promise one of my blades won't find its way to your heart by mistake."

She threw her head back and cackled, actually cackled, before disappearing behind a nearby tree. She reappeared fully clothed and still smiling a minute later.

"Briar, I swear if you're not careful you're going to make me fall in love with you." She wiped a tear from her eye and got her laughter under control. "There are worse ways to die than a blade to the heart, but I'll do my best to dodge it if need be. A worthwhile risk if you ask me."

I bent down to retrieve my dagger and sheathed it at my thigh.

"You're brave coming this far into the woods without a sword," Kenna said and reached around the tree trunk to grab her blade to secure it around her waist. "Just because we're on campus grounds doesn't mean the occasional creature doesn't break through, let alone the ones who've been trapped inside. Goddess only knows what terrors like to lurk amongst the trees."

She looked far too pleased at the prospect.

"I guess I'll just have to take my chances this time around." I wasn't walking back to campus to get another blade when I had five perfectly good ones strapped to me. I could throw them if I needed to keep my distance.

Kenna, on the other hand, must have felt differently, because the next thing she pulled from behind the trees was a bow along with a quiver of arrows.

"Kenna," I said jokingly, "Do you know about something I don't? Are we expecting a raid? I almost wonder if you're about to pull out an ax."

"You can never be too careful." She shrugged. "I'd rather be too armed than caught unaware by a threat bigger than me."

"I thought you didn't see anyone as a threat."

"I didn't say that." She corrected, "I said I don't see any

other shifter as a threat. If a few extra weapons help me ensure I stay the scariest thing in these woods, I'll carry an arsenal of them."

The shock must have been evident on my face because she tilted her head and said, "I can be lethal and know my limits, that's how I stay alive."

"I wasn't aware we were being hunted."

"Everyone in power is being hunted by those who wish to take it."

"Then consider me the huntress coming after you," I tease. I liked to be as prepared for an attack as the next person, but this felt too foreboding for a Wednesday stroll in the forest.

"I love that you think you could be," she said while looking at me like a child may look at a newborn pup, "Wishful thinking becomes you, but no. My Enforcer offer is still on the table though if you've changed your mind."

I grinned and replied, "The same offer is open to you." I meant it.

Truthfully, I wasn't sure she could be anything other than a Luna. Someone with that much dominance would struggle to fall in line to take anyone else's lead, but Enforcer was better than losing her rank altogether. Beta was too close to power for someone who craves it. I would know.

As an Enforcer I could give her a longer rope to work from. I'd keep her from going off the rails but leave her to protect the pack the way she saw fit. She must have displayed somewhat sound judgment if she'd avoided a mutiny the two years she'd been here. In my albeit limited interactions with the rest of our pack, it was obvious they held her in the highest respect, yet she always seemed to be a little bit separated, alone.

"Sure, dearie," she said, "It's good to have dreams."

"Are you just going for a stroll or planning to take a nap in the trees again?" I began walking deeper, enjoying the directionless wandering.

"I wasn't napping, I was resting my eyes," Kenna corrected, "I'm only going for a walk today though. There's something about solitude that clears the mind, don't you think?"

"I do." I nodded. "I don't want to interrupt your solitude, but you're welcome to walk with me if you want to."

"There's worse company than you I could keep." She fell into step beside me.

We walked in comfortable silence for a few minutes until the terrain changed. The woods nearest the road had been well-kept without vines or underbrush encroaching on them, but the farther we went from campus, the wilder it became. Trees had fallen. Vines criss-crossed in our path. Moss climbed the side of trees and boulders, some of them sprouting flowers.

The forest only grew more enchanting the deeper we went. Everything about it drew me in, but it was the web of rose bushes at the base of one of the boulders that stole my attention.

"Did your parents name you after the roses?" Kenna asked, tracking my gaze.

"Not exactly." I looked away from the thorny bushes and kept walking.

"Oh, come on." She bumped into my shoulder and

asked, "Not exactly? What, is it a secret known only to a select few? Don't tell me, it was your mother's favorite flower. No?"

Her grin widened as she spouted a few more far-fetched theories, smiling wider with each tale she spun. After she guessed that it had to do with my conception I raised a hand to cut her off before she could take that imagery any further.

"It was where Lucas and Ivy found me."

She came to a halt and looked at me, the smile fell from her face.

"Found you?"

"Found me."

I reached up to fiddle with a low-hanging leaf and explained, "I can't tell why my parents chose my name, or even what name they chose. Ivy and Lucas called me Briar because when they found me I was sleeping under a rose bush."

A speck of pride flared in me for rendering Kenna speechless —a feat I suspected few had accomplished. She tilted her head to one side and studied me, the intensity of her stare burning my skin.

"Why were you living under a rose bush?"

"Because the thorns helped keep the predators at bay."

Sometimes. Other times they hadn't.

Even at eight years old—based on Ivy and Lucas' guess I was a few years younger than Grayson—I'd known how to use my surroundings to survive.

"I wasn't as strong then as I am now, and even if I could've handled a weapon to defend myself, I didn't have one to wield. I used whatever advantages I could find."

"And why were you in the woods in the first place and don't you dare say because you walked there." She pointed her finger at me as she spoke, "Don't think I'm someone who cares enough about making others uncomfortable to stop prying before I find out what I want. I'm not. I can ask questions all day, but our time together will be far more pleasant if you tell me."

Because I turned an entire village to ash. Because I woke up surrounded by corpses. Because I was a monster.

"My village burned down when I was younger," I said truthfully. "I woke up to it lying in ruins. I was scared, so I escaped to the woods. I didn't know what caused the fire or if someone would come back and find me, so I fled. I was alone until Ivy and Lucas found me."

"How long were you out there?" she asked gravely, her usually strong voice barely a whisper.

A lifetime.

"I don't know. Maybe a few weeks, maybe a few months."

Time had been a blur of running from the sounds echoing through the trees, hiding when I couldn't run. When I couldn't hide, I'd done my best to fight. My best hadn't been nearly good enough.

I had the scars to prove it.

"You and your pack mates act as though you've been together your entire lives, but Grayson's been here for three years. There's no way you joined it less than five years before then, " she observed, "You couldn't have been more than what, twelve at the time and wandering the woods, surviving on your own? Maybe our duel will be even more fun than I anticipated."

"We think I was around eight when they found me," I admitted wryly.

Her head turned toward me faster than Marcus turned when a pretty girl walked by. I could've sworn it was so fast I heard the bones clang together with the force of it.

"And you're eighteen now? You were found ten years ago?"

She hadn't moved, but that sound rang out again, though it was still faint. I turned to look around but saw nothing amiss. We were the only ones out here.

"Yes," I answered absentmindedly, still looking for the source of the sound. I might've imagined it once but not twice.

"Which forest did they find you in?"

Another clang. This time the sound was clearer; somewhere in the woods weapons crossed, and a sinking feeling in my gut had me thinking it wasn't a friendly duel amongst friends.

"Briar," Kenna grabbed my arm and pulled me around to face her. "Which forest?"

A scream echoed against the trees, and I wrenched myself from Kenna's shockingly strong grip and sprinted toward it.

"Goddess if it's going to send you into a sprint, we don't have to talk about it," Kenna called as she ran after me, "I didn't know geography was such a touchy subject."

"Kenna, don't you hear that?" I asked, still running but slowing my pace to better listen for which direction the sounds were coming from.

"The wind in the trees and the pounding of your feet? Yes, I do. I have exceptional senses."

The clanging was growing louder. I pulled her behind a tree and said, "Keep your voice down, and listen." Another clash of metal against metal. We should be just close enough for her to hear it. Her brow furrowed, but she nodded. Wordlessly, she unstrapped the sword from her waist and handed it to me.

I hurried to secure it around my own and put a finger to my lips as I stepped out from behind the tree and continued forward. We cut through the trees efficiently and silently, our footsteps were light as we took care to mask our approach.

The sounds of the fight grew louder, and we crouched lower into the brush as we closed in on our potential opponents. Kenna's hand on my shoulder jerked me back a step. Her wide eyes met mine and she tapped her nose. Inhaling deeply, I froze as bile threatened to rise in my throat.

Tar and brimstone.

When I looked over, Kenna's still silent lips mirrored mine as we sank deeper into the foliage.

"Demons."

THE ROSE

They shouldn't have been here. They shouldn't have been anywhere, but they especially shouldn't have been on this half of the continent–let alone anywhere near the Academy.

The demons had been slaughtered alongside the elemental shifters when they were purged from our society like an infection burned from a wound. The few who managed to elude the legion of warriors tasked with their demise had been driven far into the Eastern Wastes.

True to its name, the decrepit land was a barren wilderness in which few entities could survive and even fewer—if any—could permanently reside. A demon, who drew its power by feeding off the corruption and malice of others, would have no hope of staying alive without access to its living prey. Furthermore, they had no hope of re-infiltrating society courtesy of the enchantment embedded throughout the borderlands. Everyone had presumed the race to be extinct—for how could parasites survive without living hosts to suck the life out of?

We were wrong.

The implications of their presence here cast an icy weight on my chest. Their last siege had been catastrophic for the Hidden Realm. Courts were overthrown. Races deemed inferior were enslaved. Hundreds of thousands of lives were lost. Entire communities were turned to ash.

If they rose to power again, what new levels of destruction could they wreak with a decade to recover from their loss? What plan could they have crafted while the rest of us fell into a false sense of security that they were gone.

How could I ever hide what I was—what I'd done—with their return?

The questions wrapped like a clenched fist around my lungs, but I pushed the feelings down until only whispers of them remained. To succumb to panic in the face of a threat was unacceptable.

We were not twenty yards from the source of the smell and clashing of blades, but we needed to get closer and gain a better view. As tempting as it was to rush into battle before my panic returned, a hint of logic in the back of my mind reminded me we needed to assess the situation before we engaged.

I didn't dare to whisper a word as I pointed Kenna to the tree on her right. She nodded, and immediately began to climb, quickly ascending its branches without rustling the foliage or making a sound. Under better circumstances I'd have paused to admire the way she embodied the stillness of night in broad daylight.

Though less graceful than my feline friend, I took care not to draw attention to myself as I began my ascent up the tree adjacent to hers. My pulse pounded in my veins and my adrenaline continued to rise, but the bark biting my fingers grounded me. I climbed higher and higher. I propelled myself over one coarse limb to another, wishing I could enjoy being engulfed by the vibrant leaves glinting from the sun. Under other circumstances—other than the sap collecting on my skin—this would be rather beautiful.

Focus. I needed to stay focused.

I kept my gaze fixed ahead of me. I ignored the light sheen of moisture beginning to gather at my palms. I dismissed the ever-increasing pace of my heart as it beat against my sternum.

Perched twenty feet in the air, I could see flashes of silver in the distance. My gesture to move ahead had Kenna and I weaving through the gossamer of tree limbs until we arrived atop the violent scene unfolding below.

There were two of them.

Their orange, gem-like eyes beamed in stark contrast against their ashen skin even from our view overhead. Both of the demons were fixated on the female trading blows with each of them. The trio's movements were a flurry of blocks and advances as they danced between the trees.

The silver-haired fighter parried each of their attacks with swift strokes of her sword. There was no questioning she was a trained warrior, but her movements were growing more sluggish by the second the longer the fight continued. She turned enough so I could glimpse her face and my heart dropped.

It was Eris.

If the heave of her chest each time she raised her blade was any indication, she wouldn't last much longer alone. Lucky for her, and potentially fatal for us, aid had arrived.

I pivoted toward Kenna and waved an arm to catch her eye. I pointed to the trees and bade her take up her post on the other side lest the demons try to escape after finding themselves outnumbered. The ideal outcome would be us killing one of them and capturing the other to interrogate. Their presence here was unnatural, and without one of them we had no way to discover if they were merely lucky survivors who'd avoided being detected all these years or if other demonic hordes had survived the purge as well.

As soon as Kenna was in place, I pointed to her and mimed shooting an arrow at the ground below. She would shoot from above while I engaged in close-quarter combat below. I sent a quick prayer of thanks for the paranoia driven artillery she carried. The moment her first arrow was notched in its quiver, I took a deep breath and took note of where I'd need to land to avoid knocking out my potential new ally. After I mapped the trio's movement, I didn't give myself another second to overthink what would come next; I dropped.

There was no time to worry about the sting radiating through my feet and into my shins as I landed in front of the cornered fighter. I was hedging my bets that Eris would quickly recognize me and, at the very least, refrain from running me through with her sword out of instinct.

My sword blocked the downward arc of one of their

blades at the same moment an arrow pierced the other's neck. The smell of tar and brimstone only grew more pungent as the blood mist splattered across us in an arc of crimson— freaking *gross*—but it did nothing to impede the relentless onslaught.

The only reaction my new comrade-in-arms displayed at my arrival was a short, sharp intake of breath before she re-engaged with the demon whose blood now donned our skin. Either Eris' nerves were too frayed from the woodland battle to give much care to a woman falling from the sky or it was exceedingly difficult to take her by surprise. Then again, I did come across her battling demons whose combined smell could be detected from twenty yards back. Maybe she was less observant than I'd thought her to be.

"You bear a striking resemblance to someone I once knew, little shifter. What an unexpected treat." The demon whose sword was crossed with mine tilted his head. The corners of his mouth lifted, one side rising slightly higher than the other, but it was too repellent to classify as a grin. "Now the true fun can commence."

"It seems like you find joy in your downfall rather easily. How fortunate for you."

I unlatched my sword from his iron blade and propelled it forward. I intended to lance his gut in hopes that his entrails would spill across the leaf-trodden ground, but he jumped back within a hair's breadth of my blade and avoided the jab entirely.

A pity.

"It's rare to come across a delicacy I find as mouthwatering as you," he continued, a smile stretching across his face as he advanced toward me. The timbre of his voice rang somewhere between melodic and eerie. "For I look into your eyes and see all you are, my ember."

Dread washed through me as I felt the blood drain from my face. He couldn't see anything in my eyes—I knew he couldn't–but he looked at me like he understood me. He looked at me like he owned me.

My brief moment of shock cost me a gash to my left arm as the demon launched into a frenzy of blows. The jolt of pain shook me from my stupefied stance enough to counter each attempted strike with my own. All the while, arrows continued to rain down around us. My bloodthirsty lion lodged no less than four arrows in the flesh of my opponent, but he showed no sign of distress or slowing his attack.

Dodge.

Strike.

Duck.

Advance.

Our movements grew faster and faster until my arms and legs were guided by instinct alone. There was no time for thinking, only countering each surge as it was launched. Behind us, the second pair was narrated by the clash of steel and the occasional grunt. The sounds of battle assured me that despite the exertion she'd expended before our arrival, Eris was still holding strong against our foe.

"Why do you deny me the pleasure of combatting your full strength?" The demon taunted me, the ever-growing smirk resolutely on his face, "Surely this is not the extent of your power. If it were, I'd find myself wholly disappointed."

I responded by swinging my sword in an arc at his neck. Of course, I was holding myself back. To do anything else would attract a plenitude of risk and a plethora of questions I couldn't afford to answer. Questions like: Why are flames shooting from your hands like you're a living volcano, Briar? Or, how did you propel a grown demon twice your weight into that tree a hundred feet away, Briar?

I was beginning to wonder if the risk would be worth it to see the miscreant's likeness etched into the wood. Maybe the force of the collision would even cause his skull to implode or at the very least silence his never-ending heckling. My temper was rising and my fingers began to burn, the temptation to give in to the flames called out to me. I couldn't answer its call, but goddess help me if I didn't want to more than I wanted a slice of chocolate cake after a grueling run.

I jumped over a fallen log to put some distance between us and regain both my lost ground and sense of control. His pursuit was immediate. He leaped over the log in one go and with far more grace than I'd demonstrated. He landed just a few feet away from where I stood. One of the perks of being close to seven feet tall, I suppose.

"Do you want to know a secret, my ember?" The demon paused and leaned back, shifting his weight to one leg. The spin of his sword in one hand was almost casual as he looked from it and back to me, "I haven't been using my full strength either."

I stumbled from the force of his next attack and was thrown off kilter. The hit would surely have taken off one of my arms had I not managed to—barely—deflect it as I found my feet. I had years of training. Years of fighting against the strongest leaders and Enforcers in the pack. As the demon renewed his barrage with even higher voracity than he'd demonstrated before, I realized even the most skilled fighter in the pack would pale in comparison to him.

The demon stole my choice from me. I had only one hope of ensuring my allies and I escaped unscathed: I loosened the leash I kept wrapped around my power an infinitesimal amount—the obsidian stone secured at my ankle aiding my control. My breath still caught at the rush of power now surging through my veins, and I pushed a stream of it out of my hand and into my blade. Sparks flew at the next collision of weapons.

"There you are. I've been waiting for you to show yourself. You've kept me waiting far too long."

I must have misinterpreted the pride and affection in his voice. Demons couldn't be affectionate. It also had to be impossible for a more gentle, subtle smile to replace the mocking smirk that had been on his lips only moments before. And yet, what other explanation could there be?

From this close of a distance, it'd be easy to get caught up in his velvety tone and full lips, but his most entrancing feature in the split seconds between battle and breath was his eyes. I hadn't noticed before, but the orbs of orange had an underlying layer of shimmer in them as if a sunstone had been covered in citrine. Looking into them filled me with a warmth I did not welcome.

"Stop," I grunted as I struck, "talking."

"But it's so rare I get the pleasure of conversing with

another real life, in the flesh —" I followed the strike of my sword with an uppercut to his jaw. He fell backward with a groan and his head cracked against the ground. My sword was lifted high to finish him once and for all, but my blade never fell.

"Briar!"

I looked over at Kenna's call just as the second demon delivered a ghastly blow to Eris' temple with the hilt of his sword. She landed in a heap amongst the fallen leaves and didn't stir.

The distance between us was far too great for me to cross in time to block the death blow the demon would surely deliver any second. I did the only thing I could: I freed two daggers from their sheaths at my thigh and sent them soaring. They cut through the air and struck true. One lodged itself into the demon's knee, sending him to the ground, where the other blade sank into his neck.

The knife in his neck was embedded to the hilt and pierced through the flesh on the other side. The demon was left sputtering as blood spilled from his mouth and his eyes so wide I wondered if they'd spill from their sockets. Kenna dropped from the trees and grasped the blade's handle firmly in her palm before raking it out the front of his throat. Her smile at the carnage was nothing short of blinding.

During his companion's demise, the remaining demon had returned to his feet, blade in hand, jaw clenched, eyes fixed firmly on mine. They were colder now than when they'd trapped me only moments ago.

"I do believe our time together is drawing to an end. I so

wish we'd had more of it." And the dance of iron and steel began once more.

With each block of my blade, each scratch I failed to avoid, I made a promise to myself. The darkness would not steal my last breath today. Every move he made was both powerful and precise. The demon was undoubtedly the most formidable opponent I'd faced in my lifetime, and he was calculated, destructive, and resilient—but so was I.

I forced myself to counter each of his advances with my own. To fail would be to doom not only myself but Kenna, Eris, and whoever may come looking for us as well. To let myself fall was one level of weakness, but to fail my pack mates was simply unacceptable.

Over the demon's shoulder, Kenna approached swiftly and silently, stalking her new prey from behind. I directed my next attacks to lure the demon toward her and pushed an extra morsel of power through my blade. He flinched at the added force. It's possible he assumed I'd already called upon my full strength, or maybe he simply didn't expect me to further risk exposure by allowing more of it to fill my veins. Whatever the case, his shock would be his downfall and my victory.

His jolt of surprise placed his neck at the tip of the arrow in Kenna's now fully drawn bow. Judging by her mild grin, I'd even wager she'd pressed it to his skin enough to draw a droplet of blood. I didn't want to risk him finding a way to turn the bow against her, so I hurried to lunge forward and press the blade of my sword against his jugular.

"Drop. Your. Sword."

"Do you plan to kill an unarmed man?" His sword fell to

the ground. "I can't say I pegged you as merciless, but I've been wrong before. I won't lie and say it wouldn't be a pleasant surprise."

"You are no man." However, if I looked past the ashen skin and crystalized eyes, I could easily think of him as one.

"I'm not going to kill you." Kenna's gaze darted up to mine as I spoke. "Yet." She sighed but nodded.

"And why ever not, might I ask?" He was fully smiling at me now, as though discussing his life and death was the most intriguing game he'd played and I was the gamekeeper.

"You're going to come with us, and we are going to have a very long chat about how two demons found themselves on the Academy's grounds and out of the Eastern Wastes. That's a tale I suspect the Hidden Council would very much like to hear." The demon's laugh disrupted the still silence of the wood that could only be found after such a disturbance.

"Do you find that funny, demon?" Kenna pressed her arrow further into his skin. He did not flinch. He ignored her question. He ignored the blood now trickling over his shoulder, down his collarbone, and into his black buttoned shirt. He instead leaned toward me, pressing into my blade until the thinnest line of crimson bloomed across his skin.

"I treasure the time we've spent together, my ember." His voice was a near whisper.

"I can't say the feeling is mutual."

His eyes fluttered shut as he rolled his shoulders back and tilted his head to one side and then the other. When he opened them again, he met my stare head-on. He wasn't smiling now.

"They're going to find you," he deadpanned. Then

Kenna and I were both gasping. He'd somehow—though I could not for the life of me explain it— straightened his neck before snapping it at an unnatural angle. A crack and pop rang through the air, and his body fell lifelessly to the ground. The forest was silent less the sound of birds singing and trees rustling once more.

THE ROSE

"What in the actual hell was that?" Kenna's eyes were nearly bursting from her head as she looked from the demon at our feet to the demon next to the still unconscious Eris and back to me.

"Right now, I truly don't know what to make of all this." I exhaled deeply in an attempt to clear my mind or at least regulate my still-pounding heart, but it did little to help.

"We should check her over."

I placed Kenna's sword in the sheath at my hip and began walking toward Eris' near-lifeless form as I pulled back the morsel of power I'd released. The loss left my arms heavy and my chest somewhat hollow.

"Poke her to see if she's dead."

"I'm not poking her." I crouched beside her to place my fingers against her neck and sighed in relief when I felt her pulse still beating.

"That's basically poking her in the neck," Kenna grumbled.

"We need to get her to a healer." I stayed crouched by Eris' side but looked up to see that despite Kenna's apathetic quip, her face had gone white.

"No one will ever believe this." Her eyes were fixed on the demon who'd snapped his neck. I couldn't blame her. If not for the combination of adrenaline and lingering fear coursing through my veins, I'd likely be doing the same.

"I can barely believe this, and I was present for it." I stood and brushed my hands against the legs of my pants. "You good?"

"Of course I'm good," she snapped. She left the demon where he lay and stood over Eris' unconscious body.

"What's her living-to-dead ratio?"

"Living-to-dead ratio?" I repeated, "What does that even mean? She's either alive or she's dead, and based on the fact that her chest is still rising and falling, I'd bet a year's worth of chocolate cake she's not dead."

"But is she mostly dead or mostly living?" she continued, "Mostly living means we have time to get her to a healer. Mostly dead means we'll be carrying dead weight back through the forest and delivering a corpse. Which, if you ask me, is both a waste of our current physical energy and our future tolerance for political absurdity because if we deliver a dead fox without explanation or proof we didn't kill her, things are going to get messy. I'm not saying I'm scared of Asher, but if I saw him at the end of a dark hallway holding a knife I'd consider taking a different route."

"First of all," I put one finger in the air, "We're not leaving someone we just battled literal demons to save to die alone in the woods because we don't want the hassle of dealing with her potential death. Second of all, even if we were okay with leaving her to die alone—which we aren't—how do you think Asher would react if he discovered we left her corpse here?"

"He wouldn't know."

"Of course, he would know."

"Not if neither of us tell anyone. We can just move her body farther back into the brush and claim innocence when we return to the scene. It's simple." She shrugged her shoulders and looked at me the way I imagined parents looked at their children when they asked silly questions.

Kenna's eyes rolled at my refusal to abandon her, but she didn't argue further.

"She didn't use her magic," I said, more to myself than to Kenna, but she replied anyway.

"She probably hasn't met her bonded yet."

"Her what?" I'd studied the foxes in school, but nothing like this had ever come up.

"Her bonded." She stressed the second word as if it were an obvious explanation. "Do they teach you nothing in the Othniel Pack? A fox's bonded is like a psychic mate, like predestined partners whose genetic makeup and powers bring balance to yours. When a bonded pair touches for the first time, it's like a vault containing their magic is cracked open."

"Cracked open but not fully available?" She nodded and began collecting arrows from the bodies and ground, wiping each bloody tip on the leather of her pants before placing them back in their quiver.

I pulled Eris onto my back as Kenna retrieved her final bloodied arrows from the demon's body. When she caught me gaping at her she shrugged her shoulders and said, "Just because they stink of demon doesn't mean they can't be reused. I'd hate to waste them."

I suspected she hated to waste anything that may one day serve her purpose. I didn't know how demon blood-encrusted arrows would benefit her, nor did I want to. The smirk on her face told me all I cared to know.

"You do know, we're never getting the blood out of these clothes, right?" I asked.She grinned and rubbed her hands into the leather a little harder. "I know. I think it serves as a nice warning, don't you?"

I shook my head and said nothing.

"At the very least, being covered in blood when we arrive will make for a memorable entrance." She placed her still blood-stained hands on her hips. She smiled widely but no joy or humor reached her eyes, they were still veiled in unease.

"I think I've had enough dramatic entrances, thank you." Goddess only knew what new rumors would fly when we arrived together, covered in blood, reeking of death, and carrying the knocked-out Viscountess from another realm. I'd been at the Academy less than a fortnight and my life had already turned to chaos.

"You might as well enjoy the attention," she said, "You're going to get it either way."

I hitched the fox higher on my back and started walking. The added weight wasn't much of a challenge, it was, however, a bit awkward to maneuver us both under low branches, around the boulders, and over fallen trees.

"I'm not offering to take a turn." Kenna looked me up

196

and down after I'd narrowly avoided falling into a burrow. I snorted.

"I never thought you would." I was surprised she'd even feel the need to clarify.

"What did he say to you, by the way?" Kenna asked. "The demon."

A thick web of ice crawled up my spine and settled in my throat, threatening to prevent the words I knew I needed to say from leaving my throat.

"Nothing worth repeating," I said, sending a quick prayer to whatever goddess would listen that I sounded convincing.

Kenna's face was solemn as she searched mine. My heart skipped a beat when her brow creased, certain she'd sensed my deception or had somehow overheard the demon's taunts amidst the chaos, but she only sighed and nodded.

I hiked Eris further onto my back and did what I'd done since the day I'd woken up surrounded by death: I kept moving forward.

"GODDESS BRIAR, how many times do you need to walk into school covered in blood before you've had enough attention?"

I turned to face Isaac just as his hands grasped my face, his fingers threading through my hair. Isaac's smile was brittle at best. The turn of his lips may have been convincing to someone else if not for the crease between his brows.

"Hopefully just twice," I wrapped my hands around his

but left them where they were. "You know I can't resist a good crowd."

He laughed shakily and nodded.

"I'm fine too," Kenna leaned in until her head was resting on my shoulder, "Thanks for asking."

"I didn't ask if she was okay. I already knew she'd walk away from any fight as the victor." Isaac took a step back, his grin turning more genuine as a twinkle of humor appeared in his eyes. "I just want to prepare myself for any future calamities or at least keep a wash basin at the ready."

"I like that answer, Isaac Cadell. I've been seeing you in a whole new light since this one arrived. Are you sure you haven't been hiding from me?" Kenna smiled widely, and I snorted when Isaac shuddered.

I turned from their exchange and looked through the open door to the foxes huddled around Eris' bed in the infirmary.

It was a good thing my natural temperature was elevated because as Asher and Fabian had brushed past us to get to their injured family member, I swore an arctic breeze had been left in their wake. The normally smiling Fabian didn't even spare us a stone-faced glance, and I wished Asher had done us the same discourtesy.

The Crown Prince's steps hadn't faltered, but his stormy gaze captured mine for more than a few moments as he strode by. He looked me up and down with calculating eyes and seemed to catalog every inch of me as he went.

I'd done nothing wrong, but he didn't know that yet. If one of my pack mates had returned bloody and unconscious in the arms of another realm, I'd be suspicious. I may even be violent depending on the circumstances. Part of me respected the foxes' self-control even as another part of me bristled at the silent accusation we'd cause another realm.

Kenna, of course, had unhelpfully murmured something about the consequences of Eris being mostly alive or mostly dead. I'd pointedly ignored her.

"Briar!" I refused to cringe at the booming voice coming at the end of the hall and glared at a sheepish Isaac accusingly.

"We had to tell him," he said, "I thought I bought us some time by asking Marcus to do it, but he is the Alpha, and this does involve his pack."

"Great," I grumbled, and Isaac leaned down to whisper in my ear.

"Plus, I knew he'd be worried about you. Try to give him a little grace. I don't think he quite knows how to handle his own emotions, especially when it comes to you."

I turned to him and started to ask, "What is that supposed to—" until a heavy hand on my shoulder spun me away from my best friend

"Goddess didn't you hear me call your name? Are you okay?" Grayson's frantic eyes jumped around looking me over, presumably for any sign of injury. Without waiting for an answer he asked, "Whose blood is this? Did you see a healer? What the hell happened to your arm?"

One of his hands slid from my shoulder up my neck until it cupped my cheek with more gentleness than I'd expected from the anger in his voice.

"And another male in my pack renders me completely invisible. How disappointing." Kenna shook her head from the corner of my eye. "If you're done fawning over her like a mother with her infant child, maybe we can answer a few of your questions. If you don't pause for a moment's breath not only will you never have your answers, but you're liable to suffocate yourself with panic. I'm not dragging your unconscious body out of the hall, so get yourself together."

"I am not panicking." Grayson dropped his hold on me and glowered at the smirking lioness.

"You keep telling yourself that." Kenna indulgently patted his shoulder. "Whatever you need to feel secure in your masculinity. Don't worry, I won't tell anyone you lost it at the sight of her covered in blood. Your secret's safe with me."

Their bickering continued, but I stopped paying attention the moment I noticed Eris was upright and speaking with her cousin and brother whose attention turned our way as she pointed toward us as she, I could only assume, recounted the day's events.

The death god stood and narrowed his eyes as he took one step in my direction and then another. Fabian, though less solemn than when he first arrived, still wore a serious expression as he rose to follow.

"Oh, goddess." Isaac's muttered curse drew Grayson and Kenna out of their back and forth.

I didn't back away as they came toward us, nor did the pack mates at my back. Asher and Fabian were less than ten feet from me now and showed no signs of slowing.

Seven feet.

Four.

After saving Eris' life, I was skeptical they meant any

harm, but my hand hovered over the sheaths on my thigh, just in case. Better to stab someone than be stabbed by someone.

When there were less than two feet left between us, a tall, tree trunk of a wolf stepped up to my side, and angled his body just a sliver in front of mine. Despite the warmth that had flooded me at his earlier concern, I reminded myself I didn't want Grayson's protection anymore. I didn't want his anything.

"Prince Asher, please accept my deepest apologies on my pack mates' behalf." My mouth fell open in shock. Any warmth I'd felt from his protective stance turned to a chill. He. Did. Not. "I'll take full accountability for their actions in putting the Viscountess in harm's way."

I wasn't sure who snorted behind me, but I considered thanking them. It assured me I wasn't the only person to find his lack of faith absurd. I didn't step in to correct Grayson's mistake. If he wanted to make assumptions and look like an ignoramus, I would happily let him. A few days of smiles and support didn't erase his offenses against me, but I had almost been convinced he was on my side–that he'd finally accepted I was stronger than he'd believed.

The death god merely stared at him with an apathetic quirk of his eyebrow and a tiny tilt of his head. It shifted a strand of charcoal hair into his eyes. He looked Grayson up and down before dismissing him entirely, offering no response to the Alpha's unwarranted apology. Instead, he squared his shoulders to look at me.

Asher stepped closer. So close I had to tilt my head back to meet his ever-cold gaze. I itched to grab my dagger when he lifted his hands, but I stayed still. I didn't need to add to the drama of today by assaulting a Crown Prince unprovoked. Without dropping his eyes from mine, he picked up my hand and slid a ring onto my middle finger. The metal was warm against my skin.

Despite myself, I looked down at the surprisingly delicate silver that now graced my hand. Silver vines twisted around each other to form an intricate band with small gems scattered throughout. The white circles flashed blue when they caught the light as I turned my hand one way and then the other.

Moonstone, how appropriate.

Two rough fingers pressed under my chin until my wide eyes met his own. I stared into his for a few seconds before I noticed he'd raised his opposite hand which sported a woven, moon-encrusted ring— the twin to the piece on my finger. When my eyes returned to him he held my gaze a moment longer before striding through the door and out of sight.

"What in the freaky fox proposals was that?" Kenna squeaked.

My sentiments exactly.

She—like the rest of us— was staring at the now empty corridor Asher had taken to depart. It was Fabian who answered, though his response was directed at me.

"Eris told us you saved her from demons in the woods. She's a strong fighter but surely wouldn't have survived without you." I ignored Grayson's sharp intake of breath and instead focused on Fabian's face. It'd grown paler as he spoke of his sister's possible demise. "We owe you a life debt. To repay your kindness and bravery, Asher has declared you to be under his, and through him all of our, protection. That ring marks it as true."

Well damn.

Did I think the ring was pretty? Exceedingly so. Was I happy that this wasn't, as Kenna put it, some kind of 'freaky fox proposal?' Also, yes. But did I particularly like someone marking me as theirs to protect, as if I could not fight my own battles? No. No, I did not.

"That's very kind of you both, but truly not necessary." Or wanted. "Anyone who came across her would have done the same. Please, don't burden yourself by feeling indebted." And please take this ring back before it causes any more rumors to circulate.

"Some people feel that needing help from someone outside of their realm is something deserving of an apology," Fabian countered, his mouth serious but his eyes laughing at his less-than-subtle jab at Grayson. "I would hate to start an inter-realm incident by not thanking the woman who saved my little sister."

His voice was pure velvet and honey as he grabbed my hand, placed a kiss on the back of it, and said, "Besides, I assure you it's my absolute pleasure to ally with the sword-wielding warrior who dropped from the sky. Welcome to our court." I extracted my hand from his but resisted taking a step back. So touchy, this male.

"It was my pleasure, and what anyone else would have done in my place," I said unconvincingly, ignoring his ever-growing smile. "As you said, some people may feel that aiding others incurs a debt, but I am not some people." I reached to pull the ring from my finger to return but he stayed my hand.

"Please don't." The teasing in his earlier tone was now absent. "For you to wear his ring is the highest honor he could bestow. We'd be grateful if you accept this token of our friendship and wear it always. To do otherwise, well. It may hurt the Prince's feelings." I was shocked he had any to hurt.

And how, exactly, could I refute that? I wasn't as well-versed in Hidden politics and history as some, but even I knew the foxes would make a powerful ally or a ruthless enemy. My hands fell to my side, and I kept the token where it was. It would seem I had a new adornment, the permanent kind. At least it was pretty.

"Very well, then," I conceded. "Thank you for this honor."

"Thank you for earning it." He gestured back over his shoulder as he said, "I should return to my sister's side, but Asher will return shortly. He had a quick matter to attend to. We'd appreciate it if you'd allow him to accompany you when you make your report to the Headmaster."

"Yes, of course. We'll stay close by."

"He shouldn't be long." He nodded in thanks, first to me, then to the wolf still brooding beside me. I may have imagined the mischief in his eyes at the latter, but I doubted it.

Once he was gone Grayson addressed me between gritted teeth.

"You didn't think to warn me it'd been Eris in peril and not you or at least intervene when I apologized on your behalf?" He scoffed. "Do you enjoy making a fool of me in front of others?"

"You didn't think to ask me before making foolish

assumptions, why should I intervene when you voice them? Your lack of faith isn't my burden to bear."

"I know your expectations around your arrival are different than what's happened, but I didn't think your frustration would manifest in disloyalty to the pack. Let the issues between us be between us, not bleed into inter-realm relations." He ran a hand through his hair and pulled at its roots. "Goddess, Briar, I didn't expect you to be this self-centered."

"Self-centered?" I drew out each syllable, reminding myself that revealing myself by setting his shirt on fire would be counterproductive.

"On a scale of dry bread to custard tart," Kenna asked me, not bothering to whisper, "How tempted are you to punch him?"

"Strawberry pie," I answered. She nodded as she considered this and took a large step away from Grayson's side.

"I'm impressed with your restraint. I'd be at a solid custard tart by now. Maybe even with scorched sugar on top."

"I'm not far off," I admitted, "But the more frequently someone disappoints you, the more you expect it to happen, and the more you expect it to happen the less your blood boils each time it does."

Kenna made a sound in agreement and started cleaning her nails with the tip of one of her daggers, apparently done discussing the subject.

"Speaking of blood," Isaac said, looking us both up and down, "you two realize you are still covered in it, right?"

"Yep." I popped my lips around the word and smiled at

him. "I think it's a nice warning to any potential adversaries, don't you?"

"I think it makes you look unhinged." Isaac's immediate observation made Grayson grin from behind him. I glared. No grinning for him.

"Aw, thanks Isaac," Kenna cooed and shifted her attention to me. "And while we're on the topic of being covered in blood, why is it that both of us are standing here, sporting the blood of our vanquished enemies, and yet you are the only one who gets a freaky fox ring? Like, was I not also there, raining down arrows of destruction and pulling daggers through a demon's throat?"

"Would you like me to go ask him for another so we can match?" I teased, "He seems rather friendly, so I'm sure the request would be well received." So well received, it would likely end with Asher turning my blood into ice, or his blade stabbing me through the heart.

"I suppose not." Her accompanying sigh could've launched a ship from the harbor on a breezeless day. "But let the record show, I am not impressed with being excluded. I mean, a girl kills a demon and what does she have to show for it?"

"Their blood soaking her skin and blade as a warning to her enemies?" I offered. Her smile brightened. "I'll get you a slice of cake later as a reward."

"Can we focus on what's important for a second instead of blood and desserts?" Grayson interjected. He leaned against the stone wall and crossed his arms over his chest.

"I find both of those things extremely important," Kenna, one finger raised in the air. Grayson ignored her.

Isaac rolled his eyes. I smiled, and she winked back at me. The stab-happy little weirdo was growing on me.

"Are you sure they were demons?" Grayson asked solemnly. "Are you certain?"

I wasn't smiling anymore. I took a deep breath and squared my shoulders before I said, "Yes. I'm certain."

His entire body tensed. He turned to Kenna who'd halted her movements, dagger still pointed under one nail. She didn't look away from the blade but nodded her confirmation.

"Damnit." The curse escaped him on an exhale, and he dropped his head back to the stoned wall, his eyes falling shut.

"You took the words out of my mouth," Isaac said under his breath.

We stood in heavy silence as the implications of the day grew even more potent in the space between us. Eventually, Grayson opened his eyes and straightened his head to be upright.

"This changes everything."

"I know." I knew more than he could begin to comprehend how very different things would be.

"Massacres," he began, "towns and villages burned to the ground, sacrifices, possession—those are just the beginning of the atrocities demons leave in the wake."

The rapid pulse pounding against the skin of his neck gave away his terror even more so than the slight tremor in his voice.

"I know," I said again, this time more gently. I hesitated, but at the dejected look in his eye, I dared to move closer to rest a hand on his arm. "I know what it means. I remember."

Except I didn't—not really—and that was half the problem. I knew of the destruction and fear. I'd woken amongst the wreckage, but I didn't know the role I'd played in creating it. What's worse? Something told me the demon I'd met today had known everything I didn't.

That he'd known me.

It was too much. My heart raced faster in my chest and that telltale sign of heat spreading from its center warned me to release Grayson's arm before my hand grew too warm to his touch.

I knew I needed to control my breathing. Calm. I needed to be—no—look calm, but under the weight of Grayson, Isaac, and Kenna's too-cunning eyes, my confidence faltered. I could not remain here and deceive them.

"I'm going to go grab some water, maybe wash some of the blood off." I gave the best excuse for my departure I could muster at the moment. "I'll be back in a few."

I didn't wait for Grayson to ask the questions manifesting in his eyes. I didn't look at Isaac who would inevitably see through me and worry. I didn't stop moving when I heard Kenna ask the others what was wrong with me. I simply walked away and prayed no one followed me.

THE ROSE

I t was too much: my arrival, the challenge, the demons, my secret, Grayson, all of it—too much.

I ducked into the first empty hallway I saw and pressed the heels of my hand against my eyes, grateful the lighting from the lanterns was dim.

One day, a handful of hours, and the decade of care I'd taken to never be discovered was put at risk. They hadn't been looking for me—for anyone before this. Why search for signs of a threat that didn't—couldn't exist? The mere whisper of demons would call the absence of elementals into question. Observations would become suspicions, suspicions would grow into questions, and questions could only lead to discovery.

Kenna already questioned the words I'd exchanged with the demons. She'd been watching me since the moment we stepped foot back on campus as if waiting for me to make a mistake or reveal some buried truth about what happened. If she discovered me, if she found out what I was, there wasn't a sliver of doubt in my mind she'd report me or take matters into her own hands. Everyone would know—the pack, Ivy, Lucas, Grayson–they would all know.

And they'd hate me for it.

I pushed away the thought and pressed into the cool stone of the wall behind me, sending a prayer to the sun and moon that it would suppress the embers beneath my skin.

If Fenrir were here he'd give me five minutes. Five minutes to panic. Five minutes to pull myself together and do what needed to be done for both the pack's survival and my own.

Five.

I could do this. I could keep my head down and get through this. Calm. I just needed to stay calm.

Four.

Tears streamed down my face without my consent. How was I supposed to stay calm through this? Even if I did manage to keep my secret, the demons had returned. What death and destruction would they bring with them?

Three.

I couldn't just keep my head down. I had to lead. I had to prove that I could lead, especially through trials and tribulations.

Two.

The pack depended on me whether they knew it yet or not. A meek leader in the face of danger would only lead to failure.

One.

Failure meant the death of the pack, and death was not an option. I would defend them. I vowed to defend them from harm, and I would not break that vow out of self-centered fear.

Zero.

My time was up. I pulled the leather cord from the bottom of my braid and shook out my hair to better obscure the remnants of tears that were sure to be present on my face. With one more fortifying breath, I opened my eyes to leave.

I wasn't alone.

Standing in the hall, leaning against the wall across from me was the death god. The low lighting did nothing to diminish the chill of his stare. He made no move to speak, showing no sign of concern or disgust at my rumpled state. He showed no sign of emotion at all.

Well if he wasn't going to speak, I certainly wasn't going to either. He was the one watching me. I hadn't sought him out or asked him to linger, and what purpose did his presence serve, anyway? Had he hoped to exploit a weakness? Catalog my vulnerability for his future advantage? Or was it the ring binding him to me?

With every new heartbeat that he watched me, electricity danced along my spine and across my skin, spreading until I felt nearly consumed by the sensation. Was this his magic? I knew foxes had their own affinities, but I'd learned very little about what they were or how they came to be.

How long would we stay this way? I didn't bother to wipe my eyes or hide my face, he'd already seen it and more. I didn't know how long he'd stood there, but I cursed us both. Him, for being eerily silent and sneaking past my senses, and myself for letting him.

If he wasn't going to say or do something, this was a

monumental waste of my time. There was no reason to act as though he held me captive. My eyes rolled at the thought before I could think better of it, and when they landed back on him, I swore the corner of his mouth had curved the most infinitesimal amount into a smirk. I straightened my shoulders and took a step to leave. He pushed off from his spot on the wall, but what he planned to do next would remain a mystery for he froze when voices from around the corner reached us.

My heart sank to my stomach. At least one of those voices was from a pack member. I'd stopped crying but the likelihood my face was splotch-free—I was not an attractive crier—was nearly impossible. I looked to either end of the hall for an exit, but in one direction came the approaching students, and the other led back to the infirmary where any of the others could be lingering.

But then I was moving backward.

My back would have crashed into the stone behind me if not for the arm now banded around my waist. The position was so similar to how he and his court had found Grayson and me on my first day, yet it felt entirely different, closer. Warmer.

Every part of my body was pressed into his. From toe to chest, he arched over me, his face hovering a few inches above mine. His forearm rested against the wall just above my head, caging me to him. Heat radiated from his skin to mine, and I wondered how someone so cold could give off so much warmth.

Asher's eyes roamed over my face, and mine did the same to him. I could see a thin ring of aqua lining his pupils from this distance, and tiny speckles of silver dotted his charcoal hair like stardust. No one could ever doubt he was a moon fox. He was the very personification of night. How many had the chance to see him from this close a distance and live to tell the tale?

"Shhh—stop!" The scuff of shoes grinding to a halt followed the man's whisper shout.

"Oh, goddess," another voice said, "Is that Asher? With a girl?"

"As if." This came from a female. "His Highness would never stoop so low as to be with an Academy girl." Well someone sounds rather bitter about that.

"That's definitely him, but who's he with?" My eyes turned to saucers, and I regained my good sense enough to push against his chest. I'd rather go back to the infirmary and risk Grayson and Kenna's too-observant eyes over this. He didn't budge. Instead, he smiled, and damn him for how stunning it was.

"I don't know, his arm's blocking her. Just walk past them and see if we can tell," The first voice suggested, "No way anyone believes this." I pushed harder against his chest as the shuffling of feet grew closer, but he only held me tighter.

Asher's smile transformed into a glower as he turned his head to look at the onlookers. He growled. They scattered. And only when they were fully out of earshot did he drop his arm and step away from me.

He'd kept me hidden, I realized much too slowly. Before I could form rational words or ask why he'd done that for me, the man quirked a single, perfectly arched eyebrow and walked out of the hallway without a word or backward glance. His only goodbye was a flick of his wrist that somehow sent a small gust of wind over my face. Was I supposed to know what that meant?

Grayson slipped past him as he left and shot a confused look between the two of us. I cleared the lingering tightness from my throat and quickly moved to wipe the tears from my face. My fingers found only dry skin. Had Asher hidden that too? Maybe the trinket on my finger had its perks after all.

"Were you just talking to the Crown Prince of Elestia?"

I pushed off of the wall but let him come to me instead of walking to meet him. "I wouldn't call it talking."

His head reared back. I took pleasure in the tightening of his jaw when he asked, "Then what would you call it?"

"Nothing to concern yourself with," I said and moved to walk away, "I don't want to do this right now, Grayson."

"Briar, wait." I didn't. I was tired of being obstructed by others today, and the command in his voice held no power over me. "Please."

That one word, on the other hand, gave me pause. Outside of requests to his mother and father, I didn't think Grayson had uttered the word please to anyone in the ten years I'd known him. Pack Princes gave orders, but they didn't make requests.

I didn't stop, not completely, but I slowed my pace. I really wanted to get to Isaac's room, wash up, and try to recover from the day's events for a few minutes before we went to see the Headmaster, but it seemed like I'd run out of time anyway.

I turned to Grayson and gave him a nod to walk with me

over my shoulder. He took one stride for every two of mine; he was at my side a moment later.

"Speak." I'd had my fill of silent conversations.

"Goddess, Bri." He chuckled and ran a hand through his hair. I decided I wouldn't say I liked his smile. "I'm only trying to check on you. Is that such a hardship to endure?"

I looked at him sideways and said nothing as I returned to my normal pace.

The fear, the panic, that had afflicted me since the demon first smiled at me was still lingering beneath my skin. I pushed it down. Fear would not save me. I may be discovered and imprisoned—or worse—by the week's end, but until then I'd be damned if I allowed my actions to be dictated by others.

"Nothing to say in response?" he continued the one-sided conversation, instilling a fleck of teasing into his voice, "That's a bit out of character don't you think? What if we went and grabbed those slices of cake? We can catch up, just like my father hoped we would. What do you say?"

He dropped a heavy arm over my shoulder to draw me near to him, but I ducked and spun away from it until there was a safe distance between us. I couldn't think when he was touching me, loathe as I was to admit it.

"I say no," I said definitively, turning to face him fully and crossing my arms over my chest. "Please explain to me which of our interactions since I arrived led you to believe I have any interest in sitting around eating cake and catching up with you?"

If I didn't know better I'd say there was a slight tinge of red atop his cheeks forming as I spoke.

"Was it when I arrived on campus and you chose not to meet me?" I continued. "Or when I came to you in the quad and the first words you spoke to me in nearly three years were undermining my ability?" The redness grew darker as his eyes grew wider.

"Oh, I know," I said, shrugging my shoulders, "It must have been just now in the hallway when you, again, assumed that I couldn't possibly be anything other than the victim in distress, the cause of this entire altercation, right?"

If I captured his expression and asked a stranger to describe it they'd say it was a man in shock. He peered at me the way I imagined I stared after biting into a peach and finding it was a carrot in disguise. Mouth agape, eyebrows lifted, head drawn back, pupils dilated from the low lighting.

"Well?" I asked. "When was it? Because as far as I could tell there was nothing remotely akin to friendship between us anymore, and that was your choice, Grayson–not mine, yours. So when did you decide I was suddenly worthy of a civil conversation?"

I knew berating him wasn't going to help anything, but goddess help me, it had been a long day and my self-restraint had disappeared along with my energy reserves.

"I was just doing what I thought was right for the pack," Grayson said each word slowly, like if he spoke too forcefully he spook me like a wild animal caught in a cage. "I'm the Alpha, it's my duty to put the pack—"

"And, what? Until I killed a demon I wasn't part of it?" Silence. "I meant nothing? We meant nothing?" My eyes jumped between each of his, searching for a shred of evidence he regretted his choices, and not just because he needed to present a united front around our adversaries and allies.

When the silence between us dragged on I said, "I guess not. You know, Gray, I didn't think we'd run into each other's arms and be the very best of friends when I got here. I'm not quite as obtuse as you seem to think, but I did expect you to at least show me the same decency you'd show to anyone else in this pack."

"You are the furthest thing from everyone else in this pack," he practically growled at me, face transforming from bewildered one second to a disbelieving glower in the next. "Don't you think if I were capable of pretending you were one of them, I would?"

And there it was. "I may not be able to transform into a wolf, a lion, or even a snake," I said emotionlessly.

"That's not what I—"

"But I found other ways to make myself a predator. I think I more than proved that today, don't you?"

"Of course you did. Briar, when Pax found me and told me you'd been in a battle in the woods, I thought that was going to be the end—your end." He put his hands atop both of my shoulders and bent so we were at eye level. "And it didn't matter he assured me you were fine. Despite every scrap of logic I told myself, all I could focus on was getting to you, holding you to prove to myself you weren't harmed. I was sure I'd find you injured or bleeding out right in front of me, but you weren't. You fought demons. You fought them and you won. If you think that didn't change how I'm looking at you, then you're not paying close enough attention."

He was good, I'd give him that. I'd be a puddle at his feet if I hadn't known the truth. He looked at me like he wanted me—needed me, but he didn't, and dammit if that didn't hurt.

"Congratulations." I stepped back, his arms falling to his sides as he straightened. "Your opinion of me changed. Unfortunately, I can't say the same for my opinion of you."

"Just give me a chance, Bri." he repeated the plea from earlier.

"Earn one. Because whatever this hot and cold game is you've been playing, I want nothing more to do with it."

Let him do the work to impress me this time around, however devious his motives may be. Let him keep his focus on gaining my trust instead of further questioning how I managed to kill the demons in the first place.

I walked away from him, and this time he made no move to stop me.

20

THE MOON

When I saw her in the hall, I told myself I didn't trace her every step or make a note of each speck of dirt and blood speckled across her skin. I told myself my heart wasn't racing to escape the confines of my chest for fear she'd be taken from me. I told myself I didn't think of her at all, but if the lies we tell ourselves have lives of their own, mine surely died the moment the word demon crossed her lips.

I could list the predators that made me uneasy on one hand, but demons were most certainly at the top of the list. They were ruthless. Invasive. Destructive. Merciless. Their power fed from the fear, anger, and despair of their opponents, only growing stronger as a battle raged on.

I'd still been a child the day they were purged from society, but I thanked every god above and below when it was done. Even then I knew that the price we paid when evil was allowed to prosper was higher than we could ever afford—than we could ever recover from losing. I knew it better than most.

And now they were back if the women were to be believed, and I had no reason to doubt Briar's and Kenna's word other than my inability to reconcile their account with what I'd thought to be true only hours prior. I was growing more impatient each minute we had to wait to hear the full story. Logically, I knew it made sense to recount it together and with everyone present. Illogically, I wanted every detail the moment I saw the blood coating their skin and battle adrenaline still shining in their eyes.

The handful of students who were still awake as we winded through the halls openly stared as we passed. Foxes and shifters weren't enemies but we certainly weren't friends. Our combined presence alone would draw a few curious eyes, but add in the women's gory appearance and I knew we'd soon be the only topic of conversation amongst the masses today.

Still, I didn't like it. An awestruck pixie had the misfortune of catching my eye after ogling one of the females a section too long. All it took for him to scatter away was the slightest narrowing of my eyes. Pathetic.

I loved the Academy, but after three years of being constantly gawked at, whispered about, and approached by other realms—either in hopes of forming an alliance or in an attempt to prove themselves stronger than us—I was well and truly done with pretending to tolerate their antics.

Leading meant playing this game they called politics, but at least the beauty of power was deciding how the game would be played. I played it by glaring at people. Simple but effective. People were less likely to speak to you if they worried you'd kill them for opening their mouths. A reputation Briar was beginning to earn for herself as well.

By the time we'd made it across campus to knock on the Headmaster's door, the whispers were like gravel grating against my skin. Isaac banged on the closed door and a nasal voice called for us to enter through the wood. Gods, I hated listening to him speak.

At his invitation, Isaac opened the door and gestured for Briar to go ahead of him. The rest of us filed in until the lot of us stood clustered in the tepid round room. According to the rules of pack decorum, the highest-ranking member should enter first, but given the circumstances, I refrained from pointing that out to her.

"Good evening, sir. We apologize for stopping in unannounced, but—"

"Briar Lennox," he drawled as he rose from his desk, "Beta of the Othniel Pack, it is so lovely to meet you. Ivy has told me such wonderful things about you over the years, I feel I know you already. Welcome to the Iolite Academy! I do hope you've been settling in well here." She gave him a small, hesitant smile, and I found myself jealous of a graying warlock.

What was running through her head when she gave it, I wondered. Why was it hesitant? Did she always shy away from compliments? Did she think herself unworthy of the accolades? Was she embarrassed by how energetically the Headmaster was shaking her hand now that he'd made it around his desk to her? I didn't know, but I wanted to. I wanted to know every thought running through her head and read every emotion hidden behind her face, and that was the problem. I shouldn't. *I couldn't.*

"Yes, it's good to meet you too, sir, but the reason we're stopping in is—"

"Yes, yes," he said as he leaned back against the front of his desk, ankles crossed and hands resting on the surface on either side. "So thoughtful of you to come and say hello. I won't keep you this evening, but you simply must join me for tea one afternoon. Ivy told me about your run-in with a troll last year; I'm dying to hear all about it." I took care not to let my face reveal my surprise.

That's a story I'd like to hear as well, but it wasn't the time and my impatience only grew each time he interrupted her. By the increasingly set line of Briar's jaw, hers wasn't far behind. Her chest rose as she took a deep breath before, again, trying to inform the Headmaster why we were here and, again, being cut off by his own pointless ramblings. Enough was enough, and if no one reined him in within the next ten seconds, I would.

21

THE ROSE

"Harold, are you planning to let her speak at some point so she can explain why she's standing in your office covered in blood, or would you prefer to continue discussing your tea?"

My cheeks heated at Grayson's intervention. It was frustrating enough to see the shock flit across his face at the Headmaster's praise, but to have him step in on my behalf because he thought I was incapable of handling the situation myself? That was worse than listening to Harold drone on about tea and trolls—though the troll story was one of my best.

The Headmaster snapped his jaw shut and cast Grayson an unimpressed glance. "Well, Mr. Pierce I prefer to welcome a new student when they arrive before diving into whatever bloody matters may need to be discussed. I understand that politeness may not be your strong suit; however, it is mine." He turned his attention back to me, an indulgent smile on his face as though we shared an understanding that Grayson didn't. "Now Miss Lennox, what is it that brings you to my door? Another ogre in the woods perhaps? I assure you, they're quite common around these parts. Nothing to worry about if you've already taken care of it."

"There's been an attack."

He stopped smiling.

I let Eris begin by recounting her journey from walking through the woods to coming across a putrid stench and her altercation with the demons. Kenna and I picked up the story from there, ending with the haunting image of the demon taking his own life.

After my account of the events was complete, silence hung like lead in the air. I watched as the Headmaster tilted his head and thought, staring at nothing while he processed what we had revealed to him.

"I understand something like this would be a very diffi-cult debacle to process," he finally said, as he looked at me, "looking at you I have no doubt a battle occurred, but demons? They've been driven out for over a decade. Are you sure that's what you saw? Is there any way you could be mistaken? Maybe you only thought they could be demons?"

He posed it as a question, but I saw it for what it was: disbelief. It was a lack of faith that three girls could identify a threat of this magnitude, even though he had praised my prowess as I entered the room only a few minutes prior.

"We are sure." Kenna's tone offered no room for debate, yet the Headmaster opened his mouth once again.

"Whether you believe us that the orange-eyed man who smelled of tar and brimstone, and could snap their necks on command are demons, or not, that doesn't change the fact that this should warrant a full investigation from the council. Don't you think, sir?"

I added the sir, as an afterthought. At that moment, I didn't feel he was worthy of the title, but I showed his due respect all the same.

"We will send a team to investigate in the morning," he said and walked back around his desk to take a seat in his leather chair.

"By morning we could lose evidence. The scene will be overrun by predators in the night." I kept my voice level, but my heart was beating ever faster in my chest. How could he look at us, hear what we had encountered, and still do nothing?

"It's not safe to leave the campus after nightfall." He dismissed the idea with a wave of his hand. "A few of the guardians will accompany you after breakfast in the morning."

To the credit of everyone who walked in with me, no one spoke as he stared at us, awaiting our confirmation. By rank and right, we had to do as he said. Confused as I may be about how he found himself on the council, he was still on it, and as such, his commands were paramount. Even when they were wrong.

He pursed his lips and clasped his hands atop his desk when our silence persisted.

"Those of you going tomorrow can meet here in the morning." He looked at each of us in turn before landing his gaze on me. "Miss Lennox, I look forward to our tea. If that will be all for this evening, I strongly suggest you get some rest before the morning's journey."

The urge to further protest must have been apparent on my face because a hand dropped to my shoulder and steered me toward the door. I looked up, expecting to see Isaac or even Grayson, but it was stormy blue eyes that looked back at me. Asher gave the subtlest shake of his head and kept his arm around me until we walked through the door.

None of us spoke as we left the room and traveled down the hallway. We dipped into a small alcove and huddled together. Kenna propped herself up to sit on the ledge of the open-air window. The foxes stood alongside her. Grayson inched closer to me, and when I looked up his glower was fixed on Asher. It could've been a trick of the light, but I'd swear the Prince's lips were slanted in the smallest of smiles.

I shouldn't find Grayson's jealousy delightful. We had more pressing matters at hand than a possessive Alpha, but I couldn't help it. His reaction pleased me.

I elbowed him and stared at him knowingly. I enjoyed every moment of the slight red tint to his cheeks when he was caught. So many blushes these days. I took pity on him and leaned into his side. All was far from forgiven, but I wasn't going to deprive myself of this brief moment. Who knew how many more we'd have?

Asher's face was stoic when I looked up again. He, like me, must have remembered the reason we'd gathered: the Hidden realm was facing a threat, and we were currently the only ones taking it seriously.

Freaking Harold.

Fabian glanced at the Moon Fox Crown Prince before clearing his throat and pushing off from his spot on the wall.

Keeping his voice low, he said, "We cannot sit idly by and trust the Academy staff to take care of this."

"Agreed," Grayson said, "We can't defy a direct order, but we don't have to stand around and do nothing either."

He directed his next question to me, "What do you want to do?"

I pretended I wasn't moved by his deference and addressed the group instead.

"We don't know if the demons were alone or if others are out there lying in wait. The Academy guards may patrol the campus border, but we were deep into the woods when we came across them—much farther than the guards typically travel. I don't think it's wise for any of us to return to the scene without reinforcements, but I do think someone needs to monitor the border tonight."

It didn't feel like an attack was imminent. From Eris' story, it didn't sound like the demons were headed toward the campus nor had they expected to come across anyone else. Still, we couldn't risk being caught unprepared if we were wrong.

"I agree," Eris interjected, "I also find the Headmaster's lack of action concerning. I don't think we can rely on whatever forces he has on patrol to handle this with urgency. Do you think he'll even raise this to the council?"

Isaac laughed humorlessly and said, "And risk his position? Not likely. He'd be displaced. If he can't secure the Academy grounds, how could he be trusted to protect the Hidden realms?"

"Then we need to warn someone else of the threat,"

Fabian added, "It's too dangerous to go unreported, and if you're sure they were demons—"

"She's sure." Grayson's voice brokered no argument, and I, once again, had to keep myself from turning to him in surprise. Where had this newfound faith come from, and why could he not have had it all along?

"Then more than just the Academy needs to know about it. They're not an enemy to underestimate."

The silence between us hung heavily in the air. Every realm had been affected by the demons regardless of whether they were aligned with the shifters against the elementals. There was no question of their malice and deceit. Their danger and destruction were widespread.

As much as I understood the council needed to know, the thought of telling them felt like a million bugs were crawling across my skin at the same time a troll sat atop my chest. I'd have to be even more diligent to keep my heritage a secret. They'd surely be on the lookout for any signs of someone like me now that my mere existence had switched from seemingly impossible to possible in a single afternoon.

I briefly considered lying—saying I was unsure or could have misinterpreted the signs. Maybe they were shapeshifters playing the part or malicious fae trying to cause unrest. It wasn't as if anyone had seen a demon in the past decade, so how could I be expected to properly identify one?

But no. Even I couldn't be that selfish.

I knew in my heart that what I reported was true. I would not be responsible for more blood than already stained my forever-crimson hands.

"Gray." His eyes softened as he looked down at me.

"We need to write to your parents and warn them. If there are more demons out there, and I think we have to work on the assumption there are, it's almost inevitable the shifters become a target. We led the slaughter against them. It wouldn't surprise me if they'd want revenge."

"Of course," he agreed, "I'll send word tonight."

"Asher, will you write to your family? Between the moon foxes and shifters, I think we'd have enough support for the council to take this seriously even if the Headmaster does try to cover up what's occurred."

He nodded. I briefly wondered if he ever spoke. Maybe he couldn't. He certainly hadn't in my presence, but maybe he didn't deem us worthy of hearing his voice. Or maybe his voice was high-pitched and scratchy. That would ruin the ice-king intimidation thing he had going for him.

"That's likely all we can do for now." Grayson ran a hand through his hair and pulled at its roots before letting the appendage fall to his side. "For everyone going tomorrow, I'll see you at dawn."

Murmurs of agreement came from everyone except Kenna who was staring off into the distance. She hadn't spoken a word since we arrived in the alcove.

"Kenna," I asked, "Do you agree?"

Her head turned sharply at her name. "Sorry, what?"

"We'll meet at dawn? I assume you're coming too."

Her answering grin was as brittle as her words. "Yes, of course. Dawn. I'll be there."

Who did they take from her, I wondered.

Kenna's mask was a good one, but I recognized the

ghosts haunting her eyes. They were the same that lived in mine.

"We'll see you all then," I said to the group, "I recommend sleeping with your weapons tonight just in case."

Kenna sounded more like herself when she looked at me incredulously and asked, "Do you usually not?" She shook her head and hopped down from her perch, "And people say I'm the odd one."

ISAAC DOVE onto the bed beside me and rested his head atop his upturned hands. "So you had a fun day, huh?"

We shouldn't joke about the day's events, but the alternative was for me to cry or start breaking things, and I'd only just proven to Isaac I was a great roommate.

I'd stick to humor for now.

"Yes," I said, turning onto my side, and propping my head up by my elbow, "Absolutely loads of fun. I just love threats of imminent death, discovery, and bloodshed, don't you?"

He nodded his head cheekily.

"Especially when they're followed up with a blindsiding betrayal from your first love." He raised an eyebrow at me, and I ground my teeth.

"Please never call him that again. He should be the least of my concerns." And yet, my mind kept replaying the moment I walked into the quad, and saw his uncaring face. The moment he heard students taunting me in the halls and did nothing. The moment he apologized at the infirmary.

Moment after moment, choice after choice, Grayson kept disappointing me. I shouldn't have been surprised he'd do it again.

"Should is the keyword of that phrase, but if you'd like us to pretend he doesn't matter for the time being, I can play along." The sign of a true friend was playing pretend upon request.

"Thank you." I took a deep breath and flopped onto my back. "Now ask the questions I know have been plaguing you since we got back." His face grew somber.

"What haven't you told me about the demons?" he asked. "I could tell you were holding back with the others. But don't hold back with me. Something spooked you more than just running into them."

"Of course, it spooked me. Need I remind you I'm only half a bloodline from being one of them? If they're back, then it feels like I'm more at risk. No one's looking for an elemental right now. Any signs they notice are dismissed or ignored because the sheer possibility of my existence is a non-factor. Once demons are top of mind again, my differences and quirks may not go unnoticed."

Everything I said was the truth. I was safer when no one thought my existence was possible, but the possibility brought scrutiny, and even if I was careful, I could still be caught. I was concerned about the risks, but that wasn't what plagued my mind, and Isaac's expectant face told me he knew it. If I remained silent he would wait for me to speak. He always did, the stubborn cat.

"I think one of them knew me," I admitted. His grin dropped and he pushed himself up until he was sitting. I did the same, leaning my back against the cool wood of the headboard behind me.

"Tell me." There was no teasing lilt left in his tone. His eyes were fixated on mine, compelling me to tell him everything I'd been withholding. So I did.

I told him about the demon's pet name for me and how he knew I was holding back my magic. I told him about his threat that they would find me before he snapped his own neck. He didn't interrupt me with questions or theories, he simply listened intently the entire way through. Towards the end, he laced his fingers through mine, and when it was over, he held both of my hands between his own.

"That would have been as jarring as fighting the demons for me had I been in your place." His thumb ran over the back of my hand. "Did it trigger anything in your memories? Did you recognize him at all?"

"No," I said and looked to the ceiling, the crown of my head thunking against the wall. "It didn't trigger anything. I still don't remember anything before wandering in the woods." Well, before I woke up in a town of ash, but that was the one secret I never shared with him.

"I don't like it."

"Neither do I."

"We have to be even more careful," he said imploringly, "if we are discovered they'll kill first, and maybe ask a few questions later."

"There is no we in that scenario." I looked him dead in the eye and pulled his hands toward me onto my lap. "If I am discovered, you will go along with whatever the pack chooses to do."

He was already shaking his head in denial before I finished speaking. Goddess, he was as stubborn as his father. What was it about the Caddell men that wouldn't let me die alone?

"You know I could never do that." He squeezed my hands in his. "I'd stay with you until the end, no matter what that end may be." And what a waste of life that would be. He deserved better than being sentenced to a traitor's death on my behalf.

"I'm asking you not to." I paused. "You didn't ask for the secret, Isaac. It was forced on you. I know that you would die for me — I would die for you too — but I'm asking you to live for me instead." Living was harder in many ways. It meant working through grief, tragedy, and disappointment, but it also meant experiencing beauty, joy, and love.

"There are many things I don't know about the world," I said, "but I do know it is a brighter place with you in it, and I refuse to be responsible for making it darker."

He didn't agree with me, or make any promises. Instead, he simply said, "Don't get caught, and we will never have to worry about it."

"That's the plan." I hoped it was a plan we could keep.

"Are we going to talk about Grayson now?"

"Absolutely not." I wouldn't even know what to say. There was nothing to say.

"You two seem to be getting along better lately." He flipped on his back and smiled at the ceiling. "Don't think I haven't noticed him trailing after you or how close you were standing in the hall earlier. Not to mention the sour look on his face every time you leave with me."

I did snicker at that. I thought I may have been over-thinking Grayson's expression when I went to Isaac's room at night, or maybe I was looking for something that wasn't there.

"He's just possessive." I wave a hand dismissively in the air. "He doesn't want me but he doesn't want anyone else to have me either. The second it suits him he'll be back to undermining me in favor of his own agenda."

Isaac rolled to his side to face me.

"There's no way you really believe that." He poked me in the side and I jerked at the contact. Curse my ticklish body. "It's more than possession and you know it."

"I don't know anything of the sort." I couldn't. "Even if there was something there, what would be the point? It could never go anywhere."

"Bri." He pushed himself up. "You don't have to spend the rest of your life alone; there's nothing wrong with leaning on someone else."

"There is when doing so puts their life at risk." I tried not to sound as sad as I felt, but I must have failed because something akin to heartbreak fell across Isaac's face. He reached for me, and I let him pull me into his arms until we were lying back down with my head cradled in the nook of his neck. I took comfort in the familiar scent of scorched sugar and rum.

"Some people are worth the risk," he said, his lips grazing the top of my head, "Some people would gladly take the risk. I'm not saying you should tell everyone what you really are. I'm not even saying you should tell Grayson what you are. I just want you to be open to the fact that someday, there may be someone you want to build a life with, and when you find that person, they won't care what you are. They'll be too in love with who you are for it to matter."

I made a noncommittal sound and nestled further into his arms, draping one of mine over his torso. We said our goodnights and soon after his breathing deepened and slowed. He'd fallen asleep.

I wish I could say I nodded off soon after but flashes of orange eyes and ash-covered ruins cycled through my mind. Maybe someone could love me despite what I am, but I knew with unbridled certainty they could never forgive what I'd done.

How could they? I couldn't even forgive myself.

22

THE ROSE

The guards didn't believe us.

That much had been obvious. It was blatantly displayed on their less-than-enthused expressions when we met them outside the Headmaster's office the following morning, and it had only grown more apparent with each minute we spent trekking through the trees.

It wasn't their disbelief that bothered me, it was the growing doubt it inspired to bloom on Grayson's face. The internal debate in his mind may as well have been printed on his face as his features grew more and more pinched the longer we walked.

He'd already been awake in the common room when I slid from Isaac's bed to sneak a cup of coffee from the kitchens before dawn. I hadn't needed to. He had a steaming mug for himself and another waiting for me. That early in the morning, when the only light and sound came from the crackling fireplace, it felt like we were back in the library, huddled in our own world behind the curtains or under one of the tables.

That I managed to hold perfectly still when Grayson reached over to brush a thumb over the already half-healed cut on my arm was an act of the goddesses themselves. When he followed the gesture by dropping his arm around my shoulder and gently guiding my body to lean into his, I gave into the flutters in my stomach and let him. Neither of us spoke as we sat on the sofa together, sipping from our mugs.

Words had felt unnecessary. Now, when it seemed he couldn't even look at me, I wished I'd asked for them. Maybe then I'd know which side of him was more likely to win: the side that made me feel cherished or the side that made me feel condemned.

The further he walked from me, and the more distant the look in his eyes, the more convinced I was it'd be the latter. I shouldn't have been surprised–I'd been the one to tell Isaac his newfound faith in me wouldn't last.

Sometimes I hated being right.

"It's just up ahead," Eris said, pointing toward a fallen tree in the distance. Just like our first meeting, her brother and cousin walked on either side of her. I would've expected the Crown Prince to place himself at the center.

"About time," Isaac grumbled while rubbing his eyes. The sun was just starting to peek above the horizon, and he wasn't one for mornings.

"I swear this path is twice as long as it was yesterday," I told him.

"Yesterday you had my riveting conversation to distract

you," Kenna offered, "I was keeping quiet because it's an ungodly hour, but I'm happy to entertain you if you're bored. Last night I was reading about this new interrogation technique where they take the space between your toes and—"

"I think we're good, Kenna," Grayson interjected. So he would talk to *her* just not to me. Noted. "Like Eris said, we're nearly there."

She paused to consider this then nodded decidedly. "I'll save it for the walk home."

"Can't wait, I've been wondering about that but haven't explored it yet." Fabian's jovial response and smile seemed genuine, and I suspected more danger lay behind it than the naked eye could see. I sent a silent thank you to the goddess we were on the same side.

Our steps slowed as Kenna called to the guards that we'd arrived. Well, what she actually yelled was they should watch their step unless they wanted their boots coated in demon blood. We learned it did, in fact, stain much to Kenna's delight, but the point of the message was the same.

They walked thirty or so feet ahead of us scanning the ground for the corpses. I knew Eris was right, this was the spot, but their scent had faded from the trees. There was but a single reason that could be possible: they weren't here.

"Is this some kind of joke to you kids?" One of the guards asked with his eyebrows drawn in, a snarl ready on his lips. "A way to kick off the start of the year by wasting the Academy's time and resources?"

"I'd be careful of who you call a kid," Kenna said, the

point of her dagger twirling on the tip of her middle finger and her tongue tracing the edge of her teeth. "Unless of course, you'd like to join me for a bit of play time."

The guard's expression remained stern, but he couldn't hide the color slowly leeching from his face. He mumbled something about troublesome students, but I tuned out of the conversation.

They had to be somewhere if not here. There must be a trace, a footprint, a trail, something! I searched, but I saw nothing. Even the grooves in the trees where our blades struck were mended as if it never happened.

"Are you sure this is the spot?" Grayson asked. Asher walked closer and titled his head in question, presumably asking the same without breaking his silence.

"Yes," I said, hands splayed out in front of me, "I'm certain this is the spot."

"Then where are they?" Grayson kept his voice low, but I didn't miss the streak of frustration running through it.

"What," I asked, "You think we made the entire thing up? Staged a fight, and even went so far as to knock Eris unconscious to gain a little attention, is that what you think?"

Asher, who'd stood at Grayson's side, took a decided step away from him and shook his head. Probably wise.

"I don't know, Briar, why don't you explain this to me then? I told the Headmaster you were sure, are you? Is it something else? Did you and the girls eat an herb or a plant in the forest that could've confused you?"

"Are you implying I was hallucinating?"

"If you weren't then where is the blood? Where are the

bodies?" He ran a hand through his hair. Maybe I should've reached out and broke it.

"I don't know, but they were here," I said emphatically, "Is it so hard for you to believe what I'm saying? Silly me, but I thought that after last night we were on the same side again. Was I wrong?"

He said nothing in response, pacing a circle and surveying the scene around us where our companions and the guards continued to search. Grayson moved until he stood a few feet in front of me, his arms folded across his broad chest.

"If you hadn't just left the bodies here, then we wouldn't even be having this debate right now. They'd be at the Academy right now as tangible proof of your story. If there were dead demons, you should have known to collect them. You should've known it'd be too difficult to believe without evidence. Otherwise, it just seems like—"

He cut himself off and ran a hand over his mouth, the other planted on his hip.

"Like what?" I dared him to continue.

"Like this was all a ploy. A poorly planned plot to prove to me—to the pack that you have the strength necessary to lead it."

The crack of my palm against his face brought all conversation around us to a halt.

I'd handled his ignorant dismissals. I'd handled his lack of faith and mood swings. I'd handled the rumors in the hallways. I'd even handled the humiliation of him claiming I was incapable of leading in front of our pack and the other realms. This? This I would not handle. At least, I wouldn't handle it gracefully.

"You disgust me," I seethed, "And if you're going to insult me with your theories, at least make them somewhat sound. Kenna was there with me. What motivation would she have to make me seem strong enough to lead the pack, which, by the way, I am?"

His wolf looked two inches from the surface when he shook his head and snarled.

"You two seem oddly close having known each other for such a short time, maybe she wanted to leave you with some dignity after defeating you in the Rite." He tossed his hands in the air. "Regardless, even if your story is true, you were wrong to leave the corpses behind. It was poor judgment and I'd expect better from a leader in this pack."

"There isn't a single word you're spewing that makes sense. If I'd brought the bodies it would've meant leaving Eris unconscious and unprotected in the forest. And who are you to pass judgment on me?" I asked quietly. "What right do you have to question my choices?"

I stepped toward him, crossing the short distance between us.

"I am the —"

"Alpha?" I asked with a humorless chuckle. "It's concerning how frequently I have to remind you that you do not outrank me, Grayson Pierce. As much as you hate it, unless the Pack Rite proves otherwise, I am the Luna of this pack, and screw you for acting otherwise. I'm done with you for today." I should be done with him forever.

The set of his jaw promised an argument, but a melodic voice halted whatever words he planned to say.

"I am exceedingly grateful you chose to get us all to the Academy safely." Eris placed a hand on my shoulder. "That was a difficult choice to make, but I thank you for making it."

"In other words," Fabian said, smirking, "Relax, Grayson. I would hate to think of you, preferring my sister, not to mention your pack mates, lingering in harm's way rather than leaving a couple corpses in the woods for a night."

"I never said I wanted them in harm's way." He straightened to his full height, an inch or two above the still smirking fox. "I trust that Briar and Kenna are more than capable of handling themselves against any threat they may come into contact with."

At that, I had to laugh. And I did, so hard that tears began streaming down my face from the sheer force of it. The foxes looked between us before backing away and joining the others as they spread out to search the surrounding area.

I could still smell traces of rot lingering in the air, but I couldn't tell the others that without raising suspicion. The bodies had to be somewhere nearby. Maybe a predator had dragged them away in the night or turned them into a meal. They deserved a far worse fate than turning into excrement scattered across the forest floor. Grayson's feet remained planted as he frowned down at me, making no move to join the others.

When I collected myself, I was able to say, "Are you serious?" I wiped my eyes. "How convenient for you to decide that when it suits your purpose. I don't even think you know what you believe anymore."

I turned toward the foxes to bid them farewell but was pulled back to the wolf in front of me, his forehead pressing into mine, eyes beginning to glow.

"Do not walk away from me, Briar."

"Why?" I whispered. "You keep walking away from me. I can't keep doing this with you Grayson. Either you trust me or you don't. Choose and choose quickly because I am two seconds from not caring what you think of me and writing you off altogether."

He released my arm as though it burned him and moved back a few steps. The movement was so abrupt I had to do a quick self-check to confirm I hadn't *actually* burned him by mistake.

"You said you wanted me to give you a chance. This is not how you earn one. This is you making me think that maybe we can't fix whatever this is between us. Maybe this is just who we are now, Gray. I made the best call that I could at the moment," I said, "Eris was unconscious, and as far as we knew the demons were dead. We had no way of knowing if others were on their way, and if they were, we had no way to know how many there would be, not to mention the other threats lurking in the woods. So, if you think I made the wrong call, I simply don't care. I would do it again because all three of us made it here alive. And there is nothing I regret about that."

He wanted to argue with me. I could see it in the muscles twitching along his jaw, but I was right, and I think he knew that too. Our quiet stare-down could've gone on for hours had Eris not spoken.

"Do you smell that?" Eris asked one of the others from behind us. Neither Grayson nor I turned until she added, "It smells like blood."

Asher was the first to reach for his weapon at her observation. He kept one hand on the hilt of his sword as one of the guards made her way to Eris and said, "Not just blood. It smells like death."

The other guards who'd only been half-heartedly searching the forest floor prior began to look in earnest. Grayson and I exchanged a brief look—his tinged with regret, mine with resolve. We separated to search in the direction Eris had been walking, the scent growing more pungent by the second.

It made sense we'd follow the trail, but what didn't make sense to me was that the scent held only the faintest hint of demon atop it, so faint I would be surprised if any of the others would be able to detect it.

The predominant stench was not the same smell that had burned to inhale the day before. When we'd tracked it another half mile it became obvious this rot was not as strong as the two demons yesterday. It was stronger, but it didn't smell of demon. It smelled of death.

Unease grew tighter in my chest as we kept moving and then the blood in my veins turned to ice. Not ten feet ahead at the edge of a small clearing, Kenna stood still as a lake on a breezeless day. Even from her side profile, the dismay was stark across her face.

She didn't turn to any of us when she shook her head and said brokenly, "I don't understand."

I froze. I wanted to steal one more moment before I saw whatever lay in wait for us. Isaac reached her first, then the guards, then Asher, Eris, and Fabian. I was still rooted in place when Grayson walked past me, brushing his hand against my side as he went.

He reached the others before I'd taken a step in their direction. In my life I'd seen Grayson happy, angry, annoyed, and murderous; I'd never seen him scared.

I took a fortifying breath and walked over to my horrified friends. Kenna said nothing, only raised an arm and pointed in the direction of her gaze. Then I was horrified too.

Arms.

Legs.

Torsos.

They were all strewn across the moss-covered plain, their blood weeping into the earth below. I hadn't noticed the smell, I'd been too distracted by the tar and brimstone, but it permeated the air now, and I doubted it'd ever leave my senses: death. So much death.

"Have you ever?" Kenna's whispered question trailed off.

"No," I said gravely. "No, I've never."

A wave of nausea threatened to drive me to my knees. I tried to push it down, to focus on something else like the mild breeze swaying the branches of the trees or how squishy the ground was under my feet. I couldn't.

Long fingers laced with mine. I'd been a young girl the last time Grayson had held my hand. I could've withdrawn from his hold, but I let his firm grip provide the grounding I couldn't find myself.

"Why would they have done this?" Kenna's question shook me from my stupor. Action. We needed to take action.

"I don't know," I answered, walking closer to the spread of body parts, taking care not to touch them.

Each end was nearly touching another. I released Grayson's hand and darted to the nearest tree. I climbed just high enough to get a view of the entire area.

"It's in a pattern," I called down to the others. "Some kind of broken spiral bordered by a hexagon." I'd never seen a symbol like it before.

"I'm coming up." I moved to a nearby branch to make space for Kenna. She climbed up quickly and curled her lip at the new view of the carnage.

"Do you recognize it?"

She shook her head and pulled her quiver of arrows to her front, grabbing the remaining few arrows and holding them out to me. "Take these." I did but looked at her questioningly until she reached into the bottom and pulled out a rolled-up, leather-bound journal and a pencil.

"You keep a notebook under your arrows?"

"You don't?" she asked, looking over at me as if I were the odd one. "Weird. What do you do when you need to write something down?" Her words held a shadow of her usual teasing.

"What would I need to write down, and why would I need to write it down in a situation involving arrows?"

"The techniques and tactics you learn from your opponent so you can study them later." This is why people gave her a wide berth in the halls. "The point is, I'm prepared, and you're welcome. Now please stop talking so I can concentrate."

Normally I'd bristle at someone else issuing me an order, but in this case, I thought it best to comply. It wasn't the moment for politics and hierarchies. I watched as she began sketching the scene in front of us, adding a separate dash in the outline for each appendage and labeling them. Her face grew more somber with each line and letter. When she was finished she released a heavy sigh and lowered the still open book to her side.

We climbed down in silence when the diagram was complete. Kenna handed her notebook to Grayson who studied it before passing it on to Isaac who passed it on to our companions in turn. When it reached the guards one of them moved to tear the journal. Kenna's blade stopped their hand.

"Does it feel like a wise choice to damage something that belongs to me?" she asked in a level voice. "I don't like people taking my things."

"We need to bring this diagram back to the Headmaster," he said without taking his eyes away from the dagger resting against his wrist, "He'll need it for us to investigate what occurred here."

The other guards were poised to reach for their weapons. I pitied the person who tried to draw it. My fellow students, on the other hand, were watching the guards—not Kenna—with keen eyes. I suspected even the guards knew who'd come out as the victor if it came to blows.

"Then I suggest you make a copy for him to keep and

give my book back to me." The guard visibly swallowed, his eyes darting between his fellow soldiers before unhanding the page and returning the journal to Kenna's care.

The guards broke away from us and began scrutinizing the massacre in earnest.

"What are they going to do with the bodies?" Eris' question broke the heavy silence.

"More than just the pattern needs to be documented before they can be moved," Grayson said, his upper lip curled as he stared at the carnage.

"They deserve to be put to rest," I added, "and identified. Their communities—their families—deserve to know their fate."

Except what was that exactly?

"Is there any chance they were already here yesterday, and none of you came across it?" Fabian asked hesitantly.

"Maybe?"

"Absolutely not."

Eris and Kenna answered at the same time. Both women turned to look at the other in surprise over the provided answer.

"I would have scented it if this were already here," Kenna said.

Eris countered, "I don't think we can be certain of that. This is at least a quarter mile from where we fought. There's no guarantee we'd have picked up the scent, especially if the kills were recent."

Except I would have. There was no chance these bodies had been here last night. Eris and Kenna continued debating their opinions while I contemplated how to take a side without drawing suspicion. I glanced at the others, expecting them to each be focused on the quarreling females, and they were, except Asher.

Asher was looking at me. A single arched brow offered a silent invitation for me to weigh in on the matter.

"It doesn't matter, does it?" The quarreling stopped. "If they were already here or not makes no difference. They're still here, the demon corpses are still gone, and we still don't know what we're up against."

I was met with silence.

"Our next steps are clear: document what we can and leave no stone or leaf unturned for any trace of who did this." And *why* they did it. "We're going to need a carriage to bring the bodies back when we've finished. Isaac, head back to the Academy and fetch one. Be discreet. Few should be awake at this hour, but we don't want to start a panic. Kenna, start collecting blood samples. It's hard to tell underneath the rot setting in, but I smell at least two different realms amongst the victims. We can't rule out that they're in a pattern. Goddess only knows what we will wish we'd documented later. We have to work under the assumption that everything is relevant from the space between the pieces to the color of hair on the limbs."

Isaac left for the Academy without delay. Kenna bristled slightly at the direction but nodded and set to work adding samples and additional detail to her diagram. Maybe the guards would document their findings but I wasn't taking any chances. The Headmaster's dismissal yesterday had set my teeth on edge and these people deserved more than a forgotten fate on a forest floor.

"I won't presume to give you orders," I said to the moon foxes with a humorless smile, "But I think there's value in the rest of us splitting up to survey the surrounding area. It'd be too much to hope we find a trail nearby, but maybe they lowered their guard with more space between them and the attack."

Fabian and Eris waited for Asher to nod before starting in opposite directions. Asher headed on his way, though notably slower than the others.

"You were right," I said the wolf standing silently beside me, "I shouldn't have left the bodies behind."

THE ROSE

A massacre had been found in the wood, demons had returned from extinction, and me? I was stuck sitting in a classroom listening to students prattle on about inconsequential rumors.

Our efforts to keep the bodies in the woods discreet had been in vain. By the time we'd documented all we could, received the go-ahead from the guards, and carefully loaded the victims into the carriage to bring back to the Academy, the halls and outer areas had been flooded with students and staff gaping at us as we passed. I briefly wondered if it was becoming more normal to see me covered in blood and smelling of death. Picking up bodies was a gory business.

To my surprise, Grayson hadn't uttered a single harsh word to me since we'd entered the death-ridden clearing. I should take it as a kindness that he hadn't pointed out I'd done exactly as he'd predicted: I'd failed. Because really, what else could I have called it?

Regardless of what I said to the others, I knew those bodies weren't there the night before. If I'd brought the corpses with us or returned to collect them, Headmaster's order be damned, then maybe those people would still be alive.

Additional enchantments were cast along the Academy's borders and a campus-wide curfew had been implemented until further notice. The infirmary had been divided into two sides: one for healing, and one for that which can no longer be healed. We'd always had a dungeon on the school grounds. We'd never needed a morgue.

But were the students surrounding me talking about these threats to life as we knew it? Was anyone plotting how they'd protect their courts from another attack? No. They were prattling on about a Prince.

"Did you hear Asher was spotted with a female last night?" I heard a girl behind me ask.

"There's no way," her friend responded, "He's been here three years, and not one person has garnered his attention. I'd check your source on that rubbish."

"It's true! Jemima saw it with her own eyes!"

"Okay," the friend said with an edge in her voice, "Then who was he with?"

"Well." She paused. "She couldn't tell who it was. She could just see Asher pressed up against someone." Relief flooded through me at the assurance I hadn't been identified as his companion. If he hadn't been pressed against– or to be more precise–hunched over me, I surely would've been, and the last thing I wanted was more eyes tracking my every step.

The stares in the hall this morning were proof enough that tales of me defeating the demons alongside Kenna had spread. Had they seen my face with Asher last night, they'd have surely named me by now. With everything else that had happened the past day, Asher being spotted with me in the hallway shouldn't even be a topic of conversation.

Naomi leaned over to me and whispered, "Who do you think was with the Prince last night?"

"Does it matter?" I asked dryly. "It has nothing to do with us."

She bit her lip and looked down. I thought she'd gained some maturity for letting it go, but she ruined it by saying, "I know but he's never seen with anyone. Aren't you the least bit curious?"

"No." I didn't need to be. "Maybe we should be less focused on handsome foxes and more focused on class. Have you done your make-up exam in herbology yet?"

"Not yet." She flopped back in her chair with a frown that turned to a smile a second later. "So you admit he's handsome, then?"

Goddess save me.

She must have heard my plea because Eris walked through the door a moment later. She took the seat beside mine and placed one of the two steaming mugs she carried on my desk.

"Someone thought you could use this today." She cradled her own mug like it was the last fire during a winter storm. I thanked her and took a sip.

Chocolate and hazelnut. My favorite.

I didn't usually drink it this late in the afternoon, but today was not a usual day.

"Oh my gods do you think it was one of those girls with Asher?"

"No way."

"I told you that was why she sat with them!"

"Oh shut up—"

"Don't be such a—"

"He would never—"

They all spoke at once, and I fought the urge to slam my dagger into their desks to demand a moment's peace.

"You know," Eris pondered aloud, "I find people's choice of conversation so insightful. I feel like it speaks to their priorities, don't you?"

"Absolutely," I agreed easily, noticing the chatter behind us had, once again, fallen silent because of her musings. Maybe I should switch my schedule to align with hers if it would bring a full day's peace. Eris' normally sweet face turned a smidge maniacal as she stared down at her coffee in thought.

"Fabian and Asher, for example, detest gossip. They say it's the first sign of poor intellect, not to mention poor character."

Gasps of indignation sounded both from the seats behind us and, less humorously, from Naomi on my left.

"I couldn't agree more."

"They may be right on one account, though." Her mouth turned up on one side in a sly grin. "My cousin would not be spotted with any mere female. Whoever she was, she must be extraordinary to garner his attention."

I hummed a noncommittal response and sent a quick prayer of thanks to whichever goddess was listening when the professor walked in a second later.

"Maybe," she continued, as the professor began taking out the day's materials, "She's so extraordinary that she can even emerge from a battle with demons unscathed, saving someone in the process."

"Eris, it's not what you think."

She leaned back in her chair, "We'll see. There's only been one other person he considered giving that ring to, and she meant a great deal to him. I wouldn't take his decision to put it on your finger lightly."

Naomi was staring at me with eyes the size of custard tarts. She opened her mouth but closed it and faced the front after one look from me.

Eris suspected something had happened between Asher and me last night. That much was obvious, but I was less certain of *what* she suspected. Nothing happened. I knew that. Asher knew that. But did she know that? If she'd sat beside me thinking her cousin's interest in me was romantic, she'd be sorely disappointed.

I wasn't sure what our encounter in the hall had been, but romantic was nowhere near the list of descriptors. It was probably him acting out of whatever misplaced sense of duty he felt toward me from giving me the damn ring that felt more and more right on my finger. I blamed the freaky fox magic, or maybe the greedy demon blood.

It was probably the demon blood.

I looked at Eris despite myself. As much as I hated to admit it, her cryptic comment about someone else made me curious to know what kind of person was capable of slipping beneath the death god's icy exterior.

"Who was she?" I asked, surprising both Naomi and myself.

Eris looked down at her hands before answering.

"She was his bonded," she said, her smile stained in sorrow. I should have left it there. I'd already pried too far into matters that were not my own.

"Is she here, at the Academy?" I hadn't seen another female with him in the halls. "Will she be angry that he gave me the ring?"

If the death god's impulsive gift put me in the middle of an inter-realm incident, I'd find his favorite belongings and burn them before scattering their ashes in the wind. He'd never know what befell them, but I would, and that satisfaction would be enough.

"She isn't anywhere." My heart dropped at Eris' answer. "She was taken from him."

I opened my mouth to apologize for overstepping but was interrupted before I could form the words.

"Eyes on me, everyone. Your attention, please," Professor Richards called. He stood at the front of the room with one foot in front of the other. His hands were placed on his hips and his chin was raised slightly in the air. The green of his shirt was so bright I was tempted to shield my eyes to avoid the glare. He had to be the most pompous person on this campus.

"As you know from reading the syllabus, we're discussing bonds. Please get out your pre-work. I'll be coming around to collect it."

I reached into my rucksack to pull out the essay I'd written the morning before and the questionnaire. To my right, Eris did the same. When I looked at Naomi the blood had drained from her horror-drawn face.

"We had pre-work?" she asked in a hushed voice as she looked around. Professor Richards had made it to the second row. "When did he assign pre-work?"

"It was in the syllabus," I said, trying to keep the growl from my voice, "Did you not read it?"

Two pink spots appeared across her cheeks.

"I mean I skimmed it, but don't the professors usually tell you ahead of time? I didn't think it was necessary!" The already rapid rise and fall of her chest only increased as the Professor drew closer. "What am I supposed to do?"

"Take whatever consequence he gives you, and start keeping track of your assignments in a journal like the responsible adult you're supposed to be."

She looked like she was close to tears, and she should be. Of all the classes in this school to miss an assignment in this was not the class. After he'd frozen half the class on our first day he'd taken to using magic on any student who either didn't meet his expectations or crossed him by way of trans-figuration, taking away one of their senses, or even freezing them the entirety of the day.

It was obvious to anyone watching that he took pleasure in it. He smiled each time a student entered the classroom with a face of fear. Crying would only make it worse, and my compassion would only make her cry harder. I needed to snap her out of it.

"Briar," Naomi reached over to grab my hand, one tear falling, "I'm scared."

"It's going to be okay," I told her, squeezing her hand, "Just take a breath. You forgot an assignment, you didn't kill someone. You need to keep yourself together, understand? You're a representative of the Othniel Shifter Pack and we do not break. Right?"

She nodded frantically and wiped at her face. "Right."

"Good." Goddess, please let her not break for both the sake of the pack's reputation and her own. Males like Professor Richards thrived on the humiliation of others. Their only real power was to abuse the powerless.

Naomi was still muttering a pep talk to herself when the pursed-lip professor reached our desks. He stopped in front of each seat with an outstretched hand. First Eris handed him her assignment to add to the growing stack he held against his hip, then me. When he stopped in front of Naomi, she stared down at her desk and mumbled something too low for even me to hear.

"If you must speak, at least do so audibly. Better yet, don't. Just hand in your assignment and spare me the rest," Professor Richards said sharply.

"I don't have it," she said only slightly louder. The professor frowned, feigning disappointment, but I saw the glee in his eyes.

"Don't have it?" he asked. She shook her head in response. "Did you forget to bring it or simply decide not to do it? Are my lessons beneath you? Do you feel you already know all there is to learn, and thus my offerings to advance your understanding are useless to you? Is that it?"

Naomi gasped as her head shot up from the desk to look at him straight on. She waved her hands in front of her and said, "No, of course not! I'm so sorry, I just forgot. I meant no offense, and I'll turn it in at our next class, I promise."

The professor's mouth turned up the slightest bit and his next words were spoken like silk. "You promise, do you? What is it you're willing to give me in return for accepting such assurances? How am I to know you'll follow through when you so clearly failed to do so when given the chance before?"

Don't do it, Naomi, I pleaded with her silently. For all that is good in the world, if you have a shred of sense, do not fall for this.

"Any—"

"Enough." I cut her off before she gave more than she was truly willing. The fae turned to me, a smile stretching from cheek to cheek. I was tempted to throw my mug at him, but that would be a waste of coffee.

"Ah, the young Luna." He looked me over. "I heard you slayed a demon in the woods. Are you an aspiring writer? Were you practicing one of your tales?"

He was baiting me. I knew it. He knew it. The silent students watching us knew it. I had two choices: back down and let him return his attention to Naomi or answer his taunts and make myself his next target.

"I wasn't blessed with the gift of storytelling." I kept my tone even—casual even. I'd be damned if I gave him the slightest reaction. He'd be disappointed if he expected to see fear or anger on my face. He waited, obviously expecting me to say more, maybe defend myself or try to prove why the report was true.

I didn't. He deserved nothing of me, so that's what I'd give him: nothing.

"No? So we're just to believe that you vanquished a supremely powerful being—an extinct powerful being at that —and walked away the victor? Really, Miss Lennox, even with Miss Lenoir at your side that's quite far-fetched."

He set the stack of papers down and placed his hands along the edge of my desk to lean over me. I shifted forward, my arms crossing atop the surface less than a foot from his hands.

"Let's be honest with each other, Miss Lennox. The like-lihood of any shifter, let alone one barely old enough to attend the Academy–one who can't even shift," he scoffed, "could defeat such a foe is next to nil. So tell me, what threat do you truly pose? What gives you the gall to interrupt a discussion between a student and her professor?"

There was something beautiful about the moment before a predator realized they'd become the prey. He was looming over me, chest puffed up, smug smile plastered on his face, eyes drilling into mine. I could've held back, I could've let it go to keep the peace. I didn't.

I laughed.

He wasn't smiling now. I heard more than one student gasp at my outburst, but I didn't look away from him as I chose my next words.

"Professor, allow me to answer your questions with one of my own." I tilted my head to one side, "Do you know why you'll never see a shifter leaning over an adversary?"

He drew his head back an inch or two, his brows nearly meeting above the bridge of his nose. He gave no answer.

"No?" I asked. It wasn't quite a taunt—I had some sense of self-preservation—but it wasn't far off. I leaned closer, nearly rising from my chair to whisper, "It exposes their throat."

24

THE ROSE

He hopped back a full foot, and it took conscious effort to keep a smile of victory off my face. A few students snickered alongside me but abruptly stopped when his fury-filled eyes looked around the class.

"Let's make a deal," I suggested. His face had grown red, the vein in his neck pulsing against the golden skin. He didn't want to entertain my offer. It would only strengthen my standing in this war between us, but if there was one thing a Fae was helpless to resist, it was a bargain.

"You want to make a deal?" he asked almost too calmly. "Didn't you prevent your friend from striking a bargain with me just now?"

"I did. I suppose it's up to you to ask yourself: Would you rather bargain with a pack member or a Pack Leader?" In other words, where do you want to fall in the hierarchy?

He considered it a moment, but I knew his answer before he spoke. What other choice could he make with the entire room watching? He may think of us as children, barely ready to leave our parents, but he did know our parents—well, other student's parents. For the students surrounding me to report he gave in to the demands of an eighteen-year-old girl would surely gall him to no end, regardless of my rank and title.

"What's your bargain?"

"Quiz me," I dared, "Ask me three questions on today's assignment of your choosing. If I get one wrong, then you can enact whatever you deem fair for Naomi's honest mistake throughout the duration of this class period. If I answer them all correctly, you'll say you won't use your magic on a single student the remainder of the school year."

Murmurs broke out across the classroom. Naomi's face had turned deathly pale in the corner of my eye. It was risky, but the alternative was for her to walk into an open-ended bargaining with a vindictive fae. The agreement could mean a lifetime of servitude. I'd seen him leave students frozen for a full day without a bargain in the mix, goddess only knew what he'd do to someone who naively entered one.

"I need neither your permission to govern my class nor your approval for my methods." He asked, "Pray tell, what exactly do I have to gain from this bargain?"

"Respect." Had a feather fallen to the floor in that moment it would've been audible from every corner of the classroom.

"I have that now." The underlying layer of violence in his voice sent chills down my spine, but I held my ground. Show no weakness. Fenrir's past advice kept me grounded. *Better to be confident in the face of a threat than uncertain. A cunning opponent will sense both but only benefit from one.*

"Do you?" I asked. Even I didn't dare blatantly disrespect a fae to his face. Plus, I did still need to survive at the Academy for four years.

"Fine," he drew out the word, "If you answer three questions correctly, I will say I won't use magic on another student for the remainder of the school year. If you answer a single question incorrectly, I get to do whatever I want to whoever I want. Agreed?"

"No," I said, leaning back in my chair and crossing my arms over my chest, "Not agreed."

"Miss Lennox, you set the terms of the bargain I was merely repeating them. Did you change your mind or do you simply enjoy wasting everyone's time?" He splayed his hands out in front of him and looked at the students gawking at us from around the room.

"It's not me wasting everyone's time, Professor," I said, "The words you spoke are not the bargain I proposed but one of your own, so how could I agree to it?" His hands fell back to the desk and his eyes narrowed just enough to confirm I'd been right. The funny thing about spending your entire memorable life deceiving everyone around you, you learned how to detect when someone else was deceiving you.

"Fine," he drew the word out, "Then why don't you say the words?"

"If I answer three questions about the content covered in today's assignment correctly, you agree to say you will not use your magic on a single student for the remainder of the school year. If I answer incorrectly, you are within your right to enact whatever consequence you deem fair on Naomi for the remainder of this class period."

The white of his teeth reflected the bright green of his shirt when he smiled and said, "I agree."

"Ask me the questions."

Naomi muttered a prayer to whatever god or goddess was listening. The gossipy girls behind us were gasping, asking if I'd lost my mind. Eris sat as the picture of composure beside me. I forced myself to be the same.

My heart beat faster in my chest every second. Professor Richards stayed silent while considering his first question. I didn't know if the heat rushing through my veins was from fire or panic—at this point, I wasn't sure which I preferred.

"How can a bond be both fated and formed by choice? Provide an example in your answer. Knowing the right answer is one thing, understanding it is another entirely."

"A bond can be fated but still requires confirmation to fully form. One example is a fox's bonded. When the two meet, one will inevitably feel drawn to the other, but it's not until they first touch that their magic begins to unlock. Unless they choose to complete the bond they'll never receive their tails and come into their full power." Bless Kenna for making me curious enough to research this. "It's fate that they find their bonded. It's a choice to keep them and complete the bond."

"And which is stronger: a bond formed by fate or a bond formed by choice?"

"Trick question." He inclined his head as if congratulating me for noticing. "It's not about the type of bond, it's about the people forming it. I know you love your examples so let's use one with a shifter's fated mate. They'll be drawn to each other when they meet, but it's nearly unheard of to find them. More often than not, we take a chosen mate and form an imprint. If we come across our fated mate after we've fully imprinted, it doesn't matter. One does not supersede the other. A brittle bond will break and a strong bond will hold."

"What are the consequences of a broken bond?"

Chills ran down my arms, leaving raised flesh in their wake.

"Unspeakable pain," I answered. "Possible insanity. Death. The deeper the bond, the more dire the consequences." A fate I didn't wish on anyone.

"Well Miss Lennox," he drawled, still leaning over my desk—some people never learned, "It seems you've adequately prepared for this class after all."

Excited whispers, maybe even a soft giggle, erupted around us.

"A bargain is a bargain." I wanted to smile as relief coursed through me. Naomi's eyes shone with happy tears beside me.

"A bargain is a bargain," he repeated, "I will not use my magic on a single student for the remainder of the school year."

Actual applause broke out amongst the class, and I did grin then, at least I did until I realized Professor Richards was still smiling. He raised a hand and snapped his fingers. Something inside me snapped with it. This was not what we agreed.

Naomi had turned to stone beside me, but she wasn't alone. I counted three, no four, other students who'd been turned into statues. Their faces were frozen in expressions of joy and disbelief.

I lunged out of my chair and growled an inch from his face, unable to take even a tiny bit of pleasure from the brief flash of panic in his eyes.

"You made a bargain." My words sounded more animal than person and I had to pull my hands from my desk for fear they'd set the wooden table top ablaze.

"And I fulfilled it," he answered, "I didn't use my magic on a single student, nor will I for the remainder of the school year. Instead, I'll use it on multiple."

"You slimy, little—"

"Careful Miss Lennox." He held up his hand. "That's no way to address your superior."

"I assure you, you'll never be mistaken for that," I snapped back at him.

"I think you'll find that when we're measured against each other, I will always come out on top."

He snapped his fingers.

And me? I did nothing but tilt my head to one side, as the satisfaction on his face gave way to rage. Eris' laugh cutting through the silence was more chilling than any angry stare the Professor could send my way. I lowered back to my seat.

"Professor, I see you haven't noticed the ring on Briar's finger," she said indulgently. Professor Richards' eyes settled on the moonstone ring wrapped around my finger. Every hint of smug satisfaction left his face. "I'm afraid your little tricks simply won't work on her. You are, after all, an expert in bonds. Surely you know what this one entails. "

She briefly looked at me to say, "Foxes are immune to Fae magic. His ring affords you the same protection," before returning her attention to the Fae in question whose fingers were beginning to leave grooves in the edge of my desk.

I was not reimbursing the Academy for those damages.

"So you convinced some unsuspecting fox to grant you their protection, have you?" His lip curled as he, again, leaned forward to tower over my still-sitting form. Some people never learned. "Will this be your approach for leading the pack? Hiding behind those around you?"

"I don't hide." Unless things started to get sparky, but really that was for the good of us all.

"You may want to, though," Eris said sweetly. Her smile was borderline angelic. "After all, when Asher finds out you threatened someone under his protection, I suspect he'll be paying you a visit."

He froze, and for a moment I wondered if his spell had rebounded. If he couldn't move to un-cast the spell, would it hold him there forever? I hoped so.

He tilted his head to one side. Damn it.

"And why would she be under Asher's protection? Since when does he care who wears one of his subject's rings?"

"Since she started wearing his." There was a second of silence and then it was as if a bind that held everyone's tongues had been undone as a chorus of disbelief sounded throughout the room.

"Oh my goddess, is she the one who—"

"There's no way Asher would single out someone like her."

"Oh, he is so dead."

"I could die of jealousy! Can you imagine?"

"She's not even powerful."

"A fox can only give that to one person!"

What felt like more exclamations than there were people in the room erupted around us. Professor Richards pushed away from the desk and turned his back on us to take his place at the front of the room.

Halfway there, he looked over his shoulder and said, "You may have a barrier around you, Miss Lennox, but you'll find those around you do not. I think I'll keep your serpent for the remainder of the day. Feel free to collect her after dinner. I will try to remember to leave the door unlocked."

He reached the front of the room and faced us fully, his back against the blackboard which only made his obnoxiously bright shirt appear that much brighter.

"Isn't it sad that the followers are always the ones to pay for the leader's mistakes?"

THE ABSOLUTE LAST thing I wanted to see when I finally burst out of the classroom at the top of the hour was Grayson, hands drawn behind him, with half the pack waiting for me in the hall. My blood was, quite literally, boiling with rage at being forced to leave Naomi behind. Seeing Grayson's smiling face had my hands itching to claw at it. I would have if the scars would achieve anything more than making him that much more handsome.

"I do not have the energy for you today," I bit out, "I think we've said more than enough to each other the past twenty-four hours. So unless you have something critical to say or lives are at stake, I'd rather we kept our distance."

Despite my best efforts, even I could hear the defeat in my voice, so I wasn't surprised when Grayson's smile dimmed. I was, however, surprised when he drew his hand out from behind his back holding a cake. He passed it to a concerned-looking Isaac beside him and strode over to meet me. The students who'd managed to make it through class with their mobility eyed us with curiosity as they filtered out of the room behind me.

"What happened?" He reached toward me to tuck my hair behind my ear, cup my cheek, or something else I'd never know because another man, fully dressed in black, slid in front of me, stealing the air that had been between us.

"You're in my way, Your Highness," Grayson growled.

Asher said nothing. He ignored the seething wolf entirely, or maybe he didn't notice he was there at all. He looked me over slowly, meticulously from head to toe.

"I'm speaking to you," Grayson planted a hand on Asher's shoulder and pulled. Still, he did—he said—nothing. There was only one focal point of his attention. Me.

"I'm not hurt," I told him. I took a step to the side, putting some space between us and re-entering Grayson's view. We'd had enough bloodshed and conflict for the day, there was no need to create it amongst ourselves.

He raised a single brow in my direction as if to say, "I'll be the judge of that" and strode into the classroom I'd just left, barely pausing to nod to Eris as he passed.

A crash followed by a high-pitched yelp sounded only moments later.

"I almost want to go back inside and watch," Eris said wryly, "But I suppose we can let him have his fun this time around."

"Did he—" I started, "Did he come here because of me? Because of what happened?" Even as I asked, I knew it was true, but didn't understand how—or why. No one had left the classroom. There was no way for him to know, and truly, I'd never been in any real danger anyway.

"You're under his protection," she stated as if commenting on the color of the sky, "He'll always sense if something's wrong with you. Didn't anyone explain this when he gave you the ring?"

"Fabian said it was a great honor when I went to take it off, but no," I said emphatically, "No one said anything about sensing me or coming to my aid when I didn't call for it. I thought it was just symbolic of an alliance or a token of respect."

"Of course he did." She rolled her eyes and said, "A moon fox can only extend their protection—their full protection—once. That ring links him to you. If you're angry, he'll find out why. If you're scared, he'll come for you. If you're sad, well, to be honest, he probably won't do much or care, but he'll be aware of that too."

"And he didn't think he should," I laugh humorously, "I don't know, ask me before gaining access to all my thoughts and emotions. What right does he have to them?"

Grayson came to stand beside me, the heat from his body extending to mine.

"It's not all of your emotions, and he can't read your thoughts." She waved a hand dismissively in the air. "It's a great honor, Briar, even more so coming from him. Besides, if you haven't noticed yet, Asher isn't the type to ask before doing anything."

The moon fox in question came back out of the room and strode down the hallway with little more than a glance.

"He's probably heading to the library," Eris commented, starting to walk in the same direction, "We saw Kenna there earlier too, but none of us have found anything on the symbol from the massacre yet. I'm going to head there and join them if you want to come after whatever this little pack gathering is."

She gave us all a half-hearted wave and disappeared after her cousin.

"I can't decide if I like them," Grayson said when she was out of hearing range. "Something about Asher sets my teeth on edge, and no one's as innocent as Eris appears."

"You mean you feel uneasy around another powerful male who may or may not pose a threat to your dominance? How surprising. I'd have never guessed," I said glibly, "Now tell me what you want and be quick about it because I'm tired, I'm hungry. Honestly, I'd love to throw knives at something for the next hour. I'm perfectly content to make that something you if you're here to volunteer."

Behind Grayson, Isaac coughed and ran a hand over his mouth to hide his grin. The others ranged anywhere from amusement, to confusion, to offense—the last being most prominent on Pax's face. I neither liked nor appreciated the challenge in his stare. I held it until he looked down. Good.

"I'm sorry."

I was still focused on his Beta and almost missed the two

words that had my gaze snapping back to Grayson. "What did you just say?" Surely I hadn't heard him correctly.

He cleared his throat, took a breath, and said, "I said I'm sorry."

I mentally added another item to the list of things I didn't expect to happen today. I was, once again, speechless. Alphas did many things. They led. They protected. They gave counsel. They made amends. They took action to acknowledge and rectify their mistakes.

The one thing they didn't do? Apologize. If they did, it certainly wasn't publicly.

My bewilderment must've been apparent on my face because after Grayson grinned and reached for the cake he'd handed to Isaac, the snow leopard placed his hand under his chin as if shutting his smiling mouth. I snapped mine closed.

"I made you this." Grayson held out the woefully misshapen cake covered in chocolate frosting. "I was hoping we could go somewhere and share it."

I wanted to say no. I should say no. He'd already proven he didn't—wouldn't—trust me. If I said yes, I'd only be setting myself up for further disappointment. And yet, the pleading, hopeful look in his eye had me wondering if just maybe, this time could be worth the risk. When I didn't speak he continued.

"I shouldn't have doubted you and I never should have accused you."

"Then why did you?" I asked.

He stepped closer and dropped his head until his mouth was right beside my ear when he admitted, "I was afraid. I was afraid of what it would mean if I let myself believe you can do this, that we can do this. Together."

He straightened his stance but didn't step away from me. I turned his words over in my mind, debating if I was willing to risk it. *A pack will crumble under weak leadership.* And I was proving each day that I was anything but weak. I never had been, even if he was only just beginning to realize it.

"Walk with me to the library," I said, not taking the cake from him, but swiping a finger along the top to place a dollop of the decadent dessert in my mouth. Delicious. "And you can tell me exactly what else you're sorry for. Maybe if I like your answer, I'll even let you sit by me when we get there."

Maybe I'd like letting him. Maybe I'd regret it and drive a dagger through his thigh. Only time would tell.

THE MOON

Nothing. An entire week of reading every tome and text we could find, and we'd found absolutely nothing. It seemed like every trace of demons had been wiped not only from the physical realm but its history as well.

We were silent after that apart from the occasional self-muttering or brief mumbled conversation about passing someone another book. Sitting in the library surrounded by the others, as beautiful as the room was, made me feel like a prisoner inside my own skin.

And why was it that libraries always felt stuffier than other rooms? Would fresh air or a cross breeze have some kind of adverse effect on the books? Or maybe it was by design. Maybe they just wanted to see us sweat while we studied as a training tactic for performing under pressure. If so, it was working.

"I hate that vindictive fae." Briar slammed a stack of books down on the table and forcefully pulled out the chair beside me to take a seat.

I continued flipping through the pages of the book in front of me. Best not to give her a reason to redirect her wrath toward me.

"I assume you're talking about Professor Richards again," Isaac, apparently a male far less wise than me asked. He closed his book and reached for another before adding, "I don't know why you let him bother you so much. He's not worth the emotional toll."

Definitely not looking up from my book now. The last couple weeks had proven Briar to be a calm, collected leader, even in the face of adversity, but if something sent her over the edge? I swear sometimes it looked like fire was half a second from pouring from her eyes and burning whoever wronged her alive.

Truthfully, I found it enchanting. Murderous rage looked lovely on her as long as it wasn't directed at me.

"I don't know, Isaac," she said, throwing her hands in the air and smacking them on the table. One of the librarians peeked around the corner to shush us but retreated when she saw who sat at the table. Smart woman. "Maybe I just take issue with someone waging injustice on the masses. Ever considered that? I don't know how he's still teaching here."

"He's supposedly brilliant," Isaac supplied, "A prodigy, or so they say. He published some discoveries on an ancient treaty that changed the fate of the Hidden Realm or something like that. That was well over half a century ago so I don't know why it matters, but apparently, it does. My father hated him when he attended here."

Mine had too.

"You mean the one that makes him act like the Solar

Court is oh so superior?" she asked. I took the opportunity to admire the column of her throat when she threw her head back to glare at the ceiling, "Thank the moon and stars we're in the Lunar court. I think I'd lose my mind if I was subjected to more people like him every day."

I nodded and turned to yet another page of text that told me nothing about what I needed to know. The problem with scrubbing an entire realm from history was sabotaging yourself from being prepared when they eventually return. Nothing stays buried—or banished in this case—forever.

"What'd he do this time?" Isaac asked, "And where is Naomi? Please tell me we're not going to have to break into the classroom to free her from whatever spell he cast again."

"Not today." Briar paused. "At least, not that I know of. She was still mobile when I left her. No, today he sewed half the class' mouth shut for speaking before the class had even started. We had to watch them claw at their lips shrieking until the twine was finished weaving through their skin. They felt every second of it."

"He's sadistic," Isaac said solemnly, "Inflicting injuries is more than a step too far."

"He shouldn't be allowed in society let alone in the school! If he were a shifter I would've challenged him by now and used his corpse as target practice."

The crack of metal splitting wood was deafening as she slammed the point of the dagger I hadn't seen her unsheathe into the table. Her chest rose and fell with every breath as that murderous glint I loved started to appear in her eyes.

"I'm just going to go ahead and take this for now." Isaac

slowly reached over to grab the blade by its hilt and pull it free.

I unsheathed my blade and held it out to her as the snow leopard looked at me in betrayal. I simply shrugged as Briar took it and began to roll it between her fingers without comment. If she wanted to eliminate the fae, I'd happily assist her or stand back and watch as she dismembered him.

"Are you getting stabby without me?" Kenna half-walked, half-danced from between two rows of books. A blood encrusted arrow had been snapped in half and stabbed through the two buns atop either side of her head. I wanted to be surprised. I wasn't. "I'd be offended if I weren't so intrigued. Who are we hurting?"

"No one," Isaac said emphatically.

"Professor Richards," Briar supplied.

"Really?" Kenna asked gleefully, "I've been wanting to end him for years. I know a place where we can dispose of the body. If we go now we'll still have time to dig the hole before nightfall."

"No!" Isaac said again, "No bodies, no disposing, no holes."

He directed his gaze at me and gestured to the plotting females. like he expected me to intervene. I shrugged instead. I was team hole.

"You take all the joy out of life Isaac," Kenna pursed her lips and looked around the table.

"He's been ruining my fun for years." Briar tilted her head to one side and said, "Nice accessories. Is that a hint of demon blood I smell?"

"I told you I'd find a use for them!" Kenna beamed. "Thank you for noticing."

Isaac stared at her in horror but quickly returned his gaze to the book in front of him when she turned her smile his way.

"We still haven't found anything, huh?" She asked with a heavy sigh.

"Nope." Briar gave me back my dagger, grabbed a book from the top of her stack, and started reading. Pity. It looked far better spinning in her hand than mine.

"Another day of trying not to sneeze from the dust amongst the pages of texts written by ancient people it is then. I don't even want to think about how many dead skin bits we've probably all inhaled."

Lovely.

Rather than getting up to find her own book, she turned her attention to mine.

"Oh look, a book, ready and available for me to scour sitting within my reach." She reached over me to grab the book I'd already gotten halfway through searching, "I'll go ahead and relieve you of this one. You must be tired of it by now."

I swatted her hand away, earning a gasp of indignation and a muttered, "Rude."

I grabbed the largest book from Isaac's stack across from me and tossed it down in front of her. The librarian, again, came around the corner ready to shush whoever caused such a ruckus and blanched when I lifted a brow in her direction.

"Ugh." Kenna flipped open the cover before propping her head up by her elbow on the table to begin flipping through the pages. "Of course, you have to give me the worst one."

"Don't worry, Ken," Briar said, placatingly reaching across me to pat her hand, and some of the tension left my shoulders at the familiar citrus and sage scent. "This just means you're only inhaling the dust from one old text written by a dead person instead of two."

Kenna paused to consider this a moment before she nodded and combed through the book more earnestly.

A hundred topics were outlined in the book I'd spent the last hour reading: necromancy, ceremonies for the spring and summer equinox, hexes, love spells, coming-of-age rituals, and yet there wasn't a single word around demons or sacrifices to be found.

And then I saw it.

There, in the margin at the very bottom of the last page was a tiny diagram, no larger than a coin, was a hexagon encasing a broken spiral.

My breath left me as I leaned back in my chair. Before I could blink Isaac had come around to our side of the table, and Briar and Kenna drew into either side of me.

"Oh goddess, that's it. That's the pattern we found the bodies," Briar whispered then pointed to each word as she read, "With death comes the rift, with fire comes rebirth, and with blood comes the reckoning."

"What does that even mean?" Isaac asked. I didn't know, but it sounded familiar and had goosebumps rippling across my skin.

"That's all it says." Kenna leaned back from the text, lips pursed together tightly.

"That's the last page of the book? There's no way. It can't be." Briar leaned over me and ran her hand along the seam of the spine, "There's a page missing."

My finger traced the spine of the tome she'd taken and felt the raised edges of paper—the ridges were slight, but undoubtedly there.

"Someone tore it out," Isaac said, more to himself than to us. "Why would someone do that?"

My heart sank as Briar spoke the only rational explanation.

"Because someone at the Academy didn't want us to find it."

26

THE ROSE

I looked at every face I passed in the hall and wondered if they'd be the death of me.

That page had not been removed by chance. Only someone with access to the Academy grounds could have done it. More than anything else, I wanted to know when they went into the library to accomplish it and how they knew it would be there. Did they know we'd find the sacrifice and come looking for it? Had they done it before the attack even took place? That book had been buried in one of the least frequented sections of the library and had taken over a week for us to find, so how did they get to it first?

It'd been four days since we found the diagram, and we'd found nothing else since. The constant nightmares that plagued me since reading the words told me their meaning was hidden somewhere in the blacked out corners of my mind. Yet each morning that I opened my eyes, I felt as lost as I had been the night before.

Poor Isaac had suffered through my tossing and turning

without complaint, but I knew I'd kept him awake. The shadows under his eyes were indisputable proof my torment was taking its toll on him as well. At least his would end after tonight. I'd be moving into the Luna suite, though knowing Kenna she'd make us both help her pack.

"Bri!" Grayson came jogging across the quad with an uncharacteristically boyish grin without care for the attention he was attracting. He laid a heavy arm around my shoulder as he fell into step beside me.

I let him. For now.

"Hi," he said, grinning down at me. The soft light of sunset somehow made the green of his eyes appear brighter. Though if there was a light he looked poorly in, I hadn't found it yet.

"Hi," I repeated.

Isaac and Marcus exited from the door leading to the main hall ahead of us. Isaac stared pointedly at Grayson's arm and grinned whereas I suspected Marcus' eyeballs might fall loose from his head if they grew just a fraction wider. It'd certainly make an interesting sight.

I felt more than saw Grayson lift his hand from my shoulder and wave them away. I stifled my smile at the outrage on Marcus' face as Isaac pulled him in the other direction.

"So I was thinking," Grayson started, "we should go somewhere."

"We are somewhere. In fact, with every step, we're somewhere different."

"Hilarious," he said in a way that assured me it was anything but. "I'm serious. Go somewhere with me."

I was intrigued, but a rumble in my stomach reminded me of what I'd been doing when he found me.

"Right now?" I asked. "I was on my way to the dining hall, do you really want to take me somewhere before I've eaten?"

"I'm not nearly that brave." I elbowed him in the side. He didn't flinch. "I promise I'll feed you if you'll just come with me. Trust me."

Like trust between us could be that simple.

"Whatever it is, I better like it."

His grin was more his wolf's than his own as he reached to grab my rucksack from my shoulder and hang it on his own.

"You'll like it, I promise."

GRAYSON WAS WRONG. I didn't like it. I loved it.

I'd been skeptical when he'd taken me down the path we'd taken for the pack run a few weeks ago—Kenna was not following in the trees this time, I checked—but he kept telling me to trust him. I'm glad I did.

We'd passed through the clearing when he slid behind me and covered my eyes with his hands. I stumbled when he drew me back against him to guide me but found my footing again quickly.

"Is this necessary?" I asked after nearly tripping on what felt like an upturned root.

"You'll thank me in a minute when we get there."

"I won't if I break an ankle first," I grumbled, then gasped when I was suddenly airborne.

Grayson had slid one hand to cover both my eyes and banded his other arm securely around my waist to lift me, my back securely pressed against his front.

"Better?" He asked the question so close to my ear I could feel his lips brush against it.

"Not really what I was thinking," I answered shakily, "But I guess it does solve the problem."

"It's not much farther now."

I'm not sure I'd have minded if it were. When we were together and he acted like this, I remembered why I would have followed him into a burning building before he left. The flames may not have harmed me, but still, it was the intention that counted. He'd been consistently thoughtful, and border-line attentive, since his apology in the hallway. Whatever doubts he'd been battling seemed to be put to rest.

I wanted to believe it would last. I wanted to believe it was real. But I'd believed he cared about me once before. All that had led to was pain and disappointment.

"Okay, keep your eyes closed," he said as he set me back on my feet. "No peeking!"

"I never peek!"

"You always peek."

It's true. I did.

As a kid, I always tried to uncover the surprises before they were revealed. There was never a present I opened whose contents I didn't already know. It drove both Grayson and his parents mad. Fenrir considered it to be a natural form of stealth training.

This time I resisted temptation and kept my eyes firmly shut. It was a near impossible task when I heard a crash followed by a soft curse and some rustling, but I didn't give in.

"Okay," he called, "Open your eyes."

My first thought was he'd pulled stars from the sky and hung them in the air. We were in the same spot I'd played with his wolf, just a few yards from the lake. There were flecks of light floating through the air, winking in and out of sight around the plush blankets and furs arranged on the ground. Someone had built an overhang of branches around them and hung lanterns no larger than the palm of my hand along the top. And the food! A spread of sandwiches, cheeses, fruits, and little cakes was laid out on the blanket just waiting to be devoured.

"So?" Grayson asked cautiously, "What do you think?"

"You did all of this," I asked, "For me?"

I could barely get the words out over the ball of emotion threading to rise in my throat. Don't read into it, Briar. You know how he feels about you. Don't make this more than the apology it was meant to be, but goddess it was hard not to.

"Of course," he said, hands in his pockets and shrugged one shoulder, "I told you before: when it comes to you, there's nothing I wouldn't do. I'd cut down any enemy in your path. If I'm willing to do that, what's a picnic by comparison?"

Everything.

It was everything.

"How did you get the floating lights?" I asked hoarsely.

"There's a cave just outside of campus," he said, "It's filled with glowing creatures at night. I relocated a few."

"We're not allowed to leave campus without permission," I said.

"I was fast. Besides, it wasn't a long journey." His eyes searched my face. "You're killing me here, Bri. I know I deserve some torment, but put me out of my misery and tell me what you think. Is it too much? Not enough?"

"No!" I said louder than I meant to. I lowered my voice and added, "I love it. Thank you for bringing me here."

He inclined his head to the lantern-lit fort and took the crook of my elbow to guide me to a seat on the plushly covered ground.

"Should I be concerned that this food has been out for however long it took you to come back to campus and bring me back here?"

He laughed and shook his head no.

"I handled everything except actually setting out the food," he admitted and ran a hand through his already tousled hair. "I had Pax run ahead and set out the food for us. He left a minute or two before we did."

I poked at the bread topping one of the sandwiches then raised it to check underneath.

"So I don't need to worry about bugs, just a bit of poison?" It was no secret Pax saw me as a nuisance despite my best efforts to limit our interactions by whatever means necessary. I didn't care to be in the same room as the jaguar but being around Grayson often meant being around his Beta.

"It's not poisoned."

"Fine." I shoved the sandwich in front of his face. "Take a bite and prove it then."

I thought he'd take it from me. He didn't. Instead, he wrapped his hand around my forearm and brought it closer until he could lean in to take a bite. I did *not* notice the way his lips grazed my fingers as he did, and I certainly didn't get any pleasure at the contact.

"See?" he asked, "Not poisoned."

"At least not with something fast-acting." I took a bite from the other side. "But at least if I die, I'll be taking you down with me."

"There's no way I'd rather go."

I couldn't think of a response to that, so I chose not to acknowledge it at all, and reached for a piece of fruit instead.

We ate without speaking. The only sounds permeating the air were the rustles of leaves from the forest and the slight whoosh of the breeze brushing over the lake and through the trees. He seemed more at ease with each minute we spent together. I, on the other hand, was stuck wondering if there'd been insects secretly living in my bloodstream who'd decided to finally stage a breakout through my skin. It wasn't until I finished off the last of the cake that he ended the silence.

"How are you feeling about tomorrow?" He moved to half-lie on his side, the weight of his torso supported by his elbow and forearm along the ground. "Are you ready for the Rite?"

I reached for one of the soft cushions to place behind me as I leaned back against the structure and another to cradle to my chest.

"What?" I asked, only half-joking. "Is this your elaborate

scheme to convince me to back out? I hate to tell you this, but it would take a lot more than pretty lights and a night under the stars to change what'll happen tomorrow."

"What would it take?" he asked softly, staring down at his hands.

"Are you serious?" Anger leaked into my voice, and shoved the cushion away to place my hands on the ground in front of me, "That's really what this was? Goddess, Grayson you never stop, and I apparently never stop hoping you will."

I pushed myself up to leave the makeshift fort. I should've known better. I did know better, yet there I was, again, feeling blindsided and betrayed by this male who never seemed to act sincerely. Was everything he did always just another tactic to get what he wanted?

"Briar, wait." He reached for my arm, but I swatted him away and took a step away from him, taking another when he rose to his own feet to follow me, taking a step for each of mine. Unfortunately, his steps were longer than mine and he had the advantage of walking forward instead of backward. He closed the distance between us faster than I'd care to admit.

"I don't know what makes you think you have the right to try manipulating me into doing whatever you want, but let me assure you, this is the absolute last—"

His hands grasped either side of my face, moving until his fingers were threaded in my hair and his thumbs pressed lightly over my mouth.

"If you would stop talking for five seconds and listen instead of walking away from me every chance you get then half of our problems would be solved by now." I tried to open my mouth to protest but he pressed harder and shook his head. "Uh-uh. I already know you're going to say I walked away first and you know what? You're right. I did. I'm sorry! I don't know how many times you want me to say it, but I'll keep saying it until you decide it's been enough. I deserve that, and I know that too, but this? This thing where you act like I've spent a lifetime disappointing you? I don't want to do that anymore. That, I did not earn and I do not deserve. Our history may not mean everything, but it should mean something."

Except none of that history had been real. He was forgetting that key point, not that he knew I was aware I'd merely been another obligation to him.

"I didn't bring you here to convince you not to enter the Pack Rite." He swiped against my lips with his thumbs until they rested on my cheeks instead. I didn't speak. I waited. "I'm allowed to wish you wouldn't compete in a challenge that could injure or kill you. I'm allowed to be afraid of watching you die, and I am allowed to tell you that instead of pretending I'm alright when I'm not. I'm here with you. I'll be there with you, but that doesn't mean I'm going to like it. Okay? I am never going to like something that puts you in harm's way, but that doesn't mean I'm not on your side."

I could still walk away. It would be smarter to walk away. Even if he was right, even if he wanted to be on my side, he never would be—never could be. Not really. If he knew the truth about me he'd walk away. All obligations to me would be absolved in seconds with one flick of my wrist to spark a flame.

If I gave in, If I went back with him and sat next to him

on this beautiful night in this beautiful place, then I was putting not just my heart at risk, but my life. If I stuck close to him, there was little doubt in my mind I could fool him forever. He was too perceptive not to eventually ask questions I couldn't answer. Right now it was just our roles as Beta and now Luna and Alpha that forced him to be in my proximity but there were walls between us.

Walls kept us—kept me—safe.

"You and I are both going to stop trying to work out everything ourselves and talk to each other from now on," he said when my silence had gone on longer than his liking, "Do you think we can do that?"

If I was smart, I would walk away now and keep this distance between us. I'd thank him for betraying me the first day and reminding me of my place—I'd take advantage of it.

Sometimes I didn't want to be smart.

"Fine," I pulled my head back and he released me from his grip. "Let's not talk about this anymore tonight. Let's just enjoy the evening as it is."

"You never answered my previous question," he pointed out.

"Which one?" There'd technically been many.

"How are you feeling about tomorrow?"

That may have been the hardest to answer.

"I'll win." And I would.

"That's not what I asked." Grayson took another step toward me until the toes of our boots were touching.

I sidestepped him and went back to the blanket-covered ground to take a seat. Small flowers were springing up between the blades of grass beside me. I smiled as I reached over to pluck them.

"Bri." Grayson prowled toward me only to stop short at the edge of the shelter and turn his face up toward the sky when I continued to gather the flowers rather than speaking.

"Fine," he said to himself. He sat beside me. There wasn't an inch of space between us. I could have moved over. I didn't. "What are you doing?"

My smile only grew. I finished tying the final flower in the crown and reached up to place it atop his head.

"Did you just put flowers in my hair?" He was less than impressed but didn't remove them.

"I did," I confirmed as I began fashioning one of my own, "I haven't made one in ages."

"I don't think I've ever seen you make one, even as a kid. Something in you decided now was the perfect moment to make one?"

"Yep," I answered. "It's as good a time as any."

"And by as good a time as any you mean you don't want to talk about the challenge tomorrow and therefore chose to focus on the surrounding flora instead?"

"Precisely." Glad he was catching on. No good would come from our previous discussion, and I was just selfish enough to delay it from happening. I knew there could only be one outcome.

"So we're pretending?" He reached for the second crown and placed it on my head, running his hands along my hair as he brought it down. Without the flowers to distract me, I had no choice but to look at his face. Curse him for being even more handsome in the starlight.

"I've never been the one pretending," I whispered. Not when it came to him.

"Bri, what are you—"

"Oh my goddess!" I stood and pointed to the sky through the gaps in the shelter, "Look!"

Streaks of light shot through the air, one stripe of white against the night sky appearing after another. I left the shelter to stand at the shoreline for a clearer view.

"The stars are falling." I'd never seen anything like it. I heard Grayson walk over to join me but my attention was fully fixated on the sight above me.

"It happens every year." He grabbed my hand and pulled me down to the bank beside him, guiding me to lie on my back for a better view. "I remember you telling me once you wanted to dance in a room full of stars. This is as close as I could get."

I looked away from the lights to turn toward him, "I was just a kid when I said that. How do you remember that?"

He adjusted his grip on my hand until his fingers were interlaced with mine. The warmth in his eyes and the soft set of his mouth made it more tempting than I could say to believe his next words as he turned to prop himself up on his elbow until he nearly hovered over me.

"When it comes to you, I remember everything." He leaned down slowly, slow enough for me to stop him if I wished. I didn't.

Just for one night, one moment, as Grayson's mouth moved over mine, I let myself forget it could never last.

THE ROSE

Whoever decided that a pack ritual in which we quite literally battled for our roles in the pack should take place before dawn's first light had never tried forcing down cooked oats at two in the morning. I scooped a glob of the brown mush from my bowl, but I couldn't make myself put it into my mouth. I slopped it back into the bowl and shoved it a few inches away.

"You have to eat something," Isaac said in a patient, measured voice, though maybe slightly less patient than when he'd said it the first or fourth time throughout our breakfast.

"If I eat one more bite of that I may as well have eaten nothing at all because I can promise you now, one more spoonful down my throat and they'll all be coming back up it." I'd done my best and finished at least half the bowl, but I gagged even thinking about putting one more gooey glob in my mouth.

Isaac released a heavy sigh and said, "Fine. But if you pass out later, don't say I didn't try my best to prevent it."

"I'm not going to pass out." I rolled my eyes. Cats could be so dramatic at times. "I've managed on far less food for far longer. Give me some credit. If you were that worried about me eating you should've picked something more appetizing."

"It was the only thing the kitchens had available this early." He frowned. "It also contains all the nutrients your body needs to function at its peak in battle."

I shook my head at him but didn't debate it further. It was too early for a lesson in the many disgusting foods that were supposedly good for my body's health. Why did they always have to be disgusting? Why couldn't a healthy food be, I don't know, cake?

"You can keep all of the nutrients to yourself." I swung one leg over the bench and turned to face him. He took a huge bite of oatmeal while looking me dead in the eyes. I gagged at the thought. When he finished he pushed his own bowl away with a grin and said, "Now I'm ready to go."

Isaac looked around the hallway before pulling me to where we were partially hidden by one of the pillars lining the walkways.

Do you think you have it all under control?" he asked in hushed tones. "If things get too tense do you feel like you can stop your fire from getting us all killed?" What an eloquent way to put that, I thought.

"Of course I can." I rolled my eyes and summoned a perfect sphere of flames just over my palm before turning it into a cube, and then a star. "I am in complete control." I always was—always had to be.

"Those are cute and all, but it would've been more impressive if you'd made a dagger or a sword. Far more handy in a fight."

"If I could use them in a fight then maybe I would have learned to form them, but given putting them into existence would mean death, I can't say the fire weapons are worth the risk."

I tossed the star of fire a few inches into the air before extinguishing it entirely with a close of my fist. I opened my mouth to tease him further, but a flash of blonde disappearing around the corner halted the words in my throat.

"What?" Isaac asked, looking behind him, "What is it?"

I paused. I could tell him what I thought I saw but if I was wrong, what good would it do for us both to worry? Even if I was right there was nothing he could do to take back what had already been seen. He could remain blissfully unaware, and me? I would do whatever I needed to do to keep him safe. Besides, I could have been wrong.

Just focus, Briar, just focus a little longer and everything will go back to normal, everything will be okay.

IT TURNS out that when one of the Hidden realms hosts an ancient fighting ritual that inevitably leads to bloodshed and the potential of death, all of the others show up to observe the event. Standing at the base of the stone amphitheater, I noticed that amongst them were sirens, harpies, and—judging the other Hidden surrounding them fervently checking their pockets—imps.

"Should I be flattered that half the student population came into the woods in the middle of the night to watch Kenna and I claw at each other?" I asked Isaac while he braided back my hair. We sat on the ground at one side of the circle. Kenna sat at the opposite end with Ainsley and Grayson.

I would be lying if I said it didn't hurt to see him on her side of the arena, especially after last night's kiss. I knew he had every right to speak to Kenna before the challenge, that I had no true claim to him, but that he stopped to speak with her before he'd even looked at me stung. While Isaac's fingers worked through my hair, I imagined the various ways I could get away with stabbing the wolf without killing him.

"No. They'd show up for any event that gives them insight into the workings of other realms, especially the more brutal ones." Instinctively I wanted to criticize their gawking, but if the roles were reversed I'd trek through a swamp to watch it.

"Are you wearing it?" he kept his voice low.

I lifted the hem of my leather pant leg in answer. "Your father asked me the same question before I left the compound. I wonder if part of him suspected this would happen." He tied the end of the braid with a leather cord and came around to my side.

"I think Dad expects the worst could happen at any moment, but I doubt he expected this. He's too loyal to the pack to think someone would undermine it with a challenge. It's probably for the best that we decided not to tell him. He'd only worry needlessly."

I hummed my agreement and pushed to my feet, dusting

the dirt from my clothes as I stood. The night was nearly at its darkest, it was almost time.

"You can handle this." Isaac placed his hands on my shoulders and blocked my view of the field. "Just win so we can move on, but don't make it look too easy. Kenna is one of the strongest shifters I've met. If you take her down too quickly people will start asking questions, especially because you're—" He flinched as he broke off.

"Latent?" I finished for him. "Avoiding the word won't change that I can't shift."

He opened his mouth to reply but the sound of approaching footsteps had him turning around to see Grayson crossing the field in our direction.

"Sure, now he comes to see me. Probably hoping to make a final plea. It's not like I could back out at this point even if I wanted to." I grumbled. Grayson continued his prowl until he stood a few feet away. I guess he only wanted me close when no one was there to see.

"I swear to the suns if you came over to ask me to stand down Grayson Pierce I will not be held accountable for the bloodshed that follows." I told myself I was irritated by the half grin that appeared on his face, and the increasing beat of my heart against my chest was purely driven by rage. It certainly had nothing to do with the way his eyes flickered with the glow of the torches surrounding the arena.

He raised his hands and said, "I didn't come here to discourage you. I understand you'll do this no matter what I say."

"Glad you're catching on." His half-grin grew.

"I just wanted to say I hope you'll be smart and safe. I

don't want to see anything happen to you." Not the message of support I was looking for, but he was trying.

"If you're going to be all worrisome and broody then you should just leave," I said, pointing to the tiered bench seats carved into the earth. "The last thing I want to hear is negativity before this fight. Maybe it'd be best for both of us if we avoided speaking until the Rite has ended."

He stepped into my space as if it belonged to him, close enough that the tips of his boots were touching mine. He reached up to cradle the back of my head, running his thumb along the nape of my neck. I took care to keep my breathing even but couldn't stop my heart from racing as he held me.

"I told you last night, don't ask me not to worry about you," he said softly, "I don't think you understand: if Kenna kills you today I'll never be able to lead with her. The pack will crumble."

"I didn't ask you not to worry about me. I asked you to believe in me, is that still so hard for you to do?"

Grayson opened his mouth, whether to defend himself or protest, I didn't know, but Isaac cleared his throat, reminding us that we were not alone and halting whatever words would leave his lips.

"We should go take our seats," he said, "the Rite is about to begin." The stones lining the perimeter of the arena were just beginning to glow in the moonlight, the lanterns starting to dim. Once the Rite began, nobody would be able to enter or exit the field until the winner was named.

Grayson clenched his jaw and nodded, giving me a long, final look. I was too tired and confused to properly interpret. Isaac leaned in and pressed a kiss to my forehead. "Try not to make it look too easy." He winked and followed his Alpha to where the pack had gathered in the stands.

I watched him bypass the empty seat next to Grayson, and plop next to an anxious-looking Naomi instead; the only sign of Grayson's displeasure was the slight purse of his lips.

As I turned away from them to focus on my opponent, a flash of silver and rose hair caught my eye. Fabian and Eris were smiling and talking cheerfully, but to their left, the Death God was ignoring their chatter. Instead, his gaze was fixed soundly on me, and I was stuck, frozen, staring into the depths of deep blue. Time felt suspended as I stood there, staring at him, wondering why the static raced along my spine. As our eyes remained locked, the stones in the ground grew incandescently bright, reminding me where I was, and where my thoughts should be focused.

When I turned away to look across the field, Kenna was pulling out her blade.

The conversation-filled arena grew still as Kenna and I walked to the center of the field and grasped each other's forearms, each of our daggers, pressing into the skin of the other. The glow from the stones raced to the ground below us. It pooled at our feet before surging up through our bodies until we shone like two stars bound together.

Together, we spoke the words, "By moon and night we hereby initiate the Pack Rite. Through blood and brawn, a Luna will arise by the first light of dawn." The light that had gathered at our joined limbs shot up and around us like a fountain, until a shimmering dome was cast over the arena floor.

Then the fight for Luna began.

Kenna tightened her grip on one of my forearms and used it to yank me toward her with one hand while the other brought her dagger down in an arc toward my head. If this was how she fought opponents she liked, I'd hate to see what she did to opponents she didn't. I blocked the blade and spun out of her hold, putting some distance between us as we began to circle each other.

It wasn't long before she was lunging toward me again and clawing at my face. I wasn't quite fast enough to dodge this time and I felt a trickle of blood against my cheek. I ducked away from her next blow, a fist aimed at my chin, and landed a kick to her side. The longer we fought the faster each move came.

Jab.

Dodge.

Kick.

Try to avoid getting stabbed.

Around and around we went, trading blows and dodging strikes in a bloody dance around the circle. I could hear the screams and cheers from the spectators filtering through the barrier, but I couldn't spare the focus to process what they were shouting.

I'd been prepared to pretend the fight was a challenge–I'd been pretending for years–but I wasn't pretending now. Kenna was incredible. The power and speed behind her attacks rivaled my own, and every moment the fight continued, I asked myself, who was this woman? The only consolation I found was she looked as perplexed as I was to find our skills were matched.

We were both breathing hard, the labored sounds

mingling between us. We were both sporting wounds dotted with blood and bruises beginning to bloom on our skin. I thanked the gods I had the bloodstone on my ankle when my fire threatened to surface.

I felt it in the growing heat of my palms and made sure to only hit her with a closed fist lest she notice the dangerously high temperature. I landed a jab to her throat and her lion roared, eyes flashing.

Kenna stepped back as the change started to come over her.

Chills ran through me as I realized if she changed into her lion, I may not win. Against a normal shifter? I could handle their animals despite my human form, but it was becoming increasingly clear that Kenna was anything but normal.

I did the only thing I could think to do: I threw my dagger at her heart. Even mid-shift, her reflexes were fast. She threw her dagger and it clashed with my own, both of them ricocheting in opposite directions. What she hadn't anticipated was the second dagger now lodged in her shoulder. It kept her from shifting, but I didn't pause to see what she would do next. I tackled her to the ground.

We tumbled heel over head, hands grasping hair and neck until finally, we ground to a halt to grapple along the ground. She landed a solid punch to my side resulting in a crack that promised me my ribs would be black and blue tomorrow. Her legs were as wild as her arms—relentlessly kicking out as we fought. The side of her boot scraped along my leg and that was when I felt it: the weight of the stone tied around my ankle fell away.

It took less than a second for the power that had been locked away to surge upward to press against my skin. It took every drop of self-control I could muster to shove it back down, but the distraction earned me a nasty gash to the side as Kenna's claws raked through skin and flesh. A wave of nausea hit me when more than one spark flickered around the wound.

Enough of this.

The longer this continued the greater the risk I'd lose control. I dug my claws into her shoulders and flung her off of me. She cried out as her head cracked against the ground, leaving traces of blood in its wake, but I didn't stop. I couldn't stop.

At some point in our battle for dominance, she must have torn through the leather cord in my hair because it came loose to form a curtain around us when I threw myself on top of her. I may not be able to shift into my animal, but I could still use my claws and fangs. I let both descend as I wrapped one hand around her neck and used the other to secure one of her wrists above her head. She relentlessly clawed at me with the other, slashing my top and leaving tears in the leather. As the neckline tore, my necklace fell free and dangled in the air between us.

Time felt suspended as the world seemed to stop.

Kenna's face lost all color and her eyes grew wider than felt natural. As they started to glow, the ground beneath us began to shake.

"It's really you," the words escaped her mouth in a pained whisper, "I never wanted it to be you."

Her head jolted back, her eyes now completely swallowed

by the light. Grooves were opening in the earth as the shaking grew stronger, and vines shot up from the dirt beneath her hands. I snatched my own away from her pinned wrist as the vines shot toward me, wrapping around my neck and torso.

"Briar!"

Grayson's scream cut through the roaring in my ears as chunks of dirt and rock broke off from the seats of the arena and tumbled toward us, knocking fleeing spectators to the ground. Some of them got up to flee. Some didn't move after their bodies fell.

There was nothing he could do for me now. The barrier would hold until dawn broke or a Luna had won. He shouldn't be focused on me, he should be getting the pack to safety. Kenna's earthquake grew more violent with each second she remained in whatever haze had taken her over.

"Kenna," I tried to say through the tightening vine, "Kenna, you have to take back control." I dug my claws into her skin and blood pooled over the punctures, painting my fingers in red. The pain did nothing to rouse her. I pressed harder. Black spots started to dot my vision. "Kenna!"

"Briar, you have to end it!" Isaac's shout was barely audible, but I knew what he wanted from me. One swipe of my claws across her throat and this would all be over, but how could I do it? The destruction around us wasn't her, not really.

I stared into her eyes, but it was only her element that looked back at me. Somewhere inside she was trapped, powerless and clawing to come back to the surface, but helpless to break through. It wasn't her fault, but I couldn't let this go on. I lifted my hand high and brought it down with all my strength in a fist against her temple.

The earth stilled.

Kenna's head lolled to the side and the vines circling me fell limp at my sides. I collapsed on top of her. I wanted to push to my feet or at least sit up, but my arms needed a minute before they'd have the strength to hold me.

The stillness of the moment was so at odds with the frenzy and rancor we'd been consumed with moments prior. It gave way to waves of panic flowing through me the longer I lay there, her words echoing through my mind with each rise and fall of my chest against hers. I reached a hand between us and tucked my necklace back into my shirt. When it was secured, I'd rolled to my back beside Kenna, and the glimmering dome concealing us fell.

"Briar!" Grayson slid to the ground beside me, his panicked face appearing over mine. One trembling hand brushed the hair out of my eyes before he snatched it back, leaving it to hover a few inches from my skin.

"I'm not going to break if you touch me."

"You might not break," he said softly, tipping his neck back at the sky, "but I might. I think you just cut my lifespan in half."

"I take no responsibility for this mess." I rolled to one side and pushed myself back to my feet, brushing my hands on my pant legs. It took more than a few seconds for the black spots clouding my vision to disappear as I stood.

"No," he agreed as he rose to stand beside me, spine stiffening when he looked at the unconscious form at our feet.

"The blame is hers to bear, and mine for failing to notice the disease festering in our pack."

His expression darkened and he drew his leg back. The crack that rang through the air as his foot crashed into Kenna's side would haunt my dreams for weeks to come.

She came to with a cough turned groan and curled on her side, legs tucked tightly to her chest. Her jade eyes scanned over her surroundings with unfocused sheen until they landed on Grayson's towering form.

"Gray—" The tremor in her voice, so at odds with the picture of her I'd painted over the past day, had my heart sinking in my chest. Her eyes pleaded with him as she struggled to pull herself to a sitting position. "Gray, you know me."

See her, I silently begged him. See her for who she is. See her for more than what she is and you fear she may become. For a brief moment, when his face crumpled and his fists loosened at his sides, I thought he would, but sometimes a moment of clarity isn't a miracle, it's just a moment.

That moment came and went, leaving nothing but disgust in its wake.

"I don't. You are a stranger to me."

Kenna's face went slack, all signs of hope or desperation leaking from her face as she watched him beckon the Enforcers who'd gathered at the perimeter to approach.

I looked around the arena at the spectators who'd gradually filtered back in since the earth became still. Was there no one willing to intervene? She'd spent the last two years praised as a Luna who'd led and protected the pack well, yet no one moved to protect her. In the crowd, I saw Kenna's Beta, face drained of color and tear tracks etched into her cheeks. Beyond her, other pack members clutched at each other as they looked down at us from the stone seats. No one moved to defend her.

The foxes, I realized, hadn't left. They were still seated exactly where I'd spotted them before the battle began. Eris' hand rested over her breastbone, eyes wide and mouth slightly agape. Her brother had wrapped an arm around her to tuck her into his side. I didn't look at Asher, save for the white-knuckled hands digging into his knees. I couldn't risk being caught in his stormy gaze. I feared what he'd uncover in mine.

A barely audible groan pulled my attention from the onlookers, and I watched as two males drew up on either side of her and hoisted Kenna up by her arms until she hung suspended between them, feet just shy gazing grazing the dirt below.

"Take the elemental to the cell block." And then Grayson spoke the words that had bile burning in my throat, "She'll be held there until her execution."

28

THE ROSE

Getting caught sneaking into the dungeon in the middle of the night would do nothing to convince Grayson I had nothing to hide, especially when we'd agreed to interview Kenna together. We'd barely spoken after Kenna had been taken away. I wanted to slink away into the night, but that was impossible before the Rite was complete.

When the ground stopped shaking almost all of the pack had returned, and a few were determined to claim their spot in the hierarchy. I'd have been impressed by their bravery if they hadn't fled from danger not twenty minutes before.

Three more challenges took place after Kenna was detained. Most of the onlookers left after the first, but several, including the foxes, had stayed through the end. One male who'd started at the Academy this year unexpectedly challenged Grayson for Alpha. He was carried from the field with a broken leg and bloodied skull not five minutes after the battle began.

Grayson stayed by my side the entirety of the other challenges, his thigh nearly pressing into mine. He kept touching me: a hand on my shoulder, his knee knocking into mine, a tug on a lock of my hair. All of them were small, thoughtless actions that had my already racing heart beating even faster against my chest.

Each touch was a small, public gesture of affection I should enjoy, should reciprocate, but I wasn't. I couldn't. Because each touch was an offering he'd surely snatch away if he knew what I was.

How long would it take him to throw me in a cell next to Kenna's? Or would he simply have my head and be done with it, no interrogation or trial needed? Yesterday I'd been collecting each brush of his warm skin over mine like gems to line a crown, but today? Today the world was spinning and Grayson's affection only made it spin faster.

When the challenges were complete, we'd tasked the Enforcers with bringing the injured to the infirmary and closed the Rite. Afterward neither of us had the energy to do more than trudge back to the pack's wing for the night. We agreed to confront Kenna after we both got some much needed rest.

It was an agreement I couldn't afford to keep.

I knew that seeing her alone, before the others could question her, would cause at least one person to wonder if I was colluding with her. Which, in some ways, I was, but it was a risk I had to take.

There was little doubt in my mind Kenna knew what, and maybe even who, I was. What I didn't know was how she knew it, and more importantly, what she planned to do with that knowledge. As no one had stormed into Isaac's room and bound me in chains immediately after the Rite, I could only assume she hadn't revealed my secret—at least not yet.

The sun would be rising soon and students, staff, and professors along with it. There were too many potential witnesses, yet there I was, skulking along corridors and dipping into shadows on the path Isaac had plotted for me. He'd begged me to stay put or to at least bring him with me, but I held firm. I needed to do this alone. My mere existence put his life at risk every day, I wasn't going to risk it further by having him accompany me. Kenna knew my secret, but she didn't know his, and I was keeping it that way.

I peeked around the last corner before I reached the dungeon's entrance, expecting a guard to be posted at the top of the stairs. Instead, it was empty, perfectly still apart from the shadows dancing down the spiral stairs, cast from the lanterns' flames.

I was cautious as I crept forward, half expecting a horde of soldiers to suddenly appear and reveal this was an elaborate trap created to catch me in the act before ordering my immediate execution. As I descended the stairs I bade the lanterns to dim ever so slightly as I passed.

The dungeon floor was dusty, and there was a chill in the air I could feel even through my boots. Cells lined either side of a long pathway, each of them housing threadbare cots and a bucket I didn't think was used for water.

"I wondered when you'd visit me." A raspy voice called from the corner cell furthest from the entrance. I quickened my pace but continued to step lightly. If a soldier or pack mate was lying in wait, I would at least make it difficult for them to know when to pounce. "You can stop your prowling, my ember. It's only you and me for now, though if you'd arrived a few minutes earlier that wouldn't have been the case."

I couldn't see her properly at first. She sat on the ground with her back against the wall, legs splayed, and bloody hands bound in front of her—was it her blood or another's? Shadows obscured her torso and down-turned face. What must have at one point been her cot lay in pieces in the opposite corner of her cell.

"Don't look so horrified, Princess," Kenna said hoarsely, "I wouldn't call it cozy, but we've both lived in worse conditions than these."

She lifted her chin from her chest, and my limbs began to go numb as pressure built in my throat. Her face was a collage of purples, blacks, and blues. Dried blood was smeared across her cheek, fading into her hairline.

"I didn't do this much damage to you in the Pack Rite."

Her chuckle was dry, humorless. "You are not the first pack member to visit me tonight. You'll never believe how vindictive some folks can be when they feel betrayed," She revealed, the implications of her broken voice settling in my mind like a weight pressing the air from my lungs. Her vacant eyes met mine as she said, "I hope you never find out."

I wanted to say that I wished she hadn't either, that I was sorry this happened to her, but there were too many questions I needed answered before I could allow empathy to rule my choices.

"You brought an amphitheater down around us, and you can't free yourself from a cell of stone?"

The walls were over a century old. The metal bars had

begun to rust. I suspected I could break free from the cell without needing an affinity for earth. For her, it should be next to nothing. Yet here she sat, bloodied and bruised.

Her smile was feral, revealing red-tinged teeth, as she raised her bound hands. "Unfortunately others were able to make that leap of logic as well. I won't be going anywhere as long as I'm bound by these little treasures." Woven into the rope were black stones flecked with red.

"Bloodstone."

She nodded. "Yes, but that wasn't what you wanted to know."

Kenna arched one elegant brow, waiting. Even facing certain death she appeared calm, in complete control. Had I not known better, I'd think the entire sequence of events had been her plan all along. That it had landed her exactly where she wanted to be: this cell.

"I've relived that fight a thousand times since it happened, and I can't understand it. What made you lose control?" I asked as I lowered myself to sit on the ground, watching her through the iron bars that separated us.

"Isn't it obvious?" She nodded at my chest. "Your marker called to me. At the worst possible moment too. We both know I was going to win that fight. If that accursed necklace hadn't popped free, I'd have had you pinned in a few more seconds."

"I see time in this cell is already eating away at your sanity," I deadpanned then said, "And what do you mean it called to you? What power could a mere trinket have?"

She tilted her head back and cackled, clutching her

bound hands to her stomach and bringing her knees off the ground.

"A mere trinket?" she asked between chuckles, "Do you think this act is convincing to me? Honestly, my ember, you've concealed yourself beautifully for all this time, but did you truly think you'd outrun them forever?" She clicked her tongue and shook her head in mock pout.

"Stop calling me that." It set my teeth on edge. "And I'll ask you again, what are you talking about? Outrun who?"

"What? Does that pet name bring back a few too many memories? Please. You're not that delicate," Kenna said, "Stop pretending. I've already proven I'm not going to spill your demonic little secret. If the blows to my face and blades beneath my nails didn't loosen my tongue, I assure you, nothing will."

"Kenna. Whatever memories you're taunting me with, they're not mine," I grasped the bars in my hands and pulled myself as close to her as they allowed, "Hear me when I tell you this: I am not pretending."

Her brows drew in and she dragged herself over the dirt-encrusted floor until she mirrored my position. Her eyes, only a few inches away, searched between mine. Whatever she found there had her shoulders falling as the breath escaped her lungs.

"You don't know." Her voice grew louder, more aggressive as she asked, "How can you not know?"

"So tell me!" My voice echoed against the stone wall, and I flinched. We both turned to the entryway and froze, listening for any sign I'd been heard. Only silence greeted us.

Kenna turned her gaze back to me, what little life I'd seen return to her face as we spoke draining.

"If you do not know, I cannot tell you."

She froze for a moment. I didn't speak for fear she'd choose not to do or share whatever it was she was considering.

"I cannot tell you what you do not know," she repeated slowly, raising her bound hands to pull at her collar, "But I can at least show you this."

She grimaced as the clumsy movement pulled at her wounds, but eventually, she managed to reveal a chain hanging around her neck.

"I don't understand," I said in a pained whisper, "How? Why?"

"What?" she asked humorously, "Did you think it was one of a kind?"

Kenna's pendant was nearly identical to my own. If it had been cast in silver instead of gold I'd think she'd stolen it from my neck.

"You're too intelligent to believe in coincidences, Briar. You have to think. You have to remember."

A scream longed to explode from my throat. I felt my temperature rise and my fire pressed against my skin in frustration, begging me to be let out. My hands grasped at the roots of my hair. If I was less vain I'd rip it from my scalp just to try to find relief.

I was so close to unearthing the truths that had escaped me since waking to a field of my own destruction. I knew there was someone—something—out there searching for me, ready to take retribution for what I'd done, I just didn't know their identity. How could I? I didn't even know my own.

"Kenna," I pleaded, releasing my hair and holding my shaking hands out in front of me, "Please. You have to tell me!"

"I can't."

"Why?" I asked. Desperation clawed at my chest as I shook the bars between us, the metal starting to glow from the heat of my hands.

"Briar, look at me." I did. "I physically cannot."

She moved her mouth but no words formed. Instead, her face turned red, her eyes bulging as she began coughing and gasping for air.

"Your tongue is bound."

She nodded, catching her breath. "I cannot give you the answers you seek."

Tears pricked behind my eyes, and I had to look away from her for a moment to collect myself. Think, Briar, think. There had to be another way. There was always another way.

"You cannot speak," I realized aloud, "But you can still give me answers." My gaze darted back to her and I pulled myself to my knees.

"I think I hit your head one too many times." She looked me over. "I doubt even you have the power to unbind a compulsion."

"No, I don't," I acquiesced, "But I don't need you to speak to indicate yes or no."

I watched as realization dawned on her face. Thousands of questions burned at the tip of my tongue, but our time was limited.

"To your knowledge are you the only other elemental at this school?"

She nodded hesitantly at first, then when her breathing remained uninhibited, more confidently.

"Did you intend to put the pack in harm's way?"

She shook her head. I prayed to the suns and stars she answered truthfully.

"Is the person you think I'm running from an elemental?"

Head shake.

"Are they a demon?"

Nod.

"Is there more than one of them?"

Nod.

"Are you working with them?" She paused for a moment, a small, sad grin crossing her face.

Nod. I didn't want to ask my next question, but I had to know.

"Is this because of me?" I asked, not meeting her eyes, focusing instead on her chin, "Do they know what I did?"

She hesitated.

"Tell me," I demanded.

She nodded.

"One final question," I asked, clearing my throat, "Will they come here?"

She nodded before dropping her head down to her chest.

My heart dropped with it.

29

THE MOON

How could I have missed a threat as dire as this? Had I grown so inattentive that evil could close in around me without notice? The signs were there. Kenna was so much stronger than the others, so confident that none of the pack members could unseat her as Luna. She hadn't shown a trace of trepidation when Briar's true rank was revealed in the quad. If anything, she was excited, a fire igniting behind her eyes at the potential challenge.

After I begrudgingly watched as Briar headed back to Isaac's room, I knew I should return to my chambers, but questions left unanswered were calling out to me. I needed to go back. So instead of climbing into bed, I trekked through the trees toward the sunken arena I hoped held the secrets I was determined to unearth.

I froze at its precipice. The enormity of the destruction had been lost on me as it occurred, muted by adrenaline and denial. Chunks of stone larger than me lay scattered, torn from the embedded benches where we'd sat. Vines brown and wrinkled, lay lifeless across the floor of the arena.

Everywhere I looked, immortalized chaos stared back at me.

I descended the steps, avoiding the loose rubble and gaps as I went. I wanted—needed—to stand where they'd stood, see what they'd seen. Maybe then a shred of reality would make sense like I thought it had a few hours before. Instead, all I felt was a growing tightness in my chest and pain lodging in the back of my throat that no amount of swallowing would dissipate. Looking up, or looking down, the scene was the same: cataclysmic.

I laced my hands behind my neck and dropped my chin to my chest. I let my eyes drift shut and tried to breathe in and out as slowly as I could manage. Maybe it was pointless to come back here. Staring at the debris wasn't going to magically explain how it was created.

I opened my eyes to go back to my room, maybe write an account of what had occurred to send to my parents. They deserved to be warned of the threat. I'd set my mind to go and do just that, but a scrap of black on a darkened patch of earth caught my eye.

I crouched to grab the torn leather and brought it to my nose. The smell of sea salt and cinder toffee greeted me. It was one of Kenna's wounds, then. Briar was more citrus than sweet. I inhaled again and the blood coursing through my veins turned to ice. It was subtle, nearly undetectable for a normal nose, but it was there: sulfur.

Any lingering doubts I may have had about Kenna's guilt left me. I didn't know when or where, but Kenna had met with a demon, and recently if the scent still clung to her clothes.

I'd been deceived, but I wasn't blind. I'd seen Kenna going off on her own, disappearing in the woods for hours on end, rejecting her Beta's counsel, deflecting any questions about herself that went past surface level. I knew there were pieces about herself she chose not to share with her pack, but I'd thought it a fair boundary to set. As a leader, I empathized with holding back parts of yourself from the ones who looked to you for direction. I'd been wrong.

"It's fascinating what secrets lie beneath battle and blood, don't you think?" Fabian's sister, Eris strode into the stone circle, and I rose to my feet, leather still grasped in my hand. "I didn't expect to find you here."

"Who else did you expect? Is investigating this incident not both my duty and my right?"

Her head cocked to one side and rose-tinged silver ringlets fell over her shoulder. She pursed her lips and looked me over, ending on my clenched hand. "I don't know who I was expecting to see, I just know I wasn't expecting it to be you."

My patience for enigmatic musings, if it ever existed, was diminished. I commended myself for keeping my eyes fixed on hers instead of letting them roll as they longed to.

"Whose vindication were you searching for when you came here?" she asked. "Yours or hers?"

"Kenna's guilt is self-evident," I said, "It became inarguable the moment she shook the ground and brought rocks down upon us." The little fox strolled along the perimeter, letting her fingertips brush the lanterns and boulders as she went.

"Then why not visit her cell and simply extract the answers you seek? You have the skill set and the stomach, so what's stopping you?"

"Contrary to what you may think, I don't relish inflicting pain on another being, even one as vile as her. I do what's required of me to protect my people. I don't think I need to remind you of what's at stake."

The last time elementals and demons infiltrated our lands entire communities had been destroyed, both of shifters and any realms who stood as their allies. The moon foxes had lost countless lives by coming to the shifters' aid.

"No," she said solemnly, "I was young, but I remember well enough." She shrugged and looked around the arena with a look of longing as if searching for something just beyond her reach.

"Why did you come here, Eris?" Her answering grin was sheepish and she toed at the dirt beneath her feet.

"I don't know, I felt drawn to come here so I did. I have no explanation to give but that." She chuckled dryly. "I'll leave you to your investigation."

As she walked away, I shifted my focus back to the bloody contents of my hand. There would be no leniency for Kenna, not with the proof of her corruption clutched between my fingers.

"Oh!" I looked up as Eris twisted to look at me over her shoulder. "One more thing. I think you misunderstood me earlier."

I snickered under my breath. "On which account?"

"It wasn't Kenna's vindication I was asking about. We both know there's only one place you'll find the truth you're searching for." The half grin that was forming on my face fell. "Enjoy the new moon."

And then she was gone, leaving me to face the question that plagued me most: how did Briar, a latent shifter, overpower an elemental on a new moon when Lunar Realms were at their weakest?

Another scrap caught my eye, this time with a flash of red. Leather-wrapped stone. Bloodstone. I grasped the strip of leather and brought it to my nose, begging whatever or whoever may be listening that its scent would be sweet.

It wasn't.

Citrus.

Sage.

Like Kenna, I knew Briar was hiding something. It didn't matter how drawn to her I was; I couldn't make the same mistake twice. Amidst Eris' oddities and ramblings, she'd said at least one thing I was certain to be true: there was only one way to find my answers.

THE ROSE

I t was because of me. Kenna, the demons, the massacre—
everything, it was all because of me.

My limbs trembled as I made my way through the darkened halls. My breath grew more ragged, more shallow with
each step. The spectators from the Rite were gone, likely
getting sleep before classes or sobbing in a corner from the
morning's events. I'd give anything to turn back time, to be
back on the shoreline watching the stars with Grayson when
the only elemental I had to worry about was myself.

I turned the corner and lunged into a shallow alcove to
hide behind the statue there at the sound of approaching
footsteps. Two sets. One from the east, one from the west.

"Pax!" Grayson's voice echoed against the stone and sent
a tremor down my spine. "Have you seen Briar? I can't find
her anywhere."

"I haven't seen the girl since the Rite." His voice dripped
with distaste as he said, "I was in the cells with *it*. Things got
a little messy. I just came from the showers."

So Pax had been the one to interrogate Kenna, not Grayson. I wasn't sure if it made me feel better or worse that he hadn't gotten his hands on her, at least not yet. On one hand, I shuddered to think of him capable of leaving Kenna bloodied and battered. On the other hand, she hadn't revealed my secret under Pax's interrogation. Something told me Grayson's could be much more persuasive if he wished it to be. It's possible she'd be incapable of telling them what I am even if she did break under the pressure, but I wasn't going to bet my life on a bound tongue.

"Did you learn anything?" Grayson asked. I could picture him running his hands through his hair in frustration.

"Nothing."

"We need to expand the interrogation to more than just her." My heart sank at his words. It was the only logical thing to do, in his shoes I'd do the same, but the weight of being under scrutiny sat heavily on my chest.

"Who else do you want to interrogate?" Pax asked Grayson. I may be imagining it but I swore there was a tinge of eagerness in his voice.

"Everyone." Came his hushed reply. "Keep it subtle at first and see who feels like they're hiding something."

"And the ones who are?"

"They'll share Kenna's fate. We have no place for traitors here."

Isaac's face flashed through my mind. I'd always known that if I were discovered he'd be sentenced alongside me, but hearing it confirmed left a metallic tang in my mouth. Pax grunted in agreement then began to speak but stopped.

"What is it?" Grayson asked. I strained to hear his response.

"I know she's from your home pack, and I don't want to overstep." My heart stilled in my chest. "But what about Briar? You told me she's a latent but she just took down an elemental in hand-to-hand, close-quarter combat—with minimal injuries. How is that possible?"

The moment Grayson took to pause aged me a lifetime.

"I don't know," he finally said, sounding somewhat reluctant to admit it, "But I'll find out."

"Should I feel her out like the others?"

"No!" Grayson barked. Then more calmly, "No, I'll stay close to her myself. If she is hiding something, she's more likely to reveal it around me than you. I've already been working on getting her to trust me again, this will seem no different. To her, it'll just be us connecting and leading like any other Alpha and Luna pair. She won't be suspicious, and if I'm wrong and she is, it won't matter. She wants to believe this, she wants to believe me. So she will."

I pressed my forehead into the cold stone of the statue until it hurt, biting my lips between my teeth to keep from making a sound. *Stupid girl*, I knew better than to believe it was real.

Pax said something in response as they started down the hall that made Grayson scoff, but I was done listening; I'd heard enough. I waited until the sound of their footsteps had disappeared completely before I left the solitude of the alcove to make my escape. The last thing I needed was for them to catch me eavesdropping or see the tears threatening to spill from my eyes.

What little control of myself I'd found since leaving Kenna's cell was rapidly deteriorating. The heat building in my palms began to spread up my arms.

Five minutes.

I'd give myself just five minutes. I could pull myself together and go back to Isaac's—no, to my—room, but goddess, it would still be filled with Kenna's things. Would they search through them, were they already? Was there something there that would link her to me?

Four.

The cool metal of my necklace burned against my skin beneath my top. She said it was what triggered her, but why? How could she have its twin? It was reckless of me to keep wearing it now, but it was the one item, one memory, I had from my life before.

Three.

I'd been stupid. Careless, not just with my own life but Isaac's. And Kenna! Did she deserve the fate that awaited her? I was living, breathing proof that not all elementals carried out the bidding of demons, but she'd already admitted she had. Did she have a choice? Did it matter? She'd be put to death either way.

Two.

I banged my head against the stone wall behind me with each question, the tears falling freely now. I slid my hand over my mouth to muffle my soft cries that still seemed to echo against the walls. Grayson and Pax would be watching me for any sign of suspicion, and I'd have to let them, pretending not to know that every graze of Grayson's hand, every offer to tag along would have an ulterior motive.

One.

One more minute, I promised—just one more. I dropped my hands from my face and tilted my head up to the ceiling, willing the tears to stop falling and my breath to regulate. I shook my head and arms along with it.

Zero.

Time to be a normal, not-at-all-infused-with-fire, Luna to avoid attracting even more suspicion, yet saltwater still leaked from my closed eyes, and I couldn't avoid the lingering sniffles. I couldn't shove down the flames begging to be free the longer the night's revelations circled in my head.

I couldn't stay here—not where anyone could come across me and not when my control was hanging on by a thread. Forsaking all stealth and silence I did the only thing I could think of: I ran.

Through the breezeway and across the quad, I pushed my legs as fast as they could carry me. Pressure was building behind my eyes but I didn't stop. I couldn't stop. Not running, not the panic, not the magic flooding my system as if it were punishing me for keeping it dormant for so long.

I cursed my own stupidity for not going back for the bloodstone after losing it in the Rite. I was too confident—too arrogant to think that keeping my fire buried for a single battle meant I no longer needed it. Stupid, presumptuous girl.

I cut through the tree line of the forest and pushed even harder to put as much distance between me and the Academy as I could before whatever brewed inside me burst through the surface.

Calm down, I urged myself as I ran, just calm down. Stay in control. Breathe.

But how could I breathe when I was drowning? How could I be calm when the world had turned to chaos? How could I control anything let alone my mind when everything was both literally and figuratively crashing around us?

It was too much. Everything was too much. Kenna. The Pack Rite. Grayson. Isaac—oh goddess, Isaac! He would be interrogated too along with everyone else. If I was discovered he'd surely pay the price alongside me.

A week ago I'd have thought there was a shred of hope, but Grayson's actions today proved nothing would stay his hand when it came to a threat against the pack—even a perceived one. How many lives would be at risk because of my failures? Even if Isaac and I came out of Grayson's investigation unscathed, Kenna had said it herself, the demons were coming for me.

They were coming to the Academy, and they were coming for me.

The first sign of a spark sputtered from my fingertips and I clenched my hands into fists to contain them.

Just keep running.

Don't think.

Don't look back.

Don't slow down.

Don't stop.

Just keep running.

I veered off the path through the underbrush as I made my way deeper into the forest. I just needed to make it over the border and I'd be safe. Branches and twigs pulled at my hair and whipped in my face but I didn't let it slow me down. What was a trickle of blood against my cheek when the alternative could be a blade through my neck? If I was discovered, it wouldn't matter if the demons came for me, I'd already be dead, and my friends would be left to fight the enemy alone.

They'd need me, I realized as I pushed myself even harder, ignoring the sharp pains beginning to spread through my legs and the cramping growing more pronounced in my abdomen.

With me, they were in peril. Without me, they'd be doomed before the battle ever began. We had barely defeated the two demons in the woods and there'd been not one, but two elementals fighting against them, even if I hadn't known it at the time.

My heart sank at another revelation: they let us win. If they were there for me, if they'd been working with Kenna, if they needed the two of us for something, they'd have no choice but to let us win. But had we? Were the two we'd fought even dead? Or were they just biding their time until we left to make their escape and report back to whatever power they served?

Flames burst from my hands and began clawing their way up my arms. Their glow was too bright not to be spotted against the blanket of night even with what had to be miles I'd put between me and the nearest campus building. I spun and searched my surroundings for any sort of protection— any kind of cover, and then I spotted it: a curtain of ivy and branches blanketing a cluster of trees. I sprinted toward it, pushed through its hanging vines, and froze.

There, carved on the trunk of a fallen tree, was the

outline of a flower. A briar rose. No. There was no way. I looked around for flashes of orange eyes watching me from the forest. I inhaled trying to detect even the subtlest hint of sulfur but there was nothing.

If this was left for me to find, it may not have been the only one. If I found this, someone else could find others. If they found the others then they'd start asking questions, and if they started asking too many questions when suspicion was already at its peak—

The last thread of my control snapped.

Then there was no tree.

No carving.

No me.

There were only flames.

31

THE MOON

I searched every building, every room, every alcove, every hallway on campus for Briar and found nothing. I could feel her pain–her panic screaming out to me, yet no matter where I searched or who I asked, no one had seen her. She was nowhere to be found.

I'd nearly broken down Isaac's door to find out if she was there. The snow leopard answered with dripping wet hair sporting only a towel and a scowl so fierce a lesser male wouldn't have dared push his way into the room.

I was not a lesser male.

I'd shoved him out of my way despite his protests that she hadn't come back yet and was likely out clearing her head after the madness of the challenge but that did nothing to stop my search. Nothing. She hadn't been there in quite some time judging by how faintly her scent still lingered.

From there I'd gone to the weapons room thinking maybe Isaac had been right. Maybe she needed to work out her aggression by throwing knives at a practice target until it was scraps of straw and fabric on the floor or for a run around the campus. Still, nothing.

I was heading to the cells on the off chance she decided to interrogate Kenna on her own when I caught her scent on a statue in the hall. It was strong and recent. She hadn't been gone long. I followed it out of the building, through the quad, and into the forest.

What was she doing in the forest? I didn't smell anyone else with her, and I was going to wring her neck for being so careless as to venture into the dark woods alone. We had no way of knowing if Kenna was the only elemental amongst us, and I didn't trust the Headmaster's warding to keep the demons entirely out of the campus grounds. She'd get the lecture of a lifetime if I could just find her first.

I felt a fresh wave of fear—of desperation—flow through me, and a flash of light appeared above the tops of trees. I pushed myself harder and called on the wind to propel the air beneath my feet, forcing myself to go even faster to get to her —fight beside her against whatever the threat she faced may be.

The closer I came to the spot the light originated the stronger the smell of burning became.

I should never have left her after the Rite.

I should never have acted like she wasn't important.

I should never have—

I pushed through a wall of ivy and every drop of blood inside me turned to ice.

Ash.

The entire world was ash. And in the middle of the sea of gray, a woman with burgundy hair was hunched over, sobbing as she looked at her still flaming hands. One of them donned a too-familiar silver ring, the blue flash of the moonstone managing to shine through the flames.

"Not you." I felt as though the words were being ripped from my gut. "It can't be you."

The woman looked up from her hands, tear tracks forming rivers of skin on her soot-covered face. Her lilac eyes widened in my direction as she fell back and gasped.

"*Asher?*"

BONUS CHAPTER

DO NOT READ BEFORE COMPLETING FORGOTTEN ASHES

24 ¹/₂

THE MOON

Briar's anger ignited the blood in my veins like a bottle of spirits tipped onto an open flame. I sat back in my seat as a corner of my mouth rose at the sensation.

She truly was magnificent.

I'd much rather be beside her, watching as she unleashed her wrath on whoever was fool enough to cross her rather than here, in a drafty classroom, listening to a professor outline concoctions of plants and herbs I'd memorized before I'd reached adolescence. Judging by the furrowed brows of my fellow students, their education had been lacking by comparison.

I'd happily spend the next forty minutes imagining what Briar was doing, what weapon she reached for—that cursed labradorite dagger the wolf had crafted for her—and what she'd use it for. Maybe she'd simply twirl it between her fingers or maybe she'd draw a pretty pattern of blood on someone's skin.

I was lost in following her emotions as they changed from fury to determination to a smug sense of joy. She'd come out victorious, then. My smile broadened at the thought, earning a gasp from a starry-eyed girl sitting to my left.

One deadened look at her and she faced the front of the classroom once again. That smile wasn't for her benefit.

I was looking forward to hearing whatever tale about Briar's conquests Eris had to share after class. My cousin had adored the little shifter from the first day she strode through the Academy's doors, and her adoration had only grown since she'd defeated the demons in the wood. So had mine. As such, convincing Eris to drop off the mug of coffee I'd prepared for her had been easier than breathing.

Every morning in the dining hall, Briar cradled her mug to her like it contained all of life's answers. The only other thing that seemed to top it was cake, but baking a cake would draw too much attention—make where I stand too obvious. She wasn't ready for it.

I wondered if she was holding the mug as she reveled in righting whatever wrong had been committed against—no. Something had shifted. Her joy was gone, replaced by a feeling of outrage that left blood simmering—both hers and mine. That she felt no fear, only frustration, defeat, was all that kept me from going to her. She wasn't in danger. It could wait. I needed to wait, but knowing that didn't stop me from analyzing every detail I could glean from our bond for the remainder of class.

Something was escaping me, yet I couldn't place what.

Then I realized, beneath the frustration and tinge of defeat there was something else.

Something that sent chills crawling across my skin.

Pain.

Briar was in pain.

My chair shot back into the desk behind me as I rose and made my way to the classroom door.

"You may not have noticed, Your Majesty, but I am in the middle of a—" Professor Soleil's protest cut off with one look cast over my shoulder as I walked into the hall. "Right, well I'm sure there's something very important you—"

The door slammed shut behind me with a flick of my wrist. I would never come into my full power—I'd accepted that—but I made use of what portion of it had been gifted to me. The gods could take every speck of it back if they'd return what they'd taken from me in exchange, but I knew it wasn't a bargain they would strike.

I would never get her back. I knew that. I'd even accepted it, but that didn't mean I hadn't dreamt of it every day since her life was stolen from me. An innocent sacrificed as a casualty of war.

I'd failed her, but I would not fail Briar.

The classroom was halfway across campus, but the walk was faster without students to push through as I made my way through the halls. The bell chimed as I turned the last corner, and then I saw her.

Briar's face was equal parts anger and defeat as she looked at the wolf expectantly—she always was. I don't know what it was she thought to gain from him, but from where I stood he'd yet to deliver.

"What happened?" Grayson reached out as if he had a right to touch her—as if he were worthy of breathing her air when half of his breath was spent doubting her. She'd more than proven herself yet he still looked at her like she'd break under the weight of her rank.

"You're in my way, Your Highness," the wolf growled behind me. As if he were capable of keeping me from her. It could be fun to let him try. I'd carved a slash into his skin for each time his choices added a fleck of pain to her eyes.

I searched every inch of Briar from the toes of her boots to the braids that kept her face from being overtaken by the waves of hair cascading down her back.

"I'm speaking to you." Why he thought I cared only the goddesses could know. If he wanted full access to her he should've blocked my path. He hadn't even tried. The hand pulling at my shoulder was a feeble attempt at best.

"I'm not hurt," she said. I would be the judge of that. She moved away from me, back into view of the wolf. His sigh of relief would've been comical if there hadn't been more important other matters needing my attention. Namely one Professor Cornelius J. Richards.

I crossed through the crowd of students filtering from the classroom, nodding to Eris as I passed. She looked entirely too smug to see me.

His face turned gray when I walked through the door. His hands raised in front his stupidly bright shirt as he took a step back behind his desk. "Now Asher, let's be calm and think reasonably about this for a moment."

I was perfectly reasonable, perfectly calm. Everything I did next, perfectly measured.

It took four steps to reach the fae.

Three seconds for him to shriek as he realized he was no match for me.

Two breaths before my hand caught him by the throat.

One crash as I slammed him atop his desk littered with shattered knick knacks and scattered papers.

"*Mine*," I growled, my face only an inch above his own. I didn't know what happened. I didn't know what he'd done. I didn't need to.

He caused her pain. I was simply returning the favor.

He struggled, limbs flailing about, but I held him there until his face neared purple and his eyes began to roll. I released his neck as I pushed away from the desk and reveled in the way he rolled onto the ground, coughing violently in his body's search for breath.

His still shuddering form looked up at me, and I repeated, "Mine," once more, lest he considered forgetting the first.

I left him there. Let him writhe on the floor for all to see.

When I reentered the hallway, Grayson stood a hairsbreadth from her. Behind him, I realized Isaac held a woefully misshapen cake. Fucking cake. I took solace that mine would have looked—and likely tasted—far better.

I'd let Grayson draw closer to her for now. It was only a matter of time before he killed any misplaced affection she had for him. Briar would see she deserved better in time. It may be a week, a month, a year, or even two years from now, but she and the wolf would part ways. They'd have to because I meant what I'd said to Cornelius.

Briar was mine.

I claimed her before I even dared to let myself admit it—before I ever slid that ring onto her finger—and goddess help anyone who tried to keep her from me.

Also by Kathryn Covens

The Iolite Academy

Forgotten Ashes

Abandoned Bonds

Standalone Publications

Ghosted by Love

ACKNOWLEDGMENTS

To my family, I love you!

To Andy & Sophie, thank you for being you! Your encouragement and support, not just during the creation of this book, but throughout my decade plus of almost but not quite going for it has meant the world to me. Thank you for encouraging me to hold onto and nourish this piece of my soul.

To my rocks Genna, Steph, & Wren:

Genna, thank you for being the only person to know the ending of the book before I wrote it, a hundred voice memo brain storming sessions, and endless encouragement.

Steph, thank you for reading and providing feedback on this story not once, but *twice*, in addition to listening to my many (often repetitive) ideas, worries, and plans.

Wren, thank you for the support, love, and encouragement you provide every day. I'm forever grateful we get to pursue our dreams together.

To my alpha & beta readers, Alice, Ashlee, Cris, Melissa, Steph, Sydney, & Z we all know this book would have been a mess without you. Thank you for the constructive comments, emoji reactions, encouragement, and excitement that turned the first draft into the final product.

To my writing group, Alice, Brit, Genna, Vanessa, & Wren, thank you for inspiring me, supporting me, and answering a million questions. You bring so much joy to this process, and I feel absurdly blessed to call you my friends.

To TGC, I love you more than cinnamon rolls and potatoes.